BRAD PIERCE
ECHOES OF DECEPTION

AETHON THRILLS

aethonbooks.com

ECHOES OF DECEPTION
©2024 BRAD PIERCE

ALSO BY BRAD PIERCE

COLIN FROST

Capital Murder

Echoes of Deception

Code of Conspiracy

———

Want to discuss our books with other readers and even the authors?

JOIN THE AETHON DISCORD!

To my parents. Thank you for teaching me how to work hard and always believe things can happen.

"A lie gets halfway around the world before the truth has a chance to get its pants on."

–Winston Churchill

PROLOGUE

September 24th, 2001

nthrax is dangerous. Alekseyev's words rang in the man's head as he carefully extracted the hermetically sealed tube from the cooler it was in. The dull hum of the fluorescent lights overhead filled the plastic enclosure around him with artificial light. Rubber gloves duct taped to his CBRN suit made his hands sweat, making him even more nervous that he would accidentally drop the white powder-filled tube. In front of him were three separate letters addressed to various U.S. politicians who he and his organization had identified as essential to kill in the coming panic.

The opening shots in this great war on America had begun in earnest only a few weeks before when brave soldiers like himself had flown four passenger jets into various targets along the east coast of the great Satan. It was now time for ambitious lone-wolf warriors like himself to step forward and destroy the United States from within. His plan was perfect, he judged, but timing was crucial at this phase.

The job he held gave him nearly unlimited access to

extremely dangerous, biowarfare-grade pathogens. However, the recent attacks against America had heightened security considerably at the United States Army Medical Research Institute of Infectious Disease. Dominick Schmidt was one of the foremost scientists in the field of virology and held several patents on experimental anthrax vaccines and pathogen delivery systems. But he also had a secret.

Dominick hated the country that he lived in. His radicalization had started several years before on a trip to the Russian caucuses on a mission of mutual proliferation. Dominick had been a part of one of the arms inspection committees tasked with assuring that former Soviet states with weapons of mass destruction either destroyed them or transferred them safely. While there, he experienced first-hand the oppression of the Muslims by the Slavic people. Subsequently, his radicalization took only the surfing of the internet to popular jihadist hangouts and videos. Or so it was meant to look.

In truth, Dominick was the farthest thing from a jihadist. He despised the Muslims and their dirty culture, but his hatred wasn't exclusive to just them. All races and cultures in his eyes that were not part of the Aryan vision laid out by Hitler and the Nazis should be stamped out. The rising tide of globalism and multiculturalism that was sweeping the world on the backs of Americans and Europeans was crushing the middle class. Good, hardworking people the world over were being screwed in droves by foreigners and liberals looking to see their communist dreams realized. But for all his anger, Dominick was not stupid, and neither was the organization that he worked for.

Dominick had not been born in the U.S. His family was of German origin and had immigrated from Argentina when he was a small child. Once in the States, they had done everything possible to assimilate themselves into the American way of life. They quickly became U.S. citizens, hosted their neighbors at barbecues, went to baseball games, and always flew an American flag on their porch in Rockville, Maryland. Dominick had actually believed he was a normal American boy until his sixth birthday.

His mind drifted momentarily from his recollection back to the task at hand. He glimpsed the childish text he had scrawled on one of the notes as he carefully distributed powder into the envelope. It instructed the reader to "take penicillin immediately" and then spoke in simple terms of the usual "Death to Israel and America." Of course, he didn't necessarily disagree with these sentiments, but the purpose of these attacks was not to make a point. He closed this envelope and moved on to the next, thinking back to his sixth birthday.

His father had come into his room to explain to him seriously that he was getting older now and becoming closer than ever to being a man. That being a man required him to understand certain truths about the world. The first was that America was not the most powerful nation in the world. Lies perpetrated by the Liberals and the Zionists propped up its reputation. These people's deceptions and bigoted hatred toward forward-thinking ideas and freedom had led them and the rest of the world to tear down the greatest empire the world had ever known. An empire that, although gone physically, was very much still alive and working toward a brighter future.

At first, Dominick had been confused. "What do you mean, Father?" he had asked. "I thought America was our home and that we live in the greatest country in the world."

"And so that is the face we must put on little one," his father had responded. "We are not American; we are German. And even more specifically, we are Aryan. Servants of the Third Reich and Fuhrer."

Dominick didn't know who that was. He had not been taught about World War Two in school yet. But his father's blue eyes shone brightly with pride beneath his pale blonde eyebrows. "Oh…" He looked out the window for a moment, longing to go and play with his friends, not really understanding what he was being told. "Can I tell my friends we are Aryan?" he asked, badly mispronouncing the word.

The slap that came from his father was not an irregular thing but was particularly vicious this time. "No! You must never tell anyone this. In time, you will learn your purpose, Dominick. You have been selected for a great honor by the Fuhrer. One that you will come to understand the gravity of as you grow older. For now, you must forget that we had this conversation. Grow big and strong, and more importantly, learn everything you can. Knowledge is power, and knowing who you truly are will free you."

As his father finished, Dominick saw him watching him intently, wanting to gauge how he would react to this. He was always being watched and, more frustratingly, tested by them. "Yes, Father," he replied. "May I go play now?"

His father nodded. "But first, I'd like you to have something for your birthday."

Dominick's father unfastened the gold watch from his wrist. He watched carefully as he slowly unscrewed the crown and removed a small red capsule from inside of it. This, he pocketed before showing the inside of the crown. Carved into the gold there was a swastika, though he didn't know what this meant at the time. "You see here, son? Though we must keep our true selves hidden for now, you may always wear your heritage proudly upon your sleeve." He handed the watch to Dominick, who inspected it eagerly. His father showed him how to screw the crown back on properly, which required twisting it in several directions to lock the cipher back in place.

"Thank you, Father," Dominick said, staring enthralled at his new possession.

"Be careful with it, son. Now run along and play with your friends."

He never saw his father take the cyanide capsule back to his room and place it securely in his nightstand.

Dominick finished the last envelope and sealed its contents inside, snapping back to the present. Soon he would deliver them to blue Post Office mailboxes across the eastern seaboard to confuse possible investigators. The return addresses on the envelopes were to fake children in various grade schools, which he hoped would entice the politicians they were being sent to to open them.

All evidence was to be pointed at a colleague who Dominick had judged to be in fragile mental health. His job now was to fade into obscurity until he could disappear back to his organization in Argentina. There he would rejoin his family as a hero of the New Reich. He had no idea that it would take him several more years, and the eventual murder, made to look like a suicide, of the man he was framing. All he knew now was that his organization needed massive amounts of money to begin their next rise to power, and they were about to make it by the billions.

1

Mexico

Narcisso Martinez was about to kill a lot of people. As the ranking lieutenant in the Descanso Eterno Drug Cartel, violent action was his main job. He was what some might call an enforcer, but that term was crude in his mind. He preferred to think of himself as a chess player. Someone who could think three moves ahead of his opponent and always get them to do what he liked. Though his moves were not moving pieces around a board, his moves were savage acts of violence aimed at Descanso's enemies. For all his cunning, though, Narcisso wasn't sure why he was about to kill all these tourists.

Killing tourists, especially Americans, usually brought undue hardship to the cartel. Kidnapping them usually worked out fine and all but guaranteed a substantial financial reward for them, but that was not his proverbial department. *No, killing Americans was stupid unless there was a very good reason,* he thought. There were some situations where this was acceptable, particularly when the person in question's family was somehow involved with the cartel and a message needed to be sent, but this was not that.

There were no names, no specific targets; their orders were simple. Walk into *this* nightclub at *this* time and kill everyone.

Narcisso knew the spot well. Poncho Villa was a popular nightclub for American college students on spring break. He and his men sometimes went there to pick up American sorority girls. *Well,* he thought, *pick up is a bit of a generous term. It's more like "drug and take advantage of them."* There would be no more of that after this. Even if the club could stay open, after the bloodshed that would ensue, no American would ever go there again.

Still, for all his thinking, Narcisso could not arrive at an answer that made sense. There was no questioning this order. It came from *El Jefe* himself, and only an idiot would disobey an order from the boss. The five men in the back of the van around him looked ordinary relative to him. This was mainly because almost anyone would have looked normal next to him. Narcisso was bald, short at about five foot five, and built like an amateur fullback. His short and squat demeanor was only amplified by the full-blown face tattoos he sported. Skeletal bones written in black ink across his face formed a grotesque and fractured skull over his almond-colored skin.

Shockingly, he was not the most curious individual in the van. A plain-looking white man with blonde hair, blue eyes, and a slight foreign accent that Narcisso couldn't place was with them as well. His gear was more advanced than that of the rest of the men. While they sported a combination of AK-47s, M4s, and one RPD machine gun, he carried something that looked to Narcisso like an M4 but was somehow different. It had a few attachments and was emblazoned with Heckler & Koch, with the words "made in Germany" on the side.

Apart from that, peeking out from beneath his flannel shirt was some kind of body armor that looked very expensive to Narcisso.

Not one to be outdone by some foreigner—who El Jefe said

was an advisor on their errand—Narcisso reached to the small of his back and pulled a gold-plated Desert Eagle pistol to inspect it. He dropped the magazine from the weapon and checked it was properly loaded. The man didn't even look at the expensive weapon, knowing it was a gift from El Jefe. Instead, he seemed singularly focused on the task at hand. Narcisso slid the weapon back into the small of his back with some difficulty due to its size and looked back at the foreigner.

"We fucking doing this or not?" Narcisso asked the foreigner.

"Not until I have confirmation," replied the foreigner in his deeply accented voice.

"Confirmation of what, Gringo?" The man stared back at him dully as if bored to be in his presence.

"Confirmation," he replied. Narcisso rolled his eyes. The only person who could order him around was El Jefe, and he was growing tired of this foreigner's lack of information eating up his and his men's valuable time.

"How about we just fucking go now because I said so?"

The foreigner seemed to consider this for a moment. "You could, but your boss would probably kill you."

This show of disrespect infuriated Narcisso. "Where's that stupid accent from?" he asked.

The foreigner didn't bother replying.

Narcisso heard a chirp from what he assumed was the man's mobile and watched him pull out a basic-looking flip phone.

The foreigner held it to his ear and waited a moment before speaking. "Ich kopiere. Ziel ist im Gebäude."

Narcisso didn't know what the man had just said, but he could tell from his body language that it was time to go. The foreigner began opening the sliding door of the van.

"Finally, let's fucking do this," Narcisso said.

The men stepped from the van onto the street in front of the nightclub. They blatantly displayed their weapons as they walked toward the club's door, which looked like the entrance to an old movie theater. In fact, the club had been an old theater in the 1950s, and entrance was still purchased through the old circular glass box office window between the two entrances. In front of them, American tourists saw the men with guns and began running.

Narcisso heard a woman scream when she saw them and trip over her drunk friends, trying to get away. Her short dress rode up her wide hips as she fell, and Narcisso was momentarily distracted by the woman's figure. He looked back at the club just in time to catch a glimpse of a man who looked very much like the foreigner who was with them. Narcisso saw the man nod at their companion as he strolled away from the club and melted into the rapidly dissipating crowd.

The two tough-looking bouncers out front took one look at them and ran away. Narcisso opted to let the men go. According to the foreigner, they were not to start shooting until they walked into the club. Electronic dance music vibrated the club's walls, and Narcisso knew the people inside would have heard nothing of the commotion going on outside. Their senses would be dulled from alcohol, drugs, and days of partying in the warm sun. The music grew louder as they approached the entrance, and the last thing Narcisso heard before stepping into the building was the charging handle of one of his men's AK-47s being racked back and forth.

When they made it inside, a scene of debauchery greeted them. Women in tight dresses, short shorts, and shirts, if you could call them that, pulsated with the electronic vibrations of the music. Men ground their bodies against the women or swilled shots of tequila in groups at the bar. Smoke machines pumped the building full of mist for green, red, blue, and purple laser lights to penetrate, and the constant strobing flashes from other lights made the dancers appear part of a fast-moving slide show.

Narcisso's men and the foreigner formed a neat line blocking the exits and waited a moment before raising their weapons in unison. If anyone had noticed them, they moved too slowly to react to the impending danger. The foreigner fired first, sending three-shot bursts into the crowd and catching random tourists by surprise. Blood sprayed over the ones lucky enough to be missed by this first volley of fire before the screaming started, and people tried to run. A few on the other side of the dance floor, closer to the bar, realized what was happening and threw beer bottles in their direction, trying to stop the shooters, but it was useless.

Before Narcisso fired his first round, a voice inside his head briefly told him that what he was doing was wrong, but he silenced it. Raising his M4, he flipped the selector switch from safe to full auto and unleashed a deadly hail of bullets in the direction the beer bottles had been thrown from. His men followed, and seconds later, Narcisso heard the unmistakable, mechanical thumping of the RPD machine gun tearing its way through the screaming college students, now begging for mercy. Bullets tore through flesh, bone, and treasured family members as the bodies began to pile up in front of them.

The sound of their guns began to level off a minute later as the targets became fewer. The man with the belt-fed RPD machine gun took the momentary lull to reload his weapon, which had run dry. A primal bloodlust had taken Narcisso at this point, a defense mechanism of his conscience to protect him from the mental damage that would occur from killing this many innocent people. His breath came hot and heavy as he discharged another burst into someone hiding behind a table. He went to fire his weapon one more time into a blonde girl who couldn't have been more than twenty-one years old, trying desperately to run from them, but his weapon clicked dry now as well, the satisfying recoil momentarily stopped.

He dropped the magazine and pulled another from his pocket.

He inserted it into the weapon and pressed the bolt catch, feeling the heavy jolt in the weapon as it was ready to fire. He lifted the weapon again, aiming at the girl, but saw her go down in a spray of blood as one of his men caught her with a round to her shoulder. Blood sprayed from the back of her arm over a stack of tequila bottles behind the bar, and the bullet buried itself in the thick wooden surface. She fell behind a table.

The foreigner walked toward her and pulled a Sig Sauer P226 from a holster at his hip. He let his modified assault rifle rest on its sling and pulled his phone from his pocket. Narcisso watched him walk up to the girl, holding the phone next to her face as he crouched down.

He seemed satisfied and stood back up, putting his phone in his pocket. Narcisso arrived at his side a moment later. The foreigner leveled the pistol at her head as she lay on the ground, bleeding to death.

"Please," she sputtered with agonizing difficulty. "My father's a senator."

The words barely left her lips before the foreigner pulled the trigger and silenced her forever.

2

Berlin, Germany

"Skull is moving again," said the man sitting at an outdoor cafe to no one in particular. The low-profile earpiece sat deep enough within his ear canal that it couldn't easily be seen by the casual passerby. A golden bubbling Pilsner sat in front of him, and he leaned back in his chair relaxedly, taking in the neat tree-lined streets of Berlin. He was quite large at six foot two with a thick but muscled body, neat, short, dirty blonde hair, and a few days of darker stubble peeking out of his face. He wore khakis that looked like something a hiker would wear, a dark flannel, Merrill sneakers, and Oakley Turbine sunglasses with blue lenses. An Osprey backpack sat next to his feet on the cobblestone ground next to the metal patio chair he was sitting on. He looked like any other late twenties adventure-type backpacking through Europe, except he wasn't.

Colin Frost, often referred to as Snowman by his teammates, led an elite black operations Echo Team working for the U.S. government. His team consisted of former elite Special Forces, law enforcement, one logistic expert, and one hacker. None of them had family, friends, close relations, or any ties to the outside world. In fact, technically speaking, none of them existed until such time they chose to leave the team.

Echo Teams were the dream child of the U.S. government's Analytical Red Cell Unit, which brought in popular writers, movie directors, and anyone else who specialized in fiction to dream up attack scenarios and solutions for the U.S. government to plan for. They were completely off the books, yet each member technically was high-ranking in every government agency, law enforcement, and military branch the federal government had to offer.

This specific Echo Team, referred to as Team Alien, specialized in counterespionage operations but flexed to cover a variety of mission profiles.

"Copy, Snowman, I'm picking him up," Colin heard through his earpiece.

He watched a man slightly shorter than himself with brown hair, green eyes, and a muscular build stepping out ten feet behind the man he had been watching. Jester, the team's second in command, strolled behind the man, pretending to stop and look at fruit from a local vendor cart. Colin heard him converse briefly with the man in German through his earpiece. Jester, like himself, was former Army Special Forces, also known as Green Berets. All Green Berets spoke another language, and Colin was no exception, being fluent in Russian.

The man ten feet in front of Jester, to whom the team referred to as Skull, was a high-end talent broker for some of the world's worst terrorist, criminal, and unfriendly intelligence agencies. The talent he represented was that of assassins, arms dealers, hackers, bomb makers, mercenaries, and, worst of all, chemical, biological, and nuclear experts. His name was Vladamir Alekseyev, and he was wanted by almost every major intelligence agency in the Western world.

Unfortunately, no agency was willing to touch Alekseyev with a ten-foot pole. The truth was that Alekseyev unquestionably sold the services of individuals inside these agencies. Whether for their expertise, skills, or secrets, catching Alekseyev would be incredibly dangerous. This was because the assets Alekseyev represented within these agencies would likely make every attempt to derail the investigation or kill Alekseyev before he could talk. And Colin needed him to talk.

Alekseyev was a veritable treasure trove of intelligence. Not only because of his contracts and relationships worldwide, but because rolling him up would likely allow the U.S. to clean up its own house in one massive sweep. In this sense, an Echo Team was the perfect asset to bring to bear in this situation. Being entirely outside the bounds of the regular system yet able to easily interact with it would allow them to take Alekseyev without fear of reprisal or spooking the turncoats inside the U.S. government. Once they broke him, they could swiftly act on the intelligence and coordinate the massive multi-agency cleanup effort.

But tracking Alekseyev had taken months of effort and had culminated in the operation they were running now. The premise was fairly simple: using the team's hacker, Charlie, they had steadily put out feelers saying Charlie was looking for extra work —the kind of work one couldn't find driving Uber or delivering meals to people. Charlie had a legendary reputation within the intelligence and black hat community for being an incredibly skilled hacker with knowledge of advanced U.S. programs. However, Alekseyev would know that Charlie was not being compensated at the level he deserved. Charlie didn't dissuade this idea when Alekseyev finally reached out to him and asked if they could meet. Charlie had told him that he was taking a short vacation to Berlin and would meet with him there.

Colin had been against the idea of using Charlie in the field at first, but eventually came around to the idea that Charlie was too juicy an asset for Alekseyev to ignore. This didn't change the fact that Colin was nervous about Charlie interacting with a dangerous international criminal. Charlie, at his core, was a computer nerd who drank way too much caffeine and was overweight.

Of course, he had been severely overweight, but he had been working diligently and had lost thirty pounds over the last year. That still didn't change how Colin felt, though. Charlie was nervous—the kind of nervous that made other people nervous— and that was not a good emotion to inject into this type of high-stakes meeting.

As if in answer to Colin's worries, Charlie came over his earpiece. "Ah... I'm in position," he said in his high-pitched voice.

"Copy," said Colin, standing up and placing a blue twenty-euro note on the table beneath a coaster so it wouldn't blow away. Colin started down the street in the direction of the man Jester was tailing. It was a cool, crisp spring afternoon with a light breeze, pale blue sky, and lazy, wispy clouds floating overhead.

"Approaching the alley," Jester said through Colin's earpiece.

"Copy. Be there in one," replied Colin. He quickened his pace now to catch up with Jester, eyeing the two private security men who followed Alekseyev. They were both tall, around Colin's six-two, and easily outweighed him by eighty pounds. They looked like former Spetsnaz operators to Colin.

"Overwatch in position and ready," Colin heard now. This was Witch—another one of their team members, a former Marine Raider, and scout sniper. His deep voice gave Colin a sense of serene calmness, as if God himself were overseeing their mission.

Colin caught up with Jester just in time to see the group of three men turn down an alleyway and proceed toward the adjacent street. The team had anticipated this movement and had intentionally chosen a small Internet cafe near the exit to this alley on the parallel street. Colin and Jester turned right and began following the men down the alley. He reached to his side and pulled his M911A1 from the concealed holster inside his pants. He saw Jester do the same as he fixed the suppressor to the end of his sidearm of choice, second only to the Special Forces Yarborough knife at the small of his back.

They were now fifty feet from the end of the alley and slowly catching up to the group in front of them. Another few seconds passed before a blue Sprinter van pulled to a squealing stop at the other end of the alley, blocking the men's exit. The driver wore a black ski mask with a skull painted on the lower half of the face, and the sliding side door opened to reveal a similarly clad figure with a suppressed MP7.

The man on Alekseyev's right fell in a quick burst of fire just as he got his weapon out. The second man, to his credit, seemed more concerned with his protectee and tried to turn with him to run down the other side of the alley. The 7.62-millimeter round from Witch's suppressed HK-417 on a rooftop a few buildings away tore through his throat and out the back of his brain stem, burying itself in the dirt between two cobblestones in a spray of blood.

Alekseyev dropped the briefcase he was carrying and put his hands up as Colin and Jester bounded toward him. Jester quickly rearranged the dead men in a poorly veiled attempt to make it look like they shot each other while Colin zip-tied Alekseyev's hands and shoved a black cloth bag over his head.

They ran him to the van with his briefcase in hand and were gone in less than thirty seconds.

3

P resident William Joyce sat back in the specially sculpted executive chair behind the Resolute Desk in the Oval Office. The lumbar support, which had been his one request to the company that manufactured the chair, pressed into him and provided some relief to his already aching lower back. *There was too much damn sitting in this job*, he thought. It was hard to go for a walk around the building talking about classified information, he knew, but he was seriously considering having them put a treadmill in the office if it kept up at this pace.

Joyce was a former Navy captain, turned successful tech businessman who had only taken up politics a few years before. He won on his keen, no-bullshit attitude, and his confident leadership style developed over years as a Navy officer. His twinkling blue eyes, soft smile, salt and pepper hair, and downright handsomeness, as one female news anchor had put it, didn't hurt either. The Secret Service codename for the president was Skipper, and he enjoyed the reference to his past. There were times he still wished that he had command of an Arleigh Burke–class guided missile destroyer rather than an entire country. But hindsight was, as they say, twenty-twenty.

The door to his right opened and his secretary poked her head in. "Mr. President, the National Security Council is here."

"Send them in, Cheryl," he said.

She stepped aside and in walked several members of the National Security Council. The full council consisted of twenty some individuals, but the president usually kept it to the few he deemed essential. In this case it was the Secretaries of Defense, Treasury, the Chairman of the Joint Chiefs of Staff, and the Director of National Intelligence. Mack Tomlin, an Army Four Star, was the Chairman of the Joint Chiefs and one of the president's oldest friends. "Hey Mack, how are you?"

"Good, Mr. President. Bit of a nightmare getting here with cherry blossom traffic, but I know a few people, and we managed to skirt around most of it. Wish it was under better circumstances, though."

"Me too, Mack. It's awful stuff. I'm hoping Wendy has some good information for us, though," he said, acknowledging the sole woman in the group as she walked in behind him. Wendy was the Director of National Intelligence, and President Joyce trusted her implicitly. "Some, Mr. President, but the facts are still extremely murky."

Everyone took their positions in the sitting area of the Oval Office and waited for the president to sit down. The president opted to wheel his desk chair over to the circle to save his lower back from sinking into one of the very comfortable plush armchairs. He caught Chairman Mack's eyes as he went. "Lower back acting up again, sir?"

"Nope, I just like this chair better," the president lied.

"I keep telling him to try yoga," said Wendy.

"I'd never meet a good woman if I got all crunchy granola in my old age," quipped Joyce. He was fifty-eight and still a bachelor, having always been a career man.

"On to business," Joyce said, resetting the conversation. "What do we know about the Poncho Villa massacre were there Americans killed?"

"I'm afraid so, Mr. President. Forty-three, including Senator Griffin's daughter," said Wendy. The sighs of disgust and anger from the group were audible. "Damn," said the president. "It's worse than that, sir. We have convincing evidence that the Descanso Eterno Cartel was responsible."

The Secretary of Defense spoke up now. "We need to send a message to these animals now. If terrorist organizations think they can kill Americans with impunity, none of our citizens will be safe."

Wendy replied, "John, you know damn well the cartels haven't been designated terrorist organizations. We can't just start drone-striking cartel leaders. We don't have the authority."

"The Mexicans certainly wouldn't be happy about U.S. military operations on their soil," interjected the Secretary of State. "I think after this massacre the American people will get behind a change in designation for the cartels," said the president.

"I'm telling you right now—the Mexicans, in their current political climate, will not allow U.S. military operations on their soil," chimed in the Secretary of State.

"Well, that's too bad for them. They're nearing failed state status, and their new president's strategy is 'hugs, not drugs.' It's a joke. We cannot allow this situation to persist, Mr. President," said the Secretary of Defense.

"I don't seriously think we're talking about an invasion of Mexico here, John," said the president, addressing the Secretary of Defense. "But I don't think we can sit idly by while they slaughter innocent Americans. They've gone too far this time. We need Congress to put a bill forward. Something with teeth that hurts the cartels and gives us the teeth we need to go after them. I'll handle that. In the meantime, I'd like to devise a plan for hurting these guys. What do we know about this Descanso Eterno group?"

Wendy answered, "Mr. President Descanso Eterno is the newest, most aggressive cartel we've seen. They seemingly sprung up out of nowhere; at least, we knew nothing about them until a few months ago. They're based out of Chiapas in southern Mexico, which is extremely rural. They're led by someone known as El Jefe, but we haven't been able to establish a firm identity on him. To date, we've had no photographs either. They traffic in the usual—people, drugs of every kind, and cyber theft. The one true unknown with them is where they got the resources to grow so fast. The quality of their product seems to be about the same as everyone else. Still, it usually takes years for a cartel to establish a customer base and grow, much like a legitimate business. The only exception being when one cartel faction splits from another, but usually we see that coming as a violent war ensues. This group has some form of outside funding, and it's enabling them to swallow up or destroy everything in their path. Not to mention, their foot soldiers seem to be better trained and equipped. Honestly, sir, they're so new we don't have much information on them."

"Mack, what are our covert options for hurting them?" asked the president.

"Well, sir, airstrikes are out, too much collateral damage, and we have no reliable targeting information on the group. I understand this Descanso group has angered some anti-drug right-wing rebels in the area, though from our intelligence briefs, is that correct, Wendy?"

"It is, Mack. There's a heavy religious presence in Chiapas and one particularly nasty rebel group, which has stopped most other cartels from setting up shop in the area. They're called Cristianos Por Un Mexico Libre, or Christians for a Free Mexico. They're actually pretty tame belief-wise compared to some of the right-wing groups in the States, but not so tame on the action side," finished Wendy.

"Then I'd recommend sending in Army Special Forces from 7th group. They'll link up with the CML rebel group and train them into a real army. From there, they can advise this force on effectively combating Descanso. It'll be low visibility and allow us to build a real intelligence network and ally within the region. From there, depending on how things go, we can launch, if necessary, more surgical strikes on the cartel."

"If necessary? I think we blow these guys to hell first chance we get," said the Secretary of Defense.

"Sir, respectfully, decapitation strikes never really work on groups like this. Believe me, we've tried. They just splinter into smaller groups, which slowly become bigger than go to war with each other. The approach with 7th group will allow us to rip the organization up by its roots and let the Mexican people feel some pride in their ability to combat the cartels."

"I like it, Mack. Sounds like a textbook Green Beret mission. John Wayne would be proud," said the president, grinning. Mack smiled in return but kept his rigid, upright posture. The president briefly thought that if anyone looked like a strait-laced military man, it was Mack Tomlin.

"Mr. President, it sounds reasonable enough. I'll need time to figure out what assets the Agency has down there so we can get the rebel group to the table with the Green Berets. It shouldn't take more than a week to set up," added Wendy.

"What can we do, if anything, to freeze their money in the meantime, Alex?" the president asked the Secretary of Treasury.

"Unfortunately, sir, we have no idea where their funding is coming from. We can start by freezing whatever their affiliate groups have here in the U.S., but it won't do much until we identify their funding source."

"Wendy, I want people on that. I'm not sure how anyone can build a drug cartel out of nowhere and pump hundreds of millions into them without us knowing about it. But I have a hunch that whoever it is, we should be keeping a closer eye on them."

The meeting broke up a few minutes later, and the president knew his day would now shift into overdrive to meet this new threat. He didn't know what he dreaded most: meeting with Senator Griffin to console him about the loss of his daughter or the new threat that was emerging on the nation's southern border.

4

Chiapas, Mexico

The mansion was not irregular on the beautiful beaches of southern Mexico. But it was by far the largest in Chiapas. If it had been easily visible to the public, questions would have been asked about who lived there, but it wasn't. The home was surrounded by nearly twelve thousand acres of private land, and the only thing visible from the road was another dirt road blocked by a gate. The armed guards who protected this gate wore clothing that would not have been out of place to the local population, and their weapons were generally kept concealed below jackets or ponchos.

The home could be found up a three-mile driveway that only became paved a mile and a half into the thick Lacandon jungle. However, what greeted visitors if they made it past the miles of armed guards was anything but quaint. The palatial twelve thousand square foot home, completed a year before, was designed to look in part like an old Spanish estate and part crumbling Mayan ruin. The jungle ran nearly up to its front, and on the other side were white sand beaches terminating in brilliant turquoise Pacific waters.

The home featured a massive infinity pool jutting up to the beach, servants' quarters, a spa, a shooting range, an equestrian center, and a large cocaine processing center, though this was in the jungle nearby. It was an understatement to say it stuck out like a sore thumb in arguably the poorest Mexican state, but it was extremely well concealed.

Ernesto Gomez had built the home as an homage to his dead wife and included everything he thought she would have wanted, except for the drug processing center. She had never been okay with Ernesto's career choice, even if he was very successful. In truth, she had fallen out of love with him before the end, though she never would have said so for her daughter's sake. Her daughter seemed to be the only thing her husband truly loved besides money.

Inwardly, Ernesto hated himself for this. Upon her death, he had split from his organization to form Descanso Eterno, and with the proper backing, his organization was rising rapidly to the top of the scrum that was Mexico's drug cartels. However, this backing was now rapidly asking him to do things that threatened his business and his family's well-being.

He tried to put this from his mind and focus on the meeting that was about to take place. His chief lieutenants were arriving as he sat pondering. Ernesto wore a colorful bathing suit with a light blue linen button-up shirt, with the sleeves rolled casually up his arms. On his left wrist was a Patek Phillipe watch, inches away from a Cuban cigar, and in his right hand was a glass of Don Julio 1942 Tequila. Today was to have been a day of leisure for him, but that was changing by the minute.

"El Jefe?" asked a man from behind the chair he sat in admiring the ocean.

Ernesto stood to embrace his chief lieutenant. The man looked slightly ridiculous in the white linen suit with the skull tattoos covering his face, but this did not phase Ernesto. "Welcome, Narcisso," he said.

"El Jefe, I'm sorry for the pain I've brought down on us. I was just following the advisor's orders. I—"

Ernesto cut him off. His men only ever referred to him as El Jefe. "Relax, Narcisso. You did well, and more importantly, you did as I said," he reassured the tattoo-faced man. Inwardly, he understood Narcisso's frustration. All of his chief lieutenants owned a piece of this enterprise and felt stewardship for ensuring that they all prospered. This massacre of American college students was costing them. Ernesto hadn't known about the senator's daughter, which only worsened matters.

"I didn't know about the American politician's girl, El Jefe."

"You did well, Narcisso; she needed to go."

"But why, El Jefe?" Narcisso prodded. "Killing Americans is bad for business at the best of times."

Ernesto wanted to tell Narcisso that he had no idea why their backers had wanted to kill all those American college students, but he couldn't give his men the idea that he had lost control. If he did, there would likely be a rebellion on his hands, and he could not allow that to happen at this stage. "In time, you will find out, Narcisso. We will speak no more of this for now."

His voice brooked no argument, and even Narcisso dared not question his boss further.

Twenty minutes later, they sat down at a round teak table by the water under a beautiful cabana. The table held a veritable feast of freshly caught seafood and delicious cooking from Ernesto's private kitchen staff. Assembled around it were five other men besides Ernesto and Narcisso. The seven began to dine, smoke cigars, drink tequila, and barely utter a word as they waited for El Jefe to speak to them.

The U.S. government had ceased a hundred million dollars in

drug shipments in the last week since the massacre. While it wasn't enough to do Descanso serious harm, it was unquestionably a serious escalation by the Americans. Ernesto watched them all, dining himself. He looked annoyed but calm. He judged it was best to display confidence to his men in a situation like this.

Finally, after twenty or so minutes, Ernesto spoke. "Hector, walk us through the numbers."

A man on the other side of the table who was, in effect, the organization's CFO, though such titles were not used, dropped a lobster claw. "In the last two weeks, the Americans have ceased approximately three tons of cocaine and one ton of assorted other products in various coordinated federal sting operations across the border to Mexico and Canada. In addition to product loss and speaking in terms of real dollars of personnel and organizational resources, I estimate the total loss to be around a hundred and twenty million American dollars in annual revenue," began Hector, reading off a printed piece of paper in a leather binder in front of him. "This represents a doubling in the projected amount of written-off revenue for the year and a miss of approximately 2 percent on annual revenue projections. As you will all remember, we projected an annual revenue of 3 billion U.S. dollars this year. I'm sure you are all aware that we own a large amount of our distribution in the U.S. and Europe, allowing us to deal directly with the end customer, meaning lower prices for them and higher revenues for us. This is a riskier tactic, but it has been successful for us. In these stings by the U.S. federal authorities, we lost two of our more profitable operations in Texas and California. And three mid-sized operations in Ohio, South Carolina, and Washington. It will take time to restore these distribution arms, and we are now projecting a 4 percent dip in our 50 percent growth projections for next year, bringing the total to 46 percent."

There were hisses around the table at this, but Ernesto held up his hand to silence them. Quiet fell instantly and allowed Hector to finish. "It appears like the Americans reached out after the recent massacre and whacked everything they could, but luckily for us, they moved too quickly and settled for the low-hanging fruit. Our larger operations appear safe for the time being," Hector finished.

The table was quiet. All the men dressed in their suave attire, and Ernesto in his bathing suit seemed solemn as if mourning the money they had lost.

"What are you hearing, Victor?" Ernesto asked Descanso's Intelligence Chief.

The bald man in shiny reflective sunglasses peaked out at the table. "Not good, my friends. The American president is in an uproar, stoking Congress into action. He wants blood for the massacre."

Narcisso spoke up. "The Americans are always talking about action. They never actually do anything. My guess is we'll hear little more after this recent escalation."

The bald man's face looked impassive through the reflective lenses of his sunglasses. "The American Congressional block known as the Veterans of Congress is involved now. And you know they have been leading an anti-drug crusade in the U.S. now under a policy of legalization of low-level, quote-unquote natural drugs. Meaning Marijuana, Mushrooms, and others. They also preach a massive increase in the amount of federal funding toward drug enforcement and declaring organizations like our own terrorist organizations, meaning the U.S. military can be used offensively against us. They have put forward a bill to sign those sentiments into law, which looks like it will pass. We must put a stop to this," Victor finished.

The men around the table looked more startled at this news. Ernesto knew this was because the predictions Victor made almost always came true. "What do you propose, Victor?" he asked.

"El Jefe, we have one American senator in a, shall we say, tough situation. The margin for the Veterans of Congress to get the bill passed is razor-thin. If we can get one senator to oppose it, we might be able to stop the bill in its tracks." The senator in question's daughter had gotten addicted to drugs, and the cartel had embarrassing videos of her that would destroy the drug hard-liner's career.

"Do it," Ernesto said.

"As you wish, El Jefe."

"And if that doesn't work?" asked Hector.

Ernesto smiled. "Then we'll have to resort to more drastic measures."

5

Berlin, Germany

The old auto-body shop on the eastern outskirts of Berlin had been a CIA safe house since shortly after the fall of the Berlin Wall. Unbelievably, the garage had never been discovered by German or Soviet agents, mainly because it had been sparsely needed over the years. The owner, an eighty-four-year-old German citizen, had been working for the American government since the OSS recruited him to spy on the Nazis in World War Two. This had morphed into helping American CIA agents escape from the Soviets in the Cold War and now simply keeping his garage available as a safe house when required. His requests were simple. His three granddaughters' college paid for who lived in the States and American candy that he couldn't get in Germany—mainly 100 Grand Bars, Reese's Cups, Butter Fingers, and Twinkies.

Colin had met Hanz Fittler, the garage owner, three years before on a mission, and the two had struck up a fast friendship. He was a gnarled old man with grease-stained hands, crooked yellow teeth from years of smoking, and a voracious sweet tooth. A smile cracked his wrinkled face when Colin handed him the large cardboard box filled with candy that he had brought with them to Germany with just this meeting in mind.

"I'm not sure if the cigarettes or the candy are worse for you, Hanz," said Colin when he and the team had hopped out of the van behind the closing garage door.

"It can't be worse for me than a bullet," Hanz shot back in a thick accent, eying the team's guns.

Colin noticed his wit hadn't slowed at all. "Good to see you, old man."

Behind Colin, Witch and Sheriff dragged a hooded and bound man from the van toward one of the hydraulic lifts and began chaining him to it. Hanz looked only half interested at the man they had brought to his garage. He had seen it all in his day and cared little for the types of people that Colin's team usually dealt with.

"I see you're still having trouble with the three hundred?" Colin was referring to the 1955 Mercedes-Benz 300SL Gullwing Coupe. A car that would go for well over two million dollars now but that Hanz had bought on the cheap and restored himself nearly twenty years ago, sitting on a lift nearby. It was one of the most beautiful cars ever made; its soft curving lines and sleek aerodynamic chase delighted the eyes, and Hanz's garage was one of the few in the area with an exceptional reputation for fixing classic Mercedes.

"She is both the love and bane of my life." Hanz smiled. "Will you need anything before I turn in for the night?" Colin considered this for a second. "Jumper cables?"

"That cabinet over there," Hanz said with a wink, and he turned to leave.

Colin heard Alekseyev grunting before he turned to see him

shirtless, hooded, and chained securely to the hydraulic lift behind him. Headphones were over the top of the black hood on his head, blasting death metal and hopefully working to disorient Alekseyev further—primal screams and grunting blasted from the headphones.

"Sure he won't go deaf?" he asked.

Witch, who was the team's interrogation expert, was busy taking quick vitals to make sure he could withstand the rigors of the enhanced interrogation he was about to endure. "Hope not," he replied with a shrug of his massive shoulders. The team hadn't had to use the technique they were about to utilize since their recent mission in Washington, D.C., unraveling a plot designed to take power in the U.S. government by a Chinese-backed U.S. politician. A plot that involved the man who had murdered Colin's sister almost two decades ago. The sights and sounds of these enhanced interrogation techniques still brought back deep scars from those events. Scars that had healed over.

Colin found comfort in those words as he watched Witch open a metal briefcase filled with black foam padding and various syringes. It was an odd contrast seeing equipment one usually saw in a hospital in the damp, oil-stained garage. However, on the scale of odd things Colin saw daily, this hardly registered with him. Interrogation was about fear more than pain or discomfort.

Experts who trained for years in the dark art came to know this above all else. The one being interrogated had to truly believe that what they dreaded most would happen if they did not answer the questions being asked. Everything from drugs, smells, mind games, and, as a last resort, physical violence could be utilized effectively. Above all else, it was the job of the interrogator to discern what that person feared, as no two people were alike. Answers would follow.

Witch had been trained for years in the military in the art of tactical questioning, though he still preferred the term battlefield interrogation. But his true education had come at the behest of a CIA Operations Directorate program known as Guiding Light. In it, he learned enough about interrogation via drugs that he could likely have worked in a hospital had his current career path not worked out.

A high-pitched voice from the office beyond the damp garage called, "Boss, we've got something interesting here."

Colin moved toward the doorway that was flooded with the artificial light of computer screens. He passed through it to see Charlie Allen drinking an extra-large coffee and eating a protein bar with German letters scrawled across the front. This was a far cry from Charlie's old ways of chugging energy drinks and slamming bags of chips. He had lost nearly forty pounds in the past year with the aid of Sarah, their operations specialist, and Jester running him through workout programs.

"Nice job out there today," said Colin.

"I just sat in a restaurant," replied Charlie. "Gotta start somewhere. What have you got for me?"

"This," stated Charlie, holding up a thumb drive.

Colin raised his eyebrows. "And this is?"

A loud slap from the garage behind them told Colin the interrogation had begun. Charlie had flinched slightly but, to his credit, tried to play it off like he was stretching his neck. "Alekseyev's little black book," said Charlie proudly.

"Shouldn't he keep that somewhere more secure?" asked Colin warily.

"Hey, don't knock the thumb drive, man. No one can access it unless it's plugged into a computer, and as long as your physical security on the device is solid, there's no chance of you getting hacked. Alekseyev is connected. Former KGB, affiliated with the Russian Mob, always has a Spetsnaz team around him. No one would dare touch him. If he kept this on a computer, we would have had it already. People think the Russians and the Chinese are always hacking people. We invented hacking people, man," said Charlie with a slight laugh, sounding very proud of his colleagues.

"Okay, you got me. Who's in there?"

"About five hundred or so names. I'm running them through our databases now to see who's who." Colin saw a document scrolling on Charlie's screen of names, photos, dates, specialties, and billable rates. Yellow highlighted text flared briefly across the pages as the program running natural language processing grabbed words and fed them into a database to speed up the process.

It would have required an army of analysts checking names and files in the old days. Charlie's army was self-made bots, machine learning, quantum computing, and artificial intelligence. Another slap disturbed the dull hum of the fans on Charlie's computer, and a fair bit of stammering and pleading filled the air. Charlie looked slightly concerned in the direction of the other room but tossed it aside when a chime from his computer told him that something had flagged.

Colin and Charlie both hunched over the screen to get a look at what the computer had found. Dominick Schmidt's name filled the top of the page. The name sounded familiar to Colin, and though he couldn't place it immediately, he kept reading. His eyes were drawn to the man's specialties, which were listed as biological warfare and pathogen development. Colin felt a chill run down his spine reading the words. Few things scared him, but weapons of mass destruction ranked high on his list. The world had had more close calls than it realized in the last twenty years. Missing nukes, stolen chemical weapons, and raided Level 5 bio-labs had all been remedied by swift and unyielding strikes by American intelligence and special operations forces.

But one mistake, and the world would fall from the knife's edge it teetered on and be changed forever. There were protocols for these things in the community. Ones that allowed Colin to bring forth the full weight of American power should one of these threats be identified. But he needed more information first. He needed to know where he had heard the name Dominick Schmidt before.

6

Argentina

The glowing sparks bloomed into the cool night air from the raging inferno of the bonfire below. Books soared from the riotous crowd, impacting the glowing embers, further adding to the maelstrom of fire illuminating the square. Drunken Germanic shouts permeated the air in a joyful but alarming tone. Men in uniforms kept the crowd at a safe distance, their khaki uniforms stained with sweat rolling down their backs, but their faces kept cool by the spring air to their front. Black armbands with red swastikas added stark contrast to their uniforms, and shining silver swastikas adorning the lapels on their collars glinted with fire.

An open-backed classic Mercedes 770 rolled through the square filled with three smart-looking men in black officer uniforms and one khaki-clad enlisted driver. The crowd looked on as they passed, and some cheered, but most, noticing the distinctive SS uniforms, chose to focus on the fire instead. It was not wise for one to be noticed by men in black uniforms in the New Reich. By day, the town was one of several Germanic-style towns built into the Argentine countryside. An impressive work of stone and German neatness that would not have looked out of place in Germany itself.

A band played German folk music in the corner of the square, adding to the celebration of the month of April. But the Mercedes continued, ignoring the crowds, plodding its way up the cobblestone hill toward the center of the town. The men inside wore serious looks befitting the black SS uniforms that adorned their fit bodies. It was not lost on them that the last times the uniforms could have truly been worn in the open was by their grandfathers over eighty years before.

Things were changing now, though. The world was slowly bending to their will, one step at a time. As members of the New Reich's elite SS, these men had undertaken hundreds of missions across the world, from targeted assassination to corporate espionage.

Of course, nobody was aware of this. In fact, the New Reich existed in no one's mind but its loyal citizens. Citizens who had been loyal since the beginning or had been born into this way of life. Most had escaped Germany before the fall of the Third Reich or else been sent abroad via ratlines set up by German Intelligence and their sympathizers. Colonel Sigfried Himmler was the ranking officer in the vehicle and was close to what amounted to royalty in the New Reich. A descendant of Heinrich Himmler himself, the architect of the so-called final solution, which resulted in the slaying of six million Jews during the Second World War. His grandmother, Margarete Himmler, Heinrich's wife, had escaped prosecution post-war and later fled the country to Argentina via one of these ratlines set up by Heinrich.

He was young for his rank within the SS. A good-looking Aryan with short-cropped blonde hair, cool blue eyes, and sharp features. An ugly scar of his own making ran from the bottom of his right eye down his cheek. SS men typically scarred their faces as a rite of passage in a way designed to intimidate their enemies. Any good looks he had came from his grandmother's side of the family. The Mercedes finally rolled into a circular driveway through a wrought iron gate flanked by two more SS guards in black uniforms. The guards, seeing the mirrored SS uniforms in the car and recognizing the faces of the men, waved them through. They were expected.

Colonel Sigfried stepped from the rear of the open-backed car and felt the hard cobblestones hit his feet. His shining boots, steel-toed and hard-soled, made a satisfying clap on the pavement that he thought would have sounded beautiful had it come from the boots of hundreds of soldiers marching. *One day,* he thought. The front door of the palatial stone mansion in front of him opened, and beams of yellow light illuminated the stone courtyard from the warm entryway within.

The mansion sat atop the hill on which the town was built. It would have looked more at home in Europe with a lord occupying it, but so would the whole town. The only risk of an outsider seeing it was by airplane, and the SS had ensured that no planes flew over this part of the country. Sigfried saw a man flanked by a beautiful woman coming through the door to greet them. She wore a tight-fitting, white silk cocktail dress; he wore a gray Nazi uniform adorned with many differently colored ribbons and markings that showcased his high rank.

Sigfried and his men snapped to, launching their right hands straight out into the air at a forty-five-degree angle, shouting in unison, "Heil Hitler."

The man returned the solute. "Heil Dominance." Heil Hitler was now only used on ceremonial occasions by the New Reich; "Heil Dominance" was the creed of choice now, but this was a ceremonial occasion—the entire month of April was for the New

Reich. Hitler's birthday marked a month of celebration culminating in the Fuhrer's birthday on April 20th, a night of massive celebrations.

"Welcome home, Sigfried. I trust your trip went well," said the man who lived in the home.

"It did, Obergruppenführer; the mission was accomplished as ordered," Sigfried replied. Of course, he knew that the Obergruppenführer knew how his mission went. The man had overseen the entire thing from his command bunker. This man knew all that happened in his command district, which in his case was South America.

"Come inside and have a drink. Your men can wait with my driver here, and I'll have some refreshments sent to them," the Obergruppenführer said, motioning him inside. Sigfried nodded at his men and followed the man inside, careful not to admire the figure of his commander's wife, who was twenty years younger than her powerful husband. The white silk cocktail dress framed perfect curves nearly as tight as the dress. Her skin was pale, if slightly tanned, to a perfect soft shade of white that matched her dress impeccably, and her blonde hair, nearly white, but Sigfried could tell it was natural, was short. She wore a pearl necklace, red lipstick, and heels.

"Drink, Sigfried?" she asked in a sweet voice.

"Tequila neat," he replied as they entered a large library. Sigfried took a leather armchair near a large stone fireplace, and the Obergruppenführer took the matching one next to him.

"Drink, my love?" the woman cooed from a bar in the corner of the room.

"Champagne, please, Eva. We are celebrating." The Obergruppenführer used the temporary absence of his wife as an opportunity to discuss business. "The senator's daughter is dead?"

"You know that, sir. You watched the footage from my body cam live."

"Yes, but are you sure it was her?"

"Her last words were 'My father is a senator,' so yes, I am sure," Sigfried replied professionally but curtly. He didn't enjoy being questioned by this man. Sigfried was a professional, and if he said a job was done, it was done properly. Adding to this was the fact that the Obergruppenführer had watched the raid live from his command bunker, and Sigfried couldn't help but feel a bit annoyed. Because of Sigfried's lineage he found himself constantly needled by the man in an effort to assert dominance.

The Obergruppenführer smiled. "Good, Sigfried. You have done well and served our great empire with honor. A testament to your lineage." Sigfried smiled but wondered internally if the man was now patronizing him. Eva returned with their drinks, and they toasted.

"To the New Reich, to Dominance, and to the Fuhrer, without whose guidance we would be nowhere," said the Obergruppenführer. Sigfried sipped the Herradura Seleccion Suprema tequila and savored the taste of the agave and deep oak barrels. Either Eva liked him enough to pour him a glass of five-hundred-dollar tequila, or the Obergruppenführer was truly celebrating. *Well, of course, she likes me. She is mine,* thought Sigfried. In his heart he knew she was his to command, but no one else could ever know. Deception was life in the New Reich.

But Eva wouldn't be one to give this away with idle doting. Eva herself was a seasoned SS operative who had killed for her empire before. Though it wasn't her mission to sleep with the Obergruppenführer, she was ambitious, and Sigfried didn't have the time to make a proper woman out of her. But his manipulation of her was deep, and her feelings for him were far deeper than the reverse. While he was off sowing chaos across the globe, she was using the information and influence gained from the Obergruppenführer to further their own position within the New Reich. It was a match of love to her and opportunity to him. Sigfried almost pitied the man, but his own dislike was enough to keep these feelings from getting too far.

"Frauline check to see that the Colonel's men have been refreshed. I must have a quick word with him in private. It's sensitive state business," he said with a slight hesitance at dismissing her. Her hooks were evidently deep inside him, and the fact that he didn't know she was an SS operative showed how deeply she had manipulated him.

"Yes, my love," she said with a wink, and she sauntered from the room, careful to let her hips sway beneath the white silk that adorned her. Sigfried's efforts to not stare were unsuccessful. It had been weeks since they had last been together. Luckily for him the Obergruppenführer was so busy staring he didn't catch him.

After a moment, he turned to Sigfried with a serious look. "It is time for the next phase of Operation Storm Light. Are your men ready?"

7

Washington, D.C.

The senior senator from Nevada stepped off the curb on Second Street Northeast and was nearly struck by a police cruiser. Besides the profuse downpour and dashes of thunder and lightning permeating the late spring afternoon sky, the only real reason the senator didn't see the cruiser coming was the phone call he had received half an hour earlier. The officer honked at him, thinking he was a staffer, but upon realizing who he almost hit, he gave a friendly wave. Alex Harkins hardly noticed as he turned left and proceeded up the street, leaving his office in the Hart building behind. He had other things to worry about.

It was a warm, humid spring day, and the rain steamed off the sidewalk as he pressed down the street toward Massachusetts Avenue and his destination. Worry crowded his mind as he walked, contemplating what he would do next. It wasn't often that Senator Harkins feared things; he had become very powerful. Some would even say he was a made man, but that meant that he owed the people who got him in this position many things.

However, the phone call he had received was not from

someone who had gotten him into this position. In fact, it was someone who had gotten his only child, a nineteen-year-old college girl named Sarah, in a bad position a year before while she attended college at Arizona State. She was a good girl with good grades, but deep down, he always knew that her proclivity for partying might eventually get her in trouble.

He turned right onto Massachusetts Avenue and proceeded down the street to a hole-in-the-wall spot with loud music where he wouldn't be overheard. He could feel his boots slapping water and dampening the bottom of his pants as he walked. A consummate Khakis and blazer man, over the more common suite on the hill, he knew the dirty street water would likely stain.

He turned through the threshold of the bar and stepped inside out of the rain, taking off his raincoat as he went. The stench of stale beer, popcorn, and disinfectants filled his nostrils. *They must have just cleaned,* he thought, possibly a first in all the times he'd been here. The bar had a green tinge to it with dark wood paneling and the occasional neon sign to interrupt the aging beer posters.

He chose a table in the back, which put a speaker between him and the bartender. A few moments later, the bartender brought him his usual Coors Light in an aluminum one-pint bottle and let him be. This was a usual place for him when meeting the occasional irregular contact, or just to think. This was because there was little chance of him running into anyone in here who might ask questions or even know who he was.

A few moments later, the door opened, and a man stepped in off the street, looking damp and annoyed at his surroundings. He turned around to leave, thinking it must have been a mistake, when he caught the senator's eye and headed toward him, stopping at the bar to order a Jameson whiskey on his way.

The man heaved himself into a chair across from him a moment later, looking thoroughly exhausted. He had thinning blonde hair, pale skin blotched red with the heat of the walk, and a bit of sag to his jowls that showed either his age or the stress of his job. His name was Tom Johnson, and he represented the organization that had ensnared his daughter a year before. "How are you, Alex?"

"Is that what we are now? Friends? If this is a social call, I'm leaving," replied the senator.

"'Fraid not. I'm here on business, as you may have guessed."

"Really, and what is it that you people want now? I've got enough going on with the NDI act." NDI stood for Narcotics Defense and Interdiction Act. A sweeping reform put forward by the president and those friendly to him in the Congress. It sweepingly legalized low-level natural drugs such as marijuana and psilocybin mushrooms while simultaneously declaring all cartels terrorist organizations. This enabled the U.S. military and intelligence communities to expend resources on dismantling these organizations. And with the lack of U.S. forces on the ground in the Middle East, there were a lot of resources to be reallocated.

"Funny you say that. That's actually what I wanted to talk to you about."

"I don't have any extra information right now outside of what's publicly available. The law's only just been written; there's been no deciding how it's going to be enforced yet." To Alex, this seemed like a perfectly normal thing to say. He physically couldn't give this man what he was asking for. All this organization had ever asked for was information on various things from a smattering of committees the man was on.

"That's not what I'm looking for. Although that request might come down the line, so I suggest you do your homework."

"What do you want, then?" asked Harkins hesitantly.

He took a sip of beer to try and stem the nervousness of whatever request might be coming. Giving information was all he had been asked to do so far, and this he didn't mind. Information was leaked to the press all the time for various reasons, and although it was technically illegal, it was fairly low risk provided one was careful. *How was this any different*, he thought. But he had a feeling the ask he was about to get was way more serious than before. The knot in his stomach grew as the carbonated beer poured down his gullet.

"We would like you to, well, vote no on that particular item."

In the background, a popping sound, followed by the familiar smell of popcorn, permeated the air and the silence. "You want me to vote no on NDI? That's insane. I'm a drug hardliner. You know that as well as everyone else. It would be out of character. The bill's already split between the two parties. It would only take one vote to torpedo the whole thing. I won't do it."

Tom smiled in an "afraid so" kind of way, which kept his teeth behind his lips.

"Well, if that's your final answer, then I'll need to get going. There are some things I'm going to need to release to the media. I'd suggest you pull your daughter out of school—things are going to get difficult for her." Tom made to stand up, but Alex grabbed his hand and pulled him down, and all color drained from his face.

"Tom, please, anything but this vote. Anything, really. You can't. I mean, she's just a kid; she made a mistake."

"You knew the deal when you were first contacted. You were to provide anything my client needed without question. That was the price for your daughter's"—he paused for a moment, searching for the word—"indiscretions not getting out to everyone."

"If I vote no on this, people will get suspicious. It's completely out of character—which means I could get investigated, and your inside man could get booted or, more likely, thrown in jail." An uncomfortable silence lingered in the air after Alex's last statement. Nothing but the last dying pops of the kernels being heated in the popcorn maker and the sound of faint nineties alternative rock interrupted the tension between them. Tom's face had gone very serious, and his age showed more than ever now.

"Will you do what my client has asked, or do I need to make a phone call?"

Alex hung his head, defeated, thinking of his daughter. She didn't deserve to go through the torture of what happened that night again, no matter his own political ambitions. Perhaps he could find some flaw in the bill and point to that as his reason for voting no on the bill. But in the back of his mind, he knew his decision would draw the ire of not only his party but the president as well. Not exactly the person he wanted to make an enemy out of in Washington.

"Is there no other way?" he asked feebly, throwing one last hail mary to try and get himself out of this situation.

"I'm not going to ask you again, Alex."

"Fine. I'll vote no on NDI," he said, resigned. "I just hope your organization can provide some type of top cover when all of this blows up in my face."

"Oh, we'll take care of you. Don't worry about that, Alex," he said, standing and turning for the door. His glass was empty, and so was Alex's Coors Light. He waved at the bartender for another, thinking he would need whatever liquid courage he could muster for what came next. In his head, he tried to put together a plan to justify his no vote, but no good reasons came to him. Thoughts bounced around of what could have been if only his daughter hadn't developed such a penitence for addiction. But it wasn't her fault. In truth, Alex knew he was being given up like a lamb for the slaughter.

8

"You're kidding me. Harkins? I thought he was a hardliner, Bob," asked President Joyce.

His Chief of Staff, Bob Mylod, a seasoned veteran of Washington Politics, was sixty-five, had thinning brown hair, pale Irish skin, and was about as pissed off as he ever got. "He is Mr. President. It was totally out of character, and we had his vote in the bag. We always knew this was going to be close even with the sympathy card on our side; it was going to be right down party lines, according to our research. But there's no reason Harkins should have flipped."

"What was his reason for voting no?" asked the president. He stood in frustration from his chair behind the Resolute Desk.

"Something about not enough funding for rehab clinics in his home state—which is total bullshit. There is room left in this bill for a follow-on piece of legislation to support drug addiction and rehabilitation funding. This was a cut-and-dry win, though, for his platform even without that. He's been a hardliner against drugs for some time now," said the president's Chief of Staff.

The fact that he swore in front of the president was an indicator of how close their relationship was. Even though the president was a former sailor, he typically detested the use of swear words in his presence, deeming them an unnecessary use of breath and finding them ungentlemanly. But Bob was something of a political father to him, so the man was allowed a certain leniency, even in the presence of the most powerful man on earth.

A Navy Steward brought in a silver tray with coffee for the two men and several additional cups.

"Expecting guests?" the Chief of Staff asked. The question was rhetorical; he knew Mack Tomlin, the chairman of the joint chiefs, and the Director of National Intelligence, Wendy Simonson, were on their way. The president was momentarily lost in thought, staring out the thick bulletproof windows onto the White House lawns. It was a cool spring day in D.C., with barely a cloud in the pale blue sky. *In a past life, I would have been outside enjoying a walk on the Chesapeake,* thought the president. The weather, though, did not match his feelings. Something felt undeniably off about this situation.

First, a sitting senator's daughter was murdered in a mass shooting while on spring break in Mexico, and now an aggressive bill to fight the cartels responsible failed because a hardline anti-drug senator, for some reason, voted no on it. Two things that were seemingly unrelated but felt strange when taken in tandem.

"You ought to know, Bob. I'm pretty sure they cleared coming with your office," said the president, turning around. He walked to the tray and held up the carafe, nodding at Bob to see if he wanted some.

"Please," said Bob. The president poured the Columbian dark roast into a white mug with a gold presidential seal on it and topped it off with some cream for his Chief of Staff. He made it a point to know his inner circle's coffee orders. Bob stood and took the saucer and mug from the president as the door opened, and Mack Tomlin, followed by Wendy Simonson, entered the Oval Office.

"Mr. President," said Mack Tomlin in his usual gruff voice.

"Mack, Wendy. Coffee?"

"Please, Mr. President," said Wendy, answering for both of them. When they all had their black coffee except for Bob, they followed the president, sat down in the comfortable sitting area of the Oval Office, and waited for him to speak. The president stayed silent in his usual manner for a moment, taking in the attitude of the room. It was clear that everyone was angry. This was good, thought the president, because what he was about to propose next would require some wherewithal.

When he spoke, his voice was measured. "Bob and I are going to get the NDI act passed. But I don't think that we can wait for Congress to get its act together. If we waited for that, we might be here forever. I want clandestine and military options to counter this threat in the meantime. We can't sit idly while Americans die, whether from bullets or narcotics. I want swift covert action to give us a running start when the bill is passed. We owe that much to Senator Griffin and his daughter. This Descanso group is more aggressive than we've seen in the past. I want to return that favor. That is why this group has gotten smaller. We are going outside the bounds of conventional authority here, and I want to keep this circle as small as possible for legal purposes."

Wendy took a sip of her coffee and placed the saucer on the table in front of her. "Mr. President, as requested, the chairman and I have come up with a plan, the specifics of which still hold even with the new political reality."

The president nodded at her, indicating she should continue.

"The agency's assets in the area are slim, as the area has been of little geopolitical significance in the past. SIGINT has been sparse as well, given the rural nature of the area. We are now, however, closely monitoring all satellite communications data coming out of the area through a DEA request to the NSA. This way, the request seems to be in line with their drug interdiction mandate. We do, however, have one asset in the area who is frankly a relic of another time, sir. He was a Cuban spy who was burned during the Cold War by the Soviets. We got him out and resettled him in Chiapas. He agreed to be of"—she paused, clearly searching for the correct word—"assistance, should we ever need him. In truth, we've hardly ever needed him. Subsequent conflicts in Guatemala never spilled over into Chiapas in the way we thought that they might."

Typically, the president knew he wouldn't have been briefed on this level about sources and means. However, he was a former intelligence officer before he got command of his warship, and everyone knew he liked as much detail as possible when it came to intelligence operations.

The president took a sip of his black coffee and placed his cup back on the white china saucer as well, scanning a brief in front of him as he went.

"That's a pretty old horse to back on this one, Wendy," he said.

"Yes, Mr. President. But we've conducted thorough research on his life since, and the CIA Station Chief in Mexico is sure he's reliable. He conducted a routine review of all assets in his AO two months ago. Paco, which is his codename, sir, was not among the 40 percent of assets deemed questionable by his staff. He has proven his worth, Mr. President."

The president caught a slight glint in her eye when she looked back at her own brief and was fairly sure he wasn't necessarily getting the whole truth, in all likelihood to insulate himself from some classified operation that was conducted using Paco or some type of blackmail they had on him. "I'm not even going to ask, Wendy," said the president, responding to their non-verbal communication.

"Thank you, sir." She smiled, then continued, "Paco will make contact with the C.M.L. rebel group and extend the

Agency's hand of friendship and assistance in taking down Descanso Eterno. Once the relationship is secure, the Agency will feed them situation appropriate intelligence and Mack's boys will take over," Wendy said, gesturing toward Mack Tomlin.

"Thank you, Wendy. Joint Special Operations Command will be loaning the Agency the 7th Special Forces Group. Until Descanso is designated a terrorist organization, the Defense Department cannot be seen to act offensively inside a sovereign nation. In effect, they will become a team inside Ground Branch with resources on loan from the army. They will insert into Chiapas via HALO jump to defeat the Mexican air defense zone and link up with Paco and his rebels on the ground. Once they make contact, they will begin training and advising the rebel force into something that can effectively combat Descanso Eterno. In addition to that, they will work with the Agency and the rebels to collate intelligence to identify the cartel's command and control apparatus for dismantlement. Once the cartel is dismantled, if the NDI act has not passed, the team will be extracted. If the act has passed, they will work with the group to expand its footprint to fight other cartels with the full resources of JSOC and the Agency behind them," said Mack.

The president noted his straight face and the slight gleam in his eyes that told him that he loved what he did. "There's a lot of moving pieces on this one. What's the contingency if everything goes haywire?" he asked.

"Preemptive neutralization of the cartel's leadership, Mr. President," said Wendy. "But I must stress that I think it imperative that we capture as much of the leadership for tactical questioning as possible. The more we dig on this one, the more we don't like what's going on down there. Someone has set up and backed a power player in Mexico, which has drastically upset the power structure. Not only that, but they have made a lot of money doing it. We're not sure how this could have happened so under our radar, but we need to figure out who is doing this, and quickly. They represent an existential threat to the security of the United States, sir."

The president sat back, taking in Wendy's words. Nothing shook that woman, which was probably how she had risen so high so young, but she was clearly shaken now. Moreover, she looked downright alarmed. Something bad was happening in Mexico, and they needed to get to the bottom of it quickly. The president nodded at both of them. "You two have the green light for Operation Southern Lance."

9

*I*t *was way too hot in this fucking jungle,* thought Carl Jones. He watched a bead of water that had pooled on a massive leaf to his left roll down its green face and splash into a muddy puddle on the forest floor. They were surrounded by tall trees, low undergrowth, and a variety of life so staggering only a rainforest could hold it. His team members, all part of the tier two army Special Forces 7th group, Operational Detachment Alpha, all referred to him as Brick. A callsign that was well earned from the massive biceps surrounding his hulking figure. At five-foot-four and two hundred and thirty pounds, he was so far outside of army regulations on height and weight that he required a special waiver on his yearly evaluations by medical staff. They happily granted one to Brick because one would be sorely mistaken for thinking his weight was anything but solid muscle. His closely shaved head, square chiseled jaw, and intense black eyes were enough to cow even the hardest enemy guerrillas. But he still hated the heat.

It wasn't so much the heat as it was the humidity in the Mexican rainforest that was getting to him, though. Very different from the high mountains and deserts of the Middle East, plagued by high daytime temperatures but low humidity. The fact that the humidity bothered him so much was a joke to his teammates, who chided him for joining the command that focused primarily on South America. The truth was his Latin American heritage, native knowledge of Portuguese, and passable Spanish made him an ideal recruit for 7th group.

The twelve-man Special Forces A team had been inserted three days ago, where they rendezvoused with the CIA asset named Paco. Then the waiting began. They built a small jungle hide and stashed their equipment while Paco met with the leaders of the rebel group referred to as the CML. Brick was nervous, which was not necessarily common for the special force's warrior.

The only other times this had happened had been before ambushes when the team had been deployed in the Middle East. Operation Southern Lance was a textbook Special Forces mission, one with which the team was extensively trained and extremely confident in their abilities to execute. But the feeling Brick had wasn't a good one. His engineer sergeant was busy building defenses around their camp with a few other team members while three of his other operators were checking out some high ground to their east. He cued his radio. "Grinch. Status check. Over."

A gruff voice replied, "We're nearly done checking out the eastern high ground. All looks clear here. Will advise when our recon is complete. Over."

Brick nodded to himself, taking in the tactical picture, wiping a drop of sweat from his brow, and triggering his radio to respond, "Copy, Grinch. Out."

The screams of wildlife around them were nearly deafening. Sun rays beat down through the high forest canopy with punishing power. All of this could serve to distract the average person. But these men were elite professionals well versed in hardship. Still,

Brick couldn't shake the feeling he had that something was off. Sure, the mission had come more quickly than was typical for a tier two special operations group, but that still wasn't it. The more Brick thought about it, the thing that was bothering him most was Paco.

The asset the CIA had assigned to them may have been a relic of another age, but the look in his eyes when Brick met him spoke to some clarity of intention that wasn't typical of older men yanked from retirement. He hadn't mistaken the look for conviction of cause; it was something else. Brick pondered this for another moment, trying to decipher any more hidden meanings, when his radio began squawking in his ear.

"Brick, vehicles inbound on our position. It looks like Paco, and he's got some company. They look well-armed." It was his engineer sergeant back at their camp.

"Copy. Keep it friendly; be there in a few. It must be the CML." Brick finished and switched to the team channel. "Grinch, finish your recon, then collapse back to the camp. We'll be greeting the CML."

"Roger that, Bossman," Grinch returned. Brick turned, signaling to his men, and moved off to the camp.

Grinch hopped over a rock and grabbed onto a particularly large vine, pulling himself up the side of the small cliff. Behind him, two other men followed in his element. Panda, the team's dog handler with his Belgian Malinois Rex, and Ford, who was a sniper by trade. Grinch crested the top of the small cliff and looked back down the hill they had just traversed. Below them a hundred yards to their front was the team's camp, and fifty yards past that, Grinch could see men exiting vehicles on a dirt road through the jungle.

"This hill didn't show up on the map," said Grinch in his gruff voice.

Ford lay down next to him and extended the legs of the bipod attached to his rifle. He peered through the scope, sighting the men on the road before saying, "The maps on this jungle haven't been updated since the fifties, and they didn't exactly have lidar to image the forest floor back then. No surprise we're running into things we didn't expect."

Grinch looked over at Ford and shrugged his shoulders with a small smile. Ford flipped his camo baseball hat around backward and leaned back into his scope, while the other man pulled out his own set of binoculars to get a closer look at the action. "Brick, be advised we've taken up an overwatch position on your meeting. We are ready to provide sniper support."

"Roger that," Brick said in Grinch's ear.

Grinch could hear the team's dog, Rex, panting behind them in the heat and knew that Panda had taken up rear security for their small element. With the basics covered, he took a sip from the Camelback straw at his shoulder and leaned into his binoculars, feeling his elbows sink a little deeper into the soft soil beneath them.

In front of him, he saw armed men exiting the vehicles with AK-47s in various states of disrepair. They were followed by two men. One elderly man, whom Grinch identified as Paco, and the other a well-dressed Spaniard in a crisp white linen shirt and pants, with high-end-looking shoes and an expensive hat. Grinch panned slightly and saw Brick and an element of Special Forces soldiers emerging from the woods.

He watched as they approached the CML rebels and stopped for a moment in front of them. Grinch thought they must have been talking. After a few moments, the men got closer, and Brick extended a hand to the well-dressed man next to Paco. Grinch flinched, and it didn't register why for another full second. As the men shook hands, Paco reached to his back and, in a flash, pulled a shiny silver pistol, pointed it at Brick's head, and pulled the trigger. Brick's head exploded with red, and they heard the shot a split second later.

Before any of them could react, the other CML rebels brought up their guns and began firing at the Special Forces soldiers. The men caught in the open barely got their weapons up before nearly thirty CML rebels massacred them.

"Fuck," said Grinch. The sounds of the automatic fire were now echoing up to their position, and Panda came running over to get a better look. Mere seconds had passed since the first shot had been fired, and already the sounds of fire in the distance were waning as the rebels finished off the rest of the Special Forces team.

Ford was about to loose his first shot after making an adjustment to his scope, but Grinch stopped him, still in shock at how fast things had happened. They were simply too far to do anything of consequence with only one sniper against such a large force.

"What, Grinch? We need to kill these fuckers now," said Ford.

"Hold. We can't engage a force of that size without air support. And look, there's something else happening," Grinch said, still in complete shock and running almost entirely on training.

Ford looked back through his scope and saw what Grinch had. A man was emerging out of the woods. He was kitted out like the special force's soldiers with high-end gear, multi-cam, and what looked to Grinch like a very heavily modified HK416. As he walked out of the foliage on the other side of the road, the men turned to look at him, and a few saluted him. He walked up to Paco and looked as if he was exchanging words with the man. Paco handed him the silver pistol he had used to kill Brick, and the man made a show of expecting it before turning it on Paco and shooting him in the head.

"What the fuck is going on?" asked Panda.

"Oh shit," said Ford. Grinch saw it, too. The man in the camo had pointed at the woods, and his men were running in their direction, now probably heading toward the Special Forces team hide sight.

"We've got to get the fuck out of here," said Grinch.

"What about the rest of our guys? There's got to be somebody left down there," Argued Ford.

"There's no one left! We've got to get out of here and regroup. We'll get back to the camp when we can be sure these assholes are gone. There's no use getting ourselves killed," said Grinch. But he saw the faces of Ford and Panda and knew that wasn't good enough.

"Look, if there is anyone left down there, we're no good to them dead. Let's get out of here and regroup, radio into command for some support, and come back once they leave to see what's left. If there is anyone, we'll get them back." Ford and Panda seemed to accept this after a moment when the calls in Spanish could be heard more audibly down the hill.

Grinch took one last look back and said, "Let's go."

10

"Mrs. Director, I believe we have a possible Star Set situation here, ma'am," said Colin into his encrypted cellphone. It took the Director of National Intelligence a moment to respond. Colin realized he hadn't sat down in over two hours, plopped down on a stack of tires behind the auto body shop, and stared at a neat brown painted fence.

The beer he had drank earlier had given him a stuffy nose, and the cool nighttime spring air was helping to clear it. As the leader of an Echo Team, Colin's only boss was the Director of National Intelligence and, on occasion, the president. This ensured his team was able to float seamlessly between the military, intelligence, and law enforcement arms of the United States government.

"Elaborate, Snowman," said Wendy Simons using Colin's callsign.

Colin took a breath and dove in. "Ma'am, we've successfully captured and begun to interrogate Vladimir Alekseyev. We've also gained access to his little black book, and my team has flagged something major. A recent deal brokered by Alekseyev for one Dominick Schmidt. His specialties include—"

Director Simons cut him off. "Did you say 'Dominick Schmidt'?"

The interruption took Colin aback. So far, the team hadn't had the chance to dig up anything about Dominick on any of the usual intelligence sources. "Ah, yes, ma'am. That is correct," said Colin. There was another brief pause, and Colin swatted a bug away from his face. He felt antsy continuing to sit, and sensing something was going on that was bigger here, he stood up.

"Fuck," said Director Simons.

Colin had never heard the director swear before and was surprised by it. Anything that could crack the polished un-reproachable veneer of Wendy Simmons was not to be trifled with. "Ma'am?".

"Do you remember around 9/11 when anonymous letters were being mailed to Americans filled with anthrax?"

Colin had been young then, but he remembered all the events surrounding 9/11 vividly. "I do, ma'am," said Colin.

"Do you know anything about the investigation surrounding the letters?" she asked. Colin closed his eyes, racking his brain and thinking for a second.

"I know the investigation was called Amerithrax, but not much past that, ma'am."

The Director of National Intelligence sighed. "Well, the short story is, after the most expensive investigation in history, Dominick Schmidt was determined to have sent the letters. The longer story is somewhat more interesting. I was a young agent at the Bureau then. When the letters began flying in the wake of 9/11, it became priority number one to find out who was sending them and to stop them as quickly as possible. Two"—she paused momentarily, searching for the words she needed—"questionable agents were selected to lead the charge. One later became the director; the other became a special prosecutor in a presidential investigation. Both, in my opinion, were far more focused on making sure their careers advanced on time than actually solving the case. Leads were scarce, and the FBI was under enormous political pressure to produce results. Corners were cut to make progress, and millions of dollars were poured into every imaginable investigative avenue."

She paused for a moment again, as if thinking about something. Colin pressed her, intrigued by where she was going with this. As a student of history, learning something new was often as good as the twist in a great book. He pressed her, "Ma'am?"

"Sorry. Something about all of that still throws me for a loop. In the end, the investigation was narrowed to one, Dominick Schmidt. He was a researcher in an army-grade Level 4 bioweapons lab with access to similar strains of anthrax that were used in the letters. The FBI closed in on him and overturned everything in his life to determine if it was him. In the end, the team was split. Half believed he was guilty on strong circumstantial evidence. Mainly him being one of the only researchers in the U.S. with access to the anthrax used in the attacks. The other half found the evidence to be lacking and was opposed to bringing an indictment."

Colin cut in, "I take it you were on the opposed half of the team?"

"I was. In my opinion, as a junior agent on the case, the evidence was so circumstantial it never would have held up in court to a remotely competent lawyer. But I wasn't in charge. In the end, the two agents who were in charge decided they were going to make their careers by closing the case and satisfying all the politicians involved at that point. Two dozen agents emblazoned in windbreakers with yellow letters moved in to arrest him, but there was a problem."

Colin found himself hanging on the edge of his seat. "What was it, ma'am?"

She proceeded. "Dominick Schmidt killed himself when they moved in to arrest him."

Colin felt his forehead wrinkle in surprise as his head cocked to the side. How could a man that Vladimir Alekseyev had just sold on contract to another group be dead? And more strangely, how were men's careers made off of the subject of an investigation's death? But Colin thought he knew the answer somewhere in the back of his mind. And it didn't make him feel any better thinking about it.

"How did the two agents who let a suspect die on their watch in such a high-profile case get so far?" he asked.

"Well, Snowman, as I'm sure you're aware, death tends to bring some finality to a situation. The agents in charge claimed the evidence against Schmidt was overwhelming, and the taking of his own life only proved what they were saying. They used their newfound political friends to ensure the case was closed and that it went in the win column for them. Several of my colleagues and I protested this, of course, but it didn't matter at that point. The letters had stopped, and the country wanted to put 9/11 behind them."

Everything about this story sounded strange and out of place to him. And he could feel his skin crawling. He ruffled his blonde hair in thought. Could there be two Dominick Schmidts? But even as he thought it, he knew it was too much of a coincidence. There was no way there were two of them in the world who each had a career in high-level bioweaponry.

As if sensing what he was thinking, the Director of National Intelligence spoke. "I don't think it's a coincidence that the name has come up again. But I do find it strange, and more than a bit surprised it's in the context of him being alive. From my understanding, a full autopsy was done to determine his cause of death. And he was buried not too far from here," she said, referring to her location in Washington, D.C.

After a few seconds more of thought Colin spoke. "There was a location on the job, ma'am, but no details. It looks like Schmidt was headed for Chiapas, Mexico. I think I'd better get Team Alien there ASAP to determine what's going on."

"Interesting," said the Director of National Intelligence.

"Ma'am?" Colin asked again.

"I happen to have a Special Forces team on the ground there now working on dismantling the Descanso Eterno Cartel." This surprised Colin. Not the fact that there were U.S. forces in Mexico but the fact that there was a cartel in Chiapas.

"I didn't think there were any cartels in Chiapas, ma'am. But the fact that there is has me concerned. If these two things are connected, it could mean a resurgence of the terrorist cartel relations the Agency stamped out years ago."

Now it was Wendy's turn to think. And she did so for a good long moment. "Somethings not right here. It stinks, and I don't like it. I think you need to get your team to Chiapas, and quickly. Link up with the Special Forces team on the ground there and find out if Dominick Schmidt is still alive and operating in their area of operations. All other priorities are rescinded, and Directive Star Set protocols will be assigned to your team. In the meantime, I think I have some digging to do on my end. And I'll let you know what that turns up."

Colin was pretty sure he knew what she meant by digging but left it alone. If it was gallows humor, it was well disguised and tastefully implemented by the Director of National Intelligence. Colin respected that. He also knew what Directive Star Set protocols meant, and not many people in the world knew what that was outside of tier-one Special Forces and NEST, more commonly known as Nuclear Emergency Support Teams. Directive Star Set meant that a weapon of mass destruction was likely in play and was suspected to be an imminent threat to the United States. It, in effect, cleared the board and gave Colin every resource the U.S. government had to find the threat and end it.

Colin prayed it wasn't too late.

11

The president waved to the press pool over his right shoulder as he proceeded down the White House's south lawn. The rain had given way to an unseasonably warm and humid day, reminding him that he truly did live in the middle of a swamp. Sometimes, the president wished he could wear shorts, but written somewhere deep within the decorum laws of American politics, he knew, for some reason, an American president couldn't be seen in shorts at the White House. *Perhaps this is a good trend to break for myself and all future presidents,* he thought. But he knew it was just weakness talking. Leadership meant leading by example.

He took a deep breath through his nose, letting the wet air do its best to refresh him, and knew he would reach Marine One soon. The solitary Sikorsky VH-3D stood hulking fifty yards to his front. A beautiful but ungainly-looking aircraft, it was undoubtedly one of his favorite parts of being president. Its white top gleamed in the hot morning sun while its green bottom did its best to blend with the tall fescue blend of grass that was mowed in pristine lines beneath it.

When I get to the chopper, I'll have them crank the air conditioning, he thought. Though internally, he wondered why he was sweating so much. In truth, Joyce was nervous about the men he had sent to Chiapas. They were late checking in, and being a former military man himself, he had a special affinity for all sent down range.

A report on their progress was due seven hours ago, yet still nothing came. Mack Tomlin assured him that if they missed one more check-in, the next he knew was in one hour, that they would adjust the mission of a new KH-13 reconnaissance satellite in geosynchronous orbit twenty-two thousand miles overhead to get some answers.

A few strides later, he reached Marine One and threw a salute at the marine guard, who returned it sharply as he walked up the stairs of the chopper. The temperature dropped nearly twenty degrees as soon as he was inside, and he was thankful for the crew, who always seemed to read his mind when it came to temperature control. He felt warm sweat turn to cold beads at the small of his back, and a slight shiver permeated his body as he sat down. The seat was soft and comfortable, and he was almost allowed to enjoy it for a full minute before his Chief of Staff, Bob Mylod, sat down across from him.

"In thirty minutes, you have a meeting with the mayor of Baltimore to discuss three new opportunity zones within the city limits, sir. Following that, you have a tour of the new Baltimore Washington High School, a meeting with a coalition of small business owners at a local coffee shop, and then you're going back to D.C. You're throwing out the first pitch at Nat's Park tonight. If all goes smoothly, we'll have you home and in bed by 10 p.m., depending on how late you'd like to stay at the game."

Bob picked up his phone the second he finished talking and began furiously typing on its screen.

The president's interest had peaked with the first pitch—something he had been looking forward to all week but had forgotten within the confines of the current crises.

Overhead, the rotors began to whine to life, and the crew chief, who also functioned like a navy steward, stepped to where they were sitting. "We should be in Baltimore in about twenty minutes, sir. Is there anything I can get you in the meantime?" The young marine before him was straight of back with a rigid muscular jaw that did nothing to betray his soft-spoken demeanor when he spoke to the president.

"A water would be great, Jackson; Bob will have the same."

Bob looked up momentarily with a look that said he needed a bourbon on the rocks but looked back down at his phone and continued tapping away.

"Anything from Mack on our boys?" the president asked Bob as the young marine stepped away to get them two bottles of water.

"Nothing yet, Mr. President. I'll let you know as soon as I get an update to the bat phone."

The president sighed, and he felt his stomach drop slightly as the helicopter lifted its way into the sky. The young marine returned with the waters on a tray for the president and his Chief of Staff.

"How's your mother, Jackson?" the president asked.

"Good, sir. Feeling much better. She can start physical therapy for her leg in another week—which is good because I think she's starting to make my dad a bit insane." The president took the water, smiling. The captain in him never really went away, and he still felt a personal responsibility to know the troops serving under him and their stories.

"Well, they'll both be happy to know I've given the commandant of the Marine Corps my personal recommendation for you to attend OCS when you finish your tour here. I have a feeling you'll be getting your package any day now," said the president with a wink. A boyish smile cracked the hardened stone jaw of the marine. It had been his dream for years to become an officer. Advancement in the Marine Corps wasn't easy, given its small size and spots were extremely limited.

"Thank you, sir," he said, beaming and at a loss for words.

"You've earned it," said the president proudly.

"Congrats," said Bob, looking up. He grabbed a remote off the table in front of him and flicked on the TV across from them, muttering as the marine retreated.

"What is it, Bob?" the president asked.

"Irene Kennedy," Bob responded in a somewhat defeated but unquestionably angry tone.

Irene Kennedy, the president knew, was a journalist who had been a painful thorn in the administration's side ever since the campaign. While the president preached about getting politics out of journalism and bringing the American people the facts so they could draw their own conclusions, she lambasted him at every opportunity she could purely because she didn't like his politics. A second later, the president knew why Bob was so angry. He looked at the screen and saw a special report plastered across the screen in red and an attractive brunette in a tight dress standing in a news studio surrounded by screens.

"The COVID-19 pandemic still conjures up feelings of horror in all of us, and though a few years have passed, the wounds are still far too fresh in our minds. Millions died, and millions more got sick. Experts warned us for years that a pandemic would happen, yet the folks in Washington never listened to them. Now standing here a few years after a vaccine that some in the world to this day have not yet received, most for their own ignorant reasons, and looking at an economy that has barely recovered, this reporter once again finds Washington blissfully unaware of what might come next. Experts are again warning that we must remain ever more vigilant of another pandemic. In the coming weeks, I will explore just how unprepared the United States is for a second pandemic, all culminating in the release of my new book, *America the Sick, America the Dead, Why Most Americans Will Die in the Next Pandemic*, in four weeks. You can pre-order now at—"

The president flicked the screen off in disgust. His administration had worked tirelessly with the country's major news organizations and the FCC to refine the way information was presented to Americans after a commission found that over 90 percent of Americans were so frightened and confused by the sheer number of opinions placed on news during the pandemic that most people had lost faith in an honest press at all.

The president may not have liked the press, but he knew they had a place in democracy. The American people needed to be informed, and the powerful needed to be held accountable by those who received that information. But if that chain was broken, democracy could easily falter. If Americans lost trust, then the republic could splinter into too many groups, and unity would never be achieved.

Most organizations had fallen in line as their ratings dipped and profits fell. But some were so engrossed with money and the legends of themselves that they couldn't see their own hands in front of their faces. The last thing the American people needed was a panic to fracture the new peace and unity that was starting to take hold. The president wasn't talking about silencing a reporter, but this was fear porn, plain and simple, designed to inflame the American people to boost ratings and sell books. Fine in a vacuum and isolated, but not fine on the national stage. A report on the national readiness for another pandemic was fine, but telling everyone in the country they were going to die was the same in his mind as yelling fire in a crowded theater. The country needed to heal fast before it was too late.

12

The water bottle toppled onto the side of the desk, drawing a nervous "Shit!" from Sarah Quinby. It was only her second week working in Representative Matt Locke's office, and she was momentarily terrified that she had just soaked all his mail with water. This being only her second job out of school, she was sure she was about to be fired immediately for her stupidity. But as she looked over, she saw that she had finished the water bottle minutes ago and that the bottle lay harmlessly dry on its side. She sighed with relief, looking up at the large old windows of the office and taking in the darkening sunlight that was coming through them.

The setting sun relaxed her; it was almost time to go home. A graduate of Clemson University and a native of Charleston, South Carolina, D.C., she was new to D.C., and she wasn't quite used to the ups and downs of the swampy weather. Senator Matt Locke had been appointed to replace the now disgraced and incarcerated Senator Rand.

Senator Locke was a favorite to win a proper election in another year. She liked him and found his deep blue eyes and parted blonde hair extremely attractive. He was also a veteran of the Marine Corps, and men in uniform had always caught her eye. Something her friends teased her about on their morning runs on the national mall, where a never-ending stream of uniformed bachelors jogged past.

She was quite fit herself and found rigorous exercise one of the best ways to deal with the stress of her new job. She was one of the many young schedulers working on the hill. Good-looking, well-educated, and underpaid, she had dreams of one day being in politics herself. Or at least she thought she did. After being on the hill for a few weeks now, she was pretty sure she wanted to meet more of the people she wanted to emulate before actually trying to be like them.

Her shining red hair flowed straight down a well-tailored Kate Spade dress with matching black shoes. She took a breath and reached out a well-toned and freckled arm to right the water bottle. She was just thinking about taking it down the hall to the fountain to refill it when something caught her eye.

The neat pile of mail had become slightly disheveled when the bottle had fallen on it, and a letter with childish handwriting had slipped the pile. As the scheduler, it was her duty to go through the mail and assess what Representative Locke needed to review and reply to. She usually waited until the afternoon to review the mail, but she needed the laugh a letter from a child usually provided. Her colleagues, the Chief of Staff, Alexa, and the Communications Director, Allie, had gone to get coffee and weren't at their desks nearby in the small office.

She picked up the letter addressed to Senator Locke in a childish scrawl and felt the weight of what must have been thicker card stock beneath the envelope. The senator's birthday had been last week, and she assumed that this must have been a late-arriving card. She grabbed a silver letter opener emblazoned with the Senate seal, something she had learned to do in her first week on the job to save her fingers, and slit the envelope open.

She placed the opener down and pulled the card from the envelope. A birthday cake was illustrated on the face of it, and she smiled opening it. In an instant, everything went wrong. White powder cascaded from the open card all over her exposed legs and hands. Smaller particles that she couldn't see filled her respiratory system as she gasped in surprise.

Panic filled her at the realization of what this was. They had been trained on opening mail when she was first hired a few weeks before, and white powder in the mail was never good. She felt her pulse quicken as the psychosomatic symptoms of whatever pathogen dusting her body filled her mind.

She began to sweat as she tried to get control of herself.

"Calm down," she said out loud to herself but found her voice to be shaking and faint. *Was this a symptom?* she thought desperately herself, panicking more and sending her pulse skyrocketing. She could feel it beating through her chest as if even her heart wanted to get away from the powder all over her body. She tried to calm herself but didn't know what to do. Images danced through her head of Covid victims clinging to life on ventilators in hospitals, something she had put out of her head since the pandemic had subsided. At that moment, she knew she was going to die.

She looked down at the card again, and printed in childish letters were the words:

Take Penicillin Now, Call 911.

She whimpered, and as she did, she heard a deep voice behind her.

"Sarah, are you okay?" It was the senator. She dared not turn around.

"Senator Locke, go back in your office and call the police," she said shakily, but with more command than she thought she could muster.

"Sarah, I've told you to call me Matt a hundred times; what's wrong? Are you okay?" he asked, starting to approach.

"Matt, please don't come any closer—" she tried to say, but he was there, and she could see the horror in his eyes as he took in the white powder all over her. They stood there in stunned silence for what felt like an eternity.

A sudden commotion by the door drew their attention. It was Allie and Alexa returning from their late afternoon coffee run.

"Stop!" Matt commanded as they reached the door. They both stood there, confused and alarmed at the sight of them and Matt's harsh military-like command. "Alexa, get the Capitol Police now and tell them that Sarah and I have opened a letter filled with white powder. It says take penicillin now and call 911. Allie, please close the door, step ten feet away from it, and make sure no one enters this office before the police arrive."

Alexa tried to argue, "Matt, what's—"

But Matt cut her off with a hand. "Alexa, now!"

The two did as they were instructed, and Sarah heard hurried footsteps behind the now-closed door. She was shaking and freezing cold. All she wanted to do was brush the powder off her, but she was too scared to move. She knew she should tell Matt to get out of the office to save himself, but somehow, his commanding presence was comforting to her.

"Sarah, put down the envelope and come sit down over here," he said, motioning to a couch a few feet away from her desk. She didn't move.

"A-am I going to die?" she stuttered, tears coming down her cheeks as she heard the words from her own mouth.

"Just come over here and sit down. Panicking isn't going to

make this any better," he said. But she was frozen to the spot, terrified of his non-answer to her question about her life.

"Am—am I going to die?!" she asked, now in full-blown hysterics. Tears ran in thick rivers down her cheeks now, and she was shaking so hard that the card fell from her hands on its own accord.

Matt grabbed her shoulders and turned her forcefully to the side, staring deeply into her green eyes. "I don't think so," he said. And he lingered there, looking into her tear-filled eyes. She felt he was trying to convey some of his strength to her in that glance, but she wasn't sure she was strong enough to have any of it at this moment.

He led her by the shoulders to the couch and sat her down. Rather than keeping his distance, he sat down next to her and put an arm around her like a father might to an upset child. She felt remarkable comfort in his touch, but her shaking did not stop. A sudden blaring siren in the building scared her back to crying once again, and a computerized voice came over the emergency alarm system. "Attention, attention, please evacuate the building in an orderly manner. A threat has been detected." The voice continued repeating itself.

Rather than the red lights of the fire system strobing, it was blue lights, which everyone knew meant something really bad must be going on. A moment later, a knock sounded at the door to the office. "Senator Locke? This is Commander Coyle of the Capitol Police. Ccan you hear me?" came a man's voice through the door.

"We can hear you! We're covered in white powder from an envelope. It says 'take penicillin now and call 911'!" Matt shouted back. The man outside the door took a second to respond.

"Okay, don't move and try not to panic!" the man shouted back. "We have a response team of doctors on the way who are coming in to help you. In the meantime, we need to seal the room."

Sarah felt something hot coming out of her nose, and she reached up to wipe what she assumed was snot away from her crying. When she pulled her hand away, she found it was blood, and she looked at Matt in terror.

13

The crystalline star-filled night thirty-five thousand feet above Chiapas, Mexico, was calm and clear. A small number of high cirrostratus clouds occasionally blocked the view of the billions of stars here with no light pollution on this moonless night, but that was fine. *This was perfect jumping weather*, reflected Colin staring out of the cockpit window. He had just spoken to the pilot to confirm the weather and to get a look at the night sky for himself before his team jumped out of the plane into it.

The flight had taken some twelve hours from Berlin to Chiapas, and the military had been kind enough to lend his team the massive C-17 Globe Master for the trip. It wasn't a Gulfstream, but if you had to make a HALO jump, this was a good platform from which to do it.

Halo, or high-altitude low-opening jumping, was extremely dangerous and required special equipment. Colin knew his team would be jumping from the upper limit of that, thirty-five thousand feet, and wouldn't open their parachutes until approximately eight hundred feet above the ground. It wasn't the Mexican air defense zone they were worried about. That was conveniently glitching out over the southern half of Mexico right now, thanks to Charlie and the NSA.

Star Set protocols certainly made things a bit simpler to pull off, he thought. In reality, it was the cartels that they were using a HALO jump to avoid. Over the last several years, the cartels had acquired their own air defense equipment, and though they didn't know much about the Descanso Eterno cartel, Colin was unwilling to take the chance of being shot out of the sky.

"Fifty minutes," the pilot said.

"Thanks for the lift," replied Colin, turning to leave the cockpit. He walked down a set of stairs to the main body of the plain, which was large enough to hold any combination of an M-1 main battle tank, one hundred and eighty-eight passengers, two combat Strikers, or two UH-60 Black Hawks.

Tonight, it held the combat element of Team Alien, which included Witch, Jester, Sheriff, and himself. There were also two Toyota Hilux pickup trucks which had been heavily modified and were ubiquitous in Mexico, and two pallets of equipment. One was filled with arms and ammunition; the other was filled with special equipment, including two small drones, medical supplies, several CBRN suits in case one was ripped, and equipment for the detection of chemical, biological, and nuclear weapons of mass destruction. In short, his team was taking no chances, and Special Operations Command, more specifically, the 10th Special Forces group, had been kind enough to lend them everything they needed for the mission.

"Can you check me, boss?" asked Jester, walking up in full multi-cam loadout and looking menacing. Colin barely heard him. He was still running calculations on supplies and scenarios in his head, double-checking that he had everything they needed. *And what did a cartel need with a biological weapons expert,* he asked himself for the thousandth time since yesterday. *Maybe they were working on some new kind of drug that killed the user unless they took more.* But that was stupid, he thought instantly. Dead addicts didn't make good customers. *Not to mention the guy the cartel had hired was supposedly dead. And where did this cartel get the resources to rise so quickly out of the scrum,* he asked himself. "Huh?" Colin asked Jester, turning.

"Can you check my chute, Bossman?"

"Yeah, sure. Sorry about that." Colin turned Jester around and checked all the straps that secured the parachute to him, then the actual parachute itself. It looked squared away. He then double-checked the reserve and the oxygen tank strapped to his leg. All looked well, but something inside of Colin had to mess with his teammate. "Fuck, man, that's bad. I wouldn't jump if I were you," he said.

Jester gave him the finger and then checked his. Jumping was a buddy sport. When they finished, it was time for supplemental oxygen for thirty minutes before they left the comfort of the plane. HALO carried risks, including decompression sickness, and the surest way to avoid it was breathing 100 percent oxygen for thirty to forty-five minutes to flush excess nitrogen from the bloodstream.

The minutes ticked down slowly as they did before any jump, and the questions that had swirled in Colin's mind before he started taking oxygen only increased as he thought more. Finally, the light turned red above them, and they knew it was time to go. They stood up, checking each other one last time. Colin faintly heard more joking but ignored it. Everyone secured their oxygen masks in place in the red light as the rear door to the C-130 opened slowly, and the roaring freezing air outside blasted through the breach.

Colin took a closer look at his team, noticing the half skulls were painted on the oxygen masks they had borrowed from 10th group. They all looked like wraiths in the dark red light. The light flicked green, and they all moved to jump. Colin was the last to the edge, making sure everyone got off okay before he plunged after them.

The sensation of falling out of an airplane always starts as sheer abject terror. Your stomach drops, and in a biological response baked into the human psyche for a millennium, you instantly want to reach around for something to catch you because falling from high things surely meant grievous bodily harm or death. This is especially true in the first seconds of free fall rather than static line jumps, which deploy the parachute nearly instantaneously.

Colin ignored this biological response, and in a few moments, the stomach drop subsided, and he merely felt like he was flying on a cushion of air. It was too dark looking at the ground for him to really understand that he was falling through the air at near terminal velocity heading toward imminent contact with the earth.

Colin didn't love jumping out of airplanes, but he didn't hate it either. He found the lead-up to the jump nerve-racking and the actual free fall almost relaxing. It was pure freedom, but like any freedom, getting to it was half the battle. Colin turned his wrist slightly to see the jump computer attached to his forearm. He was careful not to alter the position of his arm too much, as the slightest wrong movement could throw the free diver into an out-of-control spin. He had reached critical velocity.

The air whipped past his ears for what felt like ages, dulling his senses and sending his adrenal system into overtime to fight the urge to relax. Colin could no longer see the horizon and the stars; all he could see was black. The air had warmed in a linear correlation to his altitude, but he was too focused to notice. He needed to deploy his shoot at a thousand feet, which was rapidly approaching, to be beneath the cartel's air defense systems. He now stared at his jump computer, watching the altitude rapidly decreasing. Five thousand turned to two thousand, which finally hit his mark. He pulled the cord to deploy his shoot.

A moment later, though, nothing had happened. There was no snap back on his body as the canopy caught hold of the wind. Just a minor slowing of his descent. His parachute was jammed. His chances of survival had just dropped below 50 percent, and he was still falling under a thousand feet at near-terminal velocity.

His time was running out, and he knew it. Falling back on his training, Colin knew he needed to deploy his second parachute. He reached for the cord but couldn't find it.

He cocked his head slightly down to see what the problem was, but it was too dark to identify it. He pulled in his arms, feeling for his reserve line. This had the effect of sending him tumbling through the air, making finding the reserve line even more difficult. Colin began to grow dizzy as his tumble increased.

He estimated he had just crossed six hundred feet. This meant that he had precious few seconds to find the shoot and deploy it, or it wouldn't matter if he got it deployed. The parachute wouldn't slow him enough before impacting the ground, and he would die. His tumble worsened now as he fought to find the reserve parachute. Vomit swelled in his throat, threatening to explode out of his mouth and completely obscure his vision, a product of the dizziness from his fall.

Colin came to the sudden realization that he was about to burn in and die—which was fucked in his mind because after all the dangerous things that he had been through, to die from a parachute malfunction wasn't one of the ways he thought he was going to go. He prepared himself for the worst, fighting for control, when suddenly he made impact.

14

Chiapas Mexico

Ernesto Gomez sat down in a teak rocker on his back porch, taking in the palatial grounds of his estate. His eyes traced the line of blue stone from the porch to the infinity pool, which appeared to drop off into the ocean. The clear, star-filled sky reflected itself on the surface of the dark Pacific water. In the distance, he heard the crashing of waves and the screams of unknown animals from the jungle.

This is likely as close to heaven as I will ever get, he thought. But that was the price he paid for his family. He and his men had done awful things, and even if they had been done for good reasons, he didn't think any amount of confession to his priest would truly absolve him in God's eyes.

He took a sip of maroon liquid from a crystal goblet that he had set at his side. Ernesto had a passion for wine. The bottle of two thousand eight Penfolds Grange had been pulled specifically from the twenty thousand bottle cellar at his request this evening. It was a Shiraz from Australia, and he could taste the wine's deep cherries, the cellar, and the barrel it was aged in. *This was true luxury*, he thought. One he couldn't have even imagined a few years before. But there was one thing missing.

He pulled his phone from his pocket and initiated a FaceTime to the unknown number he had spoken with the previous evening. A few rings into the call, a beautiful eight-year-old girl, who was paler than she should have been, answered the call. "Papa?" she asked.

She had an American accent and sounded like she was from California. Ernesto had pushed her private school teachers and tutors in America to ensure she never lost. The world could treat you differently if you weren't like them—he knew that better than anyone. "Mija! How are you, sweetheart?" he asked his daughter.

She lay back on white sheets in a blue and white gown, sighing. "Tired. When can I go home?" she asked with pleading eyes.

Ernesto sighed himself. But his was not of fatigue but of extraordinary sadness. "Soon, Mija. You're doing very well, they tell me. Just a few more weeks, and you should be able to come home. And when you do, I'll buy you that pony we keep talking about."

The child looked back skeptically as if gauging whether he was lying. The dark circles under her eyes made her seem gaunt, but there was still fire in her eyes. "If you say so, Dad," she said. "Dr. Schmidt and I are watching cartoons."

This took Ernesto back a bit. He still hadn't grown used to the man that was treating his daughter. The doctor gave him the creeps.

"Hello, Mr. Gomez," said the man in a jubilant voice that was out of place in the girl's quiet wardroom. He sounded like a mix between a cheap radio DJ and one of the cartoons he was watching with his daughter.

"Hola, Dr. Schmidt. How is my lovely daughter doing?"

"Improving by the day. She should be out of here in no time."

Ernesto's daughter interrupted. "That's what you said last week," she said, only half-paying attention to the conversation now, her attention split between the man and the cartoons Ernesto could see on his phone screen. He paused for a second, taking a sip of wine and willing himself to relax in front of his daughter. A child takes cues from their parent's strength and emotional state. This was why Ernesto went to such pains to keep his work life separate from his daughter's life. Such violence could kill a child's mind as easily as their body.

He took a deep breath. "A word, Dr. Schmidt," he said into the phone.

Ernesto observed some shuffling on the screen and then saw the doctor's strange face with the ceiling moving above him as he left the room. The doctor had such large circles around his eyes and wide pupils that he looked like a raccoon. His mustache was untrimmed and out of order, as if he constantly ruffled it in thought. When the man finally stopped moving, he stared into the phone, looking bewildered.

After a moment, Ernesto said, "How is she really doing?"

Dr. Schmidt's face snapped back into order, understanding why he had been summoned from the room finally. "Well, we're lucky we got to her when we did. Her illness had progressed fairly far. But to date, all her markers are improving with the experimental treatments. I want to caution you that all of this is experimental, and while we are optimistic, we make no guarantees."

A bit of optimism grew in Ernesto's stomach at the doctor's words, but he crushed it as fast as it appeared. His face tightened in anger at the doctor's inability to give him a straight answer on the subject. "You'd better cure her, Dr. Schmidt. I have sacrificed an enormous amount to bring her to you. If you don't fix her, there will be nowhere on earth for you to hide."

Dr. Schmidt's face twisted as if calculating what to say. If there was anger, it didn't show through his insane face. Ernesto took another sip of wine, observing your deranged curiosity, which stared at him through the phone screen. "Are you threatening me, Mr. Gomez?"

"No, I'm simply telling you what will happen to you if anything happens to her."

The doctor stared back with a look of dawning comprehension. But there was no fear there. "I thought my employer made it clear what kind of relationship this would be, Ernesto, but it appears I was wrong. It doesn't sound like we'll be able to work together anymore, so I'll just stop the treatments and send the little girl back to her papa."

Ernesto panicked, knowing that they had his balls in a vice. He could not allow his daughter to die. She was the only good he had ever brought into this world. She was his legacy, and no amount of his pride could get in the way of her living. His powerful facade broke. "No, please," he said, utterly defeated. He could see no other way out of the situation.

"Well then, Mr. Gomez. It sounds like you'll be honoring the terms of our deal after all?"

There was a long pause. Ernesto hung his head in shame and abject defeat. All manner of liquid courage evaporating, he said, "Yes. I will do as you've asked."

"Excellent! Well, you have a lot of work to do in order to live up to the terms of our deal, so I will let you get back to it. In the meantime, we'll get Louisa all fixed up and back to you in a jiff. That is, of course, once you have satisfied your terms of the deal."

Ernesto nodded his head slowly.

"Wonderful. Well, you have a nice day now," said Dr. Schmidt.

"Wait. Let me say goodnight to my daughter, please."

"Of course, of course, Mr. Gomez. I'm not a monster. You can say goodnight to your daughter."

The screen began to blur as the doctor returned to the room. Ernesto knew damn well that the man on the other end of the phone was exactly what he claimed not to be.

15

Pacific Ocean, Off the Coast, Chiapas Mexico

The MH-60S Knighthawk flared its rotor and settled over the back of the Arleigh Burke-class destroyer named McRaven. A tribute to a recently retired special warfare admiral, the brand-new Flight III design had the latest in stealth, laser defense, experimental launchers for hypersonic missiles, and a rail gun. The ship had been completing sea trials in the Pacific Ocean when the Star Set Protocol went out, and being the closest naval vessel, the McRaven was tasked to provide support. Sarah Gonzalez had spent time on ships like this in her previous job as a support officer for DEVGRU, but it had been over two years since her last stint onboard a navy ship. The ear protection clamped tightly to the side of her head did its best to block out the steady thumping of the rotors as the chopper prepared to land on the back of the guided missile destroyer, but they could only do so much.

Looking to her left, she saw Charlie, Team Alien's hacker, looking exceptionally green as the helicopter buffeted against the rough Pacific Ocean crosswinds and tried to steady itself for landing. "You okay?" she said through the microphone attached to her ear protection.

"Well, I don't like helicopters, and I get seasick. So, I'm doing great. How about you?" he replied sarcastically. Sarah almost laughed out loud. But held it in because she could see how miserable he was.

"When we touch down, go to the railing and stare at the horizon. It will help to steady you. Then, when you're done being a girl, come inside, and I'll give you a shitload of Dramamine."

Charlie looked back at her miserably and tucked his chin into his throat like he was trying to hold down vomit. As if in answer to his prayers, Sarah felt the helicopter touchdown on the rear of the destroyer a second later. Sarah watched in amusement as Charlie knocked the crewman over, who had just slid open the side door to the aircraft in a race to get to the side of the ship and throw up. She took her headphones off and got out the side door of the aircraft just in time to see the crewman getting back to his feet.

"What's his problem?!" the young sailor yelled at her over the sounds of the aircraft powering down.

"He gets seasick."

"He just got here," replied the sailor incredulously.

Sarah shrugged her shoulders as if to say, "Yeah, no clue."

"Ma'am," she heard from behind her. She turned to see a handsome lieutenant with walnut-colored skin and blue eyes. "My name is Lieutenant Potter, U.S. Naval Intelligence. I'm to be your liaison to the McRaven while you're onboard. Our orders are to give you full access. If you follow me, we can get you set up in the ops center; the crew is at your disposal."

Sarah weighed this for a moment before responding, "Negative, Lieutenant. We'll need a private area to set up our equipment with a direct link to the ops center." Sarah knew that they would have, in all likelihood, been safe to operate in the open on a navy ship, but she was paranoid. Team Alien's specialty was counterintelligence, and she had seen far too many seemingly innocuous situations exploited. Paranoia was an occupational hazard. But that was only part of the coin. The truth was they worked much more efficiently as a small unit. It kept them free of the rampant bureaucracy and decision chains in government and the military. They could maintain this independence and call in the big guns when needed. It kept them nimble and powerful.

"Ma'am, we can get you set up in our second helicopter garage back here. Since we're just finishing trials, we still don't have the second aboard yet. It's got a direct link into ship systems, and it's private. I'll have some temporary tables and chairs brought up, and the captain will be down within the hour to greet you. He's being briefed by PACCOM." The lieutenant paused as if being interrupted. The aircraft engines had powered down to a point where he could hear Charlie retching over the side of the ship. He stared for a moment before saying, "I'll get a corpsman as well."

"That would be very helpful. Thank you, Lieutenant," Sarah said, looking at Charlie with a mild amount of amusement. Sometimes it was impressive how poor people did on boats. She stared for a minute more before looking back at the lieutenant, who hadn't moved. "Is there anything else I can do for you?" she asked.

The lieutenant paused a second before answering like he was about to say something inappropriate. "Is it true there's a WMD in play, ma'am?" he asked. *Word travels fast,* Sarah thought. But they would all need to find out eventually.

"We think so, Lieutenant. We don't have specifics yet, but I'll have a briefing for senior officers once we contact our team on the ground."

The lieutenant went quiet, and all color seemed to vanish from his face at the realization that whatever he had heard might, indeed, be very real.

Moments later, the lieutenant had dashed off, and Sarah had a good feeling that what they needed to set up would be delivered promptly. She walked over to Charlie, who was hanging his head over the railing of the ship. He was breathing shallowly, staring at the water below. She patted him soothingly on the back. "Look at the horizon, buddy. You'll be fine in a bit."

He coughed again and slowly looked up toward the sky, wiping his mouth while he did so. "It must have been the food last night," he said, slowly trying to recover.

"Some people just aren't meant for boats, Charlie."

"I've only been on the boat for about five minutes," he said.

"Some people really aren't meant for boats," she replied with a smile.

"Any word on the team?" he asked, his breath normalizing.

Sarah returned to the present, remembering that they hadn't checked in on schedule three hours ago. Not something completely out of the normal, but not something that made her feel overly comfortable as well. Her smile vanished. "Nothing yet. Let's get comms set back up fully, then start to worry. It could always be our side of things."

Charlie gave her a look. "That's only ever happened once in D.C., and I've closed all of those holes." He stood a little straighter now, the tech talk seeming to break his nausea streak. A commotion behind them drew their attention. "Looks like we've got a new home," he said.

Sarah looked back. "Just about time to go hunting again."

16

Chiapas, Mexico

If this was death, it was not what Colin was expecting. His ribs hurt like hell, and it was black and quiet. *Perhaps this is hell,* he thought for a moment as his mind cleared. That, however, didn't seem to make sense to his dazed mind. No, something had hit him really fucking hard, and by some miracle, he was now floating safely but rapidly toward the ground. He shook his head, trying to clear the cobwebs from the brief knockout, and swallowed vomit back down his throat.

"You owe me one, Snowman," Colin heard in his ear. It was Jester's voice.

"I thought you checked my chute, asshole!" he shot back, not truly angry but desperately happy to be alive.

"Yeah, I guess that's why I had to play Superman. That, and command doesn't really suit me. I'm not really the anti-social brooding type."

Colin was about to reply when he noticed how close he was to the ground. His senses were starting to come back, but he was still a little slow. He flared the parachute, pulling at cords to his left and right, and it slowed his descent long enough for him to touch down and remain standing. A moment later, he had freed himself of the parachute and was balling it up to hide. They couldn't take the parachutes with them as they would just slow them down, which meant they either needed to be burned or buried.

"Team, this is lead stash chutes and rally on my position." He heard three rogers in return and stashed his own under some nearby rocks.

"Death Star, this is Snowman. We are on the ground. Requesting sitrep," he said into his mic. He gritted his teeth slightly, having to call them Death Star. Charlie had bothered them for a codename for their command unit for months following their compromise in Washington, D.C., and Colin had finally caved to appease him. It wasn't that Colin didn't enjoy *Star Wars*. It was more that Charlie had been so adamant in picking the nerdiest call sign ever.

Even if Colin admitted to himself begrudgingly, it actually sounded kind of cool saying it out *loud*. He pulled a tablet from his pack and put it on his lap. When he opened it, a map appeared with the location of their two care packages of gear that had been dropped with them. It would be about a mile hike to get to them in the deep rainforest. Not a surprise, Colin figured his free fall hadn't put them precisely on course.

A moment later, Colin repeated his call for a sitrep but got nothing in return. *Fucking trees,* he thought. Colin had luckily come down in a small clearing, one of several the team had identified throughout their drop area. The Lacandon Jungle was one of the largest rainforests in North America. It was also a huge target for illegal loggers and others exploiting its natural resources.

The team had studied satellite imagery to find recently running illegal logging operations to locate clearings to parachute into. Colin was standing in one such clearing now. *Luckily,* he thought. Having to cut himself out of a hundred-and-fifty-foot tree and climb down was not how he had wanted to start this mission. Then again, his parachute malfunctioning wasn't exactly how he planned it either.

The trees were likely interfering with their communications, and until they could get a drone up to relay their comms to the ship off the coast, they would likely be in the dark. *One problem at a time,* Colin thought. It would be light in two hours, and they needed to locate their gear and hide themselves before they became easy targets. Colin flipped down his four monocled GPNVG-18-night vision goggles from his Ops-core FAST helmet and scanned the area.

Something he should have done as soon as he landed, but he'd give himself the small break after his mid-air collision had rattled his brain around.

Someone was walking in his direction through the trees. It was either a very kitted-out enemy or one of his guys. Colin trained the IR laser on his Sig Spear rifle on him, and the man, without even looking up, gave him a wave and then a middle finger. *Jester,* thought Colin. A bad guy who wasn't wearing night vision wouldn't have been able to see the laser, and a bad guy that was would have ducked or started shooting. The middle finger also helped to confirm the identity of the approaching man.

A few moments later, Jester joined him at the edge of the clearing, looking only a little worse for wear. "Thanks for the assist," Colin said, pointing upward.

"My fault. Happy we made it work."

"Witch and Sheriff are approaching from the south."

Five minutes later, the team had met and was off heading west toward their equipment. The jungle had grown thick as soon as they had left the clearing behind. The elevations were even more surprising, even if they had seen the topographical lines on the maps before they had jumped. The Chiapas portion of the Lacandon Jungle was centered on a series of deep valleys flanked by the eastern mountains, rivers, and the ocean. Much of the forest was part of the Montes Azules Biosphere Reserve—which carried heavy penalties for logging, up to and including planting three thousand trees. Judging by the clearings they had jumped into, the loggers were doing just fine. But Colin was sure policing one point nine million Hectares wasn't exactly easy.

It took them forty-five minutes to make it the mile to their equipment. The noise in the nighttime jungle was immense—a mixture of monkeys, growls, and other unidentified wildlife. The journey was an exercise in contrast within the rainforest. They had found more clearings flanked by seemingly untouched rainforest. But the most surprising thing was where their equipment had touched down. It lay nestled within a patchwork of ruins flanked by dense vegetation.

Vines and shrubbery covered much of it, but apart from that, it looked to be untouched by human hands. While his team went about checking the two pallets, both about fifty feet from each other, Colin checked out the ruins under the guise of security. Random stone walls that must have been hundreds, if not thousands, of years old rose from the forest floor. No roofs covered anything, but some of the walls and stone ground had strange markings on them. The markings looked like some kind of ancient language scrawled into the eroding stone.

Colin knew the Lacandon was famous for its Mayan ruins sites, like the Bonampak and the Yaxchilan. He had read about both on Wikipedia, but Colin was always a student of history. Everything about it fascinated him. One of the more intriguing things he had read was that supposedly hundreds of undiscovered sites were buried in vegetation throughout the massive jungle. Colin suspected this might be one of them.

He flipped up his night vision goggles as the morning light was beginning to make them irrelevant. There was no sun yet, but it was easy enough to see clearly now. He turned, wanting to continue checking out the site, but something caught his eye without his night vision on. He approached a wall that had a small outcropping on top. Colors were peeking out from underneath a dense thicket of vines.

Carefully, he began removing them, wanting to see what was underneath. It took him a few moments to get them down, and when he did, he had to step back. Beneath was a moderately well preserved mural on the wall. It took Colin a second to grasp the meaning behind it. It appeared to be depicting some kind of human sacrifice, judging by the headless human over an altar and the clear red marks. Some brown on top of the red made Colin wonder if the painter had also used real blood.

A few moments later, Colin tore his eyes away from the ominous mural and tried to bring his mind back into the present. The walk and the history had helped to clear his head, but he still had a mild headache from his rescue. He began to check out the rest of the ruins, placing small cameras from his pack as he went around. This would have to serve as their supply stash for now until more suitable accommodations could be found. The cameras would serve as added eyes due to their lack of manpower. He entered another area flanked by stone steps. As he walked, he saw a small eroded stone pillar about waist height in the middle of the area. The top was brown, and the stone didn't match the others. Judging by the pattern, the stone looked to have been stained by blood long ago.

An ominous feeling in Colin's gut returned. He heard buzzing as the team launched a drone some twenty yards away. This was the alter from the mural. Colin just hoped it wasn't a sign of things to come. A sudden snapping to his right told him he might be wrong. *Shit,* he thought, *Gunfire.*

17

The president took a bite of the hot dog and savored the flavor. Ketchup and raw onions were his preferred toppings. He washed it down with a sip of Miller Light just in time to see the Nationals hit a line drive down the second plate and finally get their first run of the game. He cheered with the rest of the crowd. The sun was just setting behind the stadium, and the bright game lights combined with the brilliant orange swirls in the sky created a truly serene night. The temperature had even cooled down from the unseasonably hot day, making it into a truly special night. This was one of the times he felt like a normal person.

Normal except for the hundreds of Secret Service agents and personnel surrounding him, most dressed like fans. There was also the fact that he was sitting conveniently next to a ground-floor exit with even more bodyguards and his convoy of vehicles close to that. There were staff who wanted him to throw out the first pitch and leave, but President Joyce didn't like his motorcade moving around during rush hour. It was unfair to all the hard-working people in D.C. who just wanted to get home to see their families.

That and he loved sports. Any opportunity he got as president to go to a game was one he took, and he usually had a TV he brought into the Oval Office when he worked late at night so he could catch a game. His first pitch had been surprisingly good as well. Well, *at least I hadn't embarrassed myself,* he thought.

"Smile, Bob, and enjoy the game. What a perfect night. We don't get to do this often," he said to his Chief of Staff seated next to him. Bob was furiously typing away on his phone as per usual.

"Whatever you say, Mr. President," Bob replied, not even looking up from his phone.

Some people don't know how to relax, the president thought. He turned to Wendy, who was wearing a pink Nationals hat and looked to be enjoying herself. "Any updates?"

Wendy had been trying to hide that she was also checking her phone constantly, but she at least looked up and tried to take in some of the game. "Nothing of consequence yet, Mr. President."

The trouble in Chiapas wasn't far from the president's mind, but he found that he needed occasional distractions to keep his mind sharp. Not even the president could be on twenty-four hours a day.

"Wendy, try to relax. I'm sure you'll be updated if—" He stopped short as a sudden calamity erupted around him. Everywhere, Secret Service agents sprang into action. Leaping up and surrounding him in a wall of Nationals jerseys, weapons drawn, eyes scanning the crowd. Two agents bracketed him through the scrum, one being his lead agent, Tom Corrigan. The man wasted no time grabbing him by the collar, yanking him up, and pulling him out of the row.

"Mr. President, we need to go right now. There's a serious threat," Tom said, pulling him around the corner and into a tunnel. They were running now, and agents formed around his left and right as they sprinted toward the waiting vehicles.

"What the hell is going on?" William tried to say, but the agents ignored him in full protection mode.

When they reached the presidential limousine referred to as the beast a moment later, the door was already open, and they pushed him in Tom right behind him before the door was slammed and the massive vehicle jolted forward. "What's going on?" the president asked again, slightly out of breath and trying to regain his composure.

"Mr. President, there's been some kind of biological incident at the Capitol. We're moving you to Camp David immediately," replied Tom. Then he placed his finger to his ear and said, "Move to alternate extraction one. Bring in the helos. Initiate chain protection and containment protocols."

"Tom, take me to the White House; I'm not leaving the city in a state of panic."

"I'm sorry, Mr. President. We need to sweep the place for contaminants, and that's going to take the rest of the night. We need to get you to a safe location outside of the city to protect the continuity of government until we have a handle on the situation."

William sat there stunned as the vehicle made erratic turns, moving to some unknown location. They were turning back into Navy Yard by the looks of it and heading toward shipping containers. He remembered the place from doing campaign speeches there before. It was a bar next to Nat's Park called the Bullpen and was a large outdoor venue for concerts and drinking. They made another turn on a street blocked off to pedestrians and pulled up to the entrance, which was just a hole in the shipping containers.

"If you're going to haul me out of here, make sure Wendy and Bob also make it there. Get Mack Tomlin to Camp David as well."

"Wendy and Bob are in the car behind us, sir. I'll make sure Mack gets there as well. They'll be on the next bird out. People were running out of the bullpen now, looking drunk, confused, and scared. Suddenly, he heard thumping overhead. It was Marine One coming into land in the gap between the shipping containers, which was impressive but also downright dangerous at the speed the chopper was moving.

"Hold here one moment, Mr. President. We need to deploy the mobile landing pad."

"Any updates from the Capitol?" the president asked.

"We're hearing Anthrax, but information is spotty at best at the moment. The Capitol Police are only just getting a handle on the situation."

The president was stunned. What the hell was happening? He knew Star Set Protocols were in place, but they thought it was still early, and they had the chance to intercept any attack before it reached the United States. Were they in the middle of it right now? If so, his administration had failed in its solemn duty to protect the American people, possibly worse than on 9/11.

"Choppers ready, sir. Let's move," Tom said as the door to the beast flew open, and he was rushed out of it. He ran to Marine One surrounded by Secret Service agents with their weapons drawn, the rotor wash flinging empty beer cans and cups around the outdoor bar. The president briefly caught a look at one of the giant screens overhead playing scenes from him being rushed out of the game and a headline saying *Breaking News: Nationals Park Is Being Evacuated.*

He reached the helicopter and was pushed into a seat, with five agents following and taking seats around him. He had barely sat down before the helicopter began lifting off into the twilight. When they got high enough, William saw Marine Two landing to pick up his staff while Marine Three formed up with One to help protect it in the event of the attack. They didn't wait for Marine Two as they flew north to Camp David.

"What the hell happened, Tom? I need information!"

"We're not sure, sir, but there looks to have been a biological attack on the Capitol."

18

The team clearly heard the shots, too, because, in seconds, he saw them charging toward the low stone walls of the ruins to get to cover. Colin sprinted the twenty feet to where Sheriff was and peered out behind the wall.

"Everyone stay down and do not engage until I give the say so. We don't know what we're dealing with here, and I don't want us in the middle of anything," he said into his mic. The sound of an engine—*or possibly two,* thought Colin—could be heard whining in the distance. Followed by what was unmistakably a fifty-caliber machine gun cutting through the air.

Colin pulled a set of binoculars from a pouch on his experimental Mithril body armor vest and watched the top of the ridge line. The seconds took what felt like an eternity before Colin suddenly saw three figures running for their lives appear running toward them. Colin trained the optics on them and was surprised. He knew the man leading the way. With no time to spare, Colin spotted the old Jeep coming over the top of the hill. A gunner at the back began to pivot the fifty caliber toward the men.

"Witch, kill that gunner now," said Colin to the team's best marksman. A second later, the gunner's head exploded in a cloud of pink mist just as he got the first shot off. The men sprinting toward them paused in surprise. Colin stood up from his perch and put both of his fingers in his mouth, whistling as loud as he could. The sprinting men turned back toward him just as the driver's head exploded with another crack, and the Jeep went careening into a nearby tree. Not wasting another second, the men sprinted toward them and jumped behind the wall where they were hunkered down.

The leader of the men stared at Colin like he had seen a ghost, all the color gone from his face. "Frost?" he said between haggard breaths. "I thought you were dead."

"I thought you were in a wheelchair ,Grinch," Colin replied.

The man smiled, pulling up his pant leg for his old teammate. "Miracle of prosthetics. Apparently, I cost too much for the army to put out to pasture. That doesn't explain how you were worth enough for the army to bring back to life because I was always a better shot."

"Listen, this reunion is great and all, but first things first. What the hell are we dealing with behind you?"

"One other Jeep and about ten more guys on foot. The rest we either killed or lost in the jungle."

With no time to spare, Colin relayed instructions to his men. "Jester, get the LAW and take out that next vehicle. Witch, ten more guys are going to come over that hill. We're going to take them out. Sheriff. See to these guys—" Before he could finish, Colin spotted a man with an AK-47 emerging from behind a low wall of the ruin twenty yards behind him. Before he could get his weapon up, a streaking missile of brown fur closed the gap to the man in less than three seconds and leaped from the ground to his neck. In another three seconds, the man was on the ground, attempting to scream as the dog tore his throat apart with a series of vicious bites and snarls.

Colin looked at Grinch. "The fur missiles ours. We'll secure the rear while you deal with the guys to the front," he said, standing up and moving toward the dog. Colin nodded and turned, pivoting to his knee and raising his rifle. He sighted a target and centered the reticle on the man's head. Pressing the trigger, he watched as the bullet missed wide three feet to the right of the man's head. *Shit, optics must have gotten knocked out of whack on the jump in,* he thought. He re-centered the optic to the man's left and pressed the trigger again. This time he was rewarded with death as the man's head snapped backward and tumbled to the earth.

Within ten minutes, the team had cleaned up the rest of the resistance and launched a handheld UAV to keep an eye out for more. It was now time for a proper conversation between old friends.

"Do you want to explain to me how you're not dead?" Grinch asked Colin. He thought about this for a moment. The last time Grinch had seen Colin was in Kandahar when their teams had been deployed several years before. Colin and Grinch had become fast friends and had spent months playing video games and hitting targets together, living the Gucci life in some of the worst areas in the world. When Colin's brother had gone missing, presumed dead, back home, and his last familial link to the world had been severed, Colin had been quietly recruited onto the Echo Teams, and his death had been faked on a nighttime operation to capture an HVT.

Interestingly enough, this had been the first time he'd been recognized since his new life began.

Colin decided to tell the truth. "For all intents and purposes, I am dead, and you're imagining this. I really can't say more than that for now, except that we were sent in on Star Set protocols to figure out why a cartel hired a biological weapons expert from a Russian talent broker."

Grinch raised his eyebrows. "Woah, spooky. That's some

black ops shit if I've ever heard it. Except we've got one problem. I just lost half my team when an allegedly solid asset just betrayed us to a group we thought were supposed to be friendly to us to take out that same cartel's leadership. So, you're going to need to explain to me what the fuck we're in the middle of and how a textbook Special Forces mission now has WMDs involved in it."

"Honestly, I don't know yet. We stumbled onto this from the Russian angle and came to find out more, but it sounds like we should team up to get some answers on what the hell is going on here," replied Colin.

Grinch smiled in a pained sort of way. "As long as we can get some revenge, we're fine with that. But we get to put the bullet in the assholes head who did this."

"Fine with me. But we have no idea who or where the leadership of the cartel is. We were hoping the indigenous group would have teamed up with you all when we got on the ground, and we'd have some intel. What was your backup plan in the event the CML didn't pan out as a partner to take out the cartel?" asked Colin.

Grinch shrugged. "Wait for the Spooks to find some cartel sites when their satellites get overhead. Hit them, possibly make it look like another cartel to draw out a lieutenant who knows something, capture them, and politely ask questions until we figure out who leads them and where they are. Then storm said location, kill everyone there, and send said leader directly to the afterlife."

Colin's eyes widened at the plan. But the more he thought about it, the more it made some kind of insane sense. Satellites should be overhead now and should give them at least some idea of something to hit. Making the cartel think it was another one was an interesting point. If they could, they might cause enough chaos to encourage them to make some mistakes.

They needed to jump their way up the chain of command if they wanted to get to the route of the issue quickly. Also, it was their only current option on the table unless Charlie and the spooks located something quickly. Causing chaos would also have the benefit of the cartel moving pieces of its operation around, which would help the spooks to pinpoint their nexus more quickly. *It just might work, Colin* thought.

19

Chiapas Mexico

E rnesto Gomez sat behind the well-appointed mahogany desk of his first-floor home office. Bermuda shudders veiled the view of the ocean enough to make one forget they were at a beachfront paradise. This was very much intentional. *One could hardly be expected to work with paradise outside,* Ernesto thought. A cup of coffee sat next to him, imported from a farm that he owned in Columbia. Coffee was one of his great pleasures in life, next to alcohol, and a bad cup was not one of the things that he was willing to tolerate.

The office was an exercise in contrast. On one wall, hundreds of leather-bound volumes decorated a handsome bookshelf. Leather smoking chairs, a red oriental carpet, and various knick-knacks that wouldn't have been out of place at an exclusive members-only club in Downton London rounded out the look. But Ernesto had never opened any of the books. The two large Apple Studio Displays on his desk received far more action than the literature, and several iPads lying around the room ate up the rest of his time there. Ernesto didn't allow smoking or drinking by himself or his lieutenants in this office. This was a place of business.

Ernesto took a sip of coffee, savoring the taste of the beans, dark chocolate, and smoke; he thought and scrolled his news feed. The Americans were in an uproar. Not one, not two, but three congressmen, all who had voted for the aggressive drug measures in Congress, had received anthrax-riddled letters. The American Capitol building was completely locked down as their authorities investigated.

The fact that the letters had made it through at all was a small miracle. When Ernesto's masters had demanded his assistance, he had first balked. "What difference do new American laws make," he had asked. "They don't enforce the ones they have, and posturing from some new administration never leads to anything anyway." But they had the trump card, and the anthrax had been their idea. One simple reference to his little girl was all it had taken to strip the last shreds of resistance from him. *This deal is getting worse all the time*, he thought.

The deal, which had started innocently enough, was both the start of Ernesto's and Descano Eterno's meteoric rise to the top of the cartel scrum. Ernesto had been a high-ranking lieutenant in a Sonora-based cartel that was in the process of erupting in the wake of its leader's death. Several higher-ranking members than him were in a desperate struggle for control. Ernesto had taken a back seat with the death of his wife and his young daughter's illness when he was approached by a mysterious organization that offered him the answers to all his prayers. They would pay for the most high-end experimental treatments for Louisa from the best doctors in the world that weren't available to the general public. In exchange, Ernesto would relocate and, with the capital they provided, start a new organization.

He was to acquire the product and build distribution channels and large networks to smuggle his wares into the United States. "What's the catch?" Ernesto had asked. A 30 percent profit share had been the catch, in addition to agreeing to help them with certain other unspecified activities. Ernesto had been skeptical, but his daughter's health was failing, and he was a desperate man. In the end, his resistance broke down, and he agreed.

That was three years ago, and his daughter was still alive, which was more than he could have hoped for. He had also built one of the largest cartels in Mexico and become quite rich in the process. Louisa had been home with him for a time, but six months ago, her doctors had approached him with a new treatment, one that might be able to permanently cure her rather than have her just survive between treatments.

He had agreed, and she was sent to a hospital with a location that he didn't know due to security reasons. It became very clear to him shortly after she left that this was partially a tactic of control by his backers. A reminder that they were in charge, and he worked for them. All attempts to locate his daughter had failed, and his backer's requests kept growing as the months passed. But he still had hope. His daughter looked better every call, and according to the reports he received, she was improving every day.

Ernesto took another sip of coffee. It had cooled with his thoughts. He pressed a button on his desk and requested another from the kitchen. Getting the letters into the Capitol had been quite easy. The cartel had made a huge business out of the wide-open American border. Sneaking migrants across it was a growing source of revenue for them. One of the contracted cleaning services for the post office that handled Congress's mail had a taste for cheap labor from illegal immigrants. One of these immigrants had snuck the envelopes into the mail cart post-security inspection under threat to her family's life. She had also died in a car accident after work that day. *Once you start doing business with us, you're never off the hook. Shame, though,* Ernesto thought.

A FaceTime call brought him back; it was Louisa. He answered eagerly, "Hello, Mij—" but stopped when he saw Dr. Schmidt's face.

"Hello, Mr. Gomez. I'm sorry if you thought it was your daughter," the man said too jubilantly.

"What can I help you with, Dr. Schmidt?" Ernesto responded in a strained way.

"Do you want your daughter to die, Ernesto?"

"What did you say to me?" El Jefe asked, his anger growing.

"It's just if you want us to keep her alive, cure her. In fact, I would think you would be doing everything in your power to accomplish the tasks you're being provided?"

"I have accomplished them. And if you ever threaten me or my daughter's life again, I'll cut off your—" Ernesto started, but the doctor cut him off.

"Don't shoot the messenger, Mr. Gomez. Especially not when if he stops treating your daughter, she will die immediately!" he said with a deranged smile. "Now, you were supposed to be testing our new cocaine out on your customer base quietly. Why have you stopped these tests?"

Ernesto frowned. "Because all the customers died. Whatever you gave them killed them. And killing off my customers is bad for business. Is bad for your bottom line."

Dr. Schmidt smiled as if contemplating what he had said, but only in the way a lunatic contemplates an insane action. "Did we tell you to stop testing the batches on your customers?"

"No, but—"

"Ah, you see, that's the problem right there! You didn't do what you were told. Now either resume the tests and do what you were instructed, or I'll have to stop doing what I was told and stop curing your daughter."

Ernesto didn't say anything. He was trying to control his anger. He didn't know what they were doing to the drugs that were killing his customers, but he knew the argument resulted in the death of his daughter. He was one of the most powerful men in his corner of the world, and he could do nothing against this lunatic doctor or his associates. It wasn't even like he could go to authorities for help finding his daughter. Being a cartel boss had its pros and cons. "Fine, I will resume the testing, but the more of my customers you kill, the more it hurts your bottom line. And what of this American Special Forces team hiding in the jungle?"

"Ah! Happy you asked, Mr. Gomez! We're pleased to inform you that we killed all of them yesterday, and our sources in the American military will let us know if any more are on their way."

This stopped Ernesto in his tracks for a second. The American Special Forces were elite troops with mythical status across the world. This man's organization had killed them so easily? The mystery deepened in his mind around who these people really were. Sources in the American military were hard to come by, especially ones placed close to their Special Forces and intelligence operations. He tried not to let his surprise show. "Good, please inform me if more come into the area."

Ernesto had put together close to one hundred of his cartel's soldiers to fight the American team sent to the jungle when they had informed him they were coming. Now he found out they had been eliminated. It was good but disturbing. "Please let me speak to my daughter now, Dr. Schmidt."

"Unfortunately, she's unavailable at the moment, Mr. Gomez. However, I have a feeling that by the time you resume testing the drugs on your customers, she will be ready for a nice long chat with you! Now, you have an excellent day, Ernesto, and I'm sure we'll talk soon!"

The doctor hung up on him, leaving him sitting there like a petulant child. He picked up his coffee mug and hurled it across the room at the wall, where it shattered into a thousand pieces, leaving the coffee to drip down his wall. He then swallowed his pride, picked up his phone, and sent a message to resume testing the drugs.

20

"Snowman, this is Death Star. Do you copy?"

"I read you, Death Star; good to hear your voice!" said Colin with a sigh of relief. He was starting to get worried that the drone would never get high enough to relay its signal to the destroyer.

"Snowman, please provide a status update," came Sarah's voice through his headset.

"Death Star, we've linked up with what's left of the Green Berets on the ground. The CML betrayed them and killed most of their team. We've made contact with the enemy pursuing them and have destroyed them. We're requesting targeting packages off the new satellite imagery so we can start hitting targets down here. Has the bird made a pass yet?"

"Copy, Snowman. The bird has made a pass. We've started pulling apart the photos and have several sites that may be of interest to you," replied Charlie.

"Good, copy. Please send the packages through to my tablet."

"Snowman, we have a few updates for you as well. Several attacks were just carried out in the Capitol, targeting various congressmen who voted for the new Drugs Act. Three separate congressmen that we know of received what we believe to be anthrax-laced letters, and it gets weirder. The notes in the letter were the exact same as the ones received shortly after 9/11 in the attacks Wendy Simons worked on. No one died yet, but the ones affected are in bad shape."

Colin sat down against one of the walls of the ruins that was their temporary home. As he sat, he felt the pain in his ribs from where he'd been hit during descent. *How is it even possible for anthrax-laced mail to make it through the screeners, especially at the Capitol, Colin thought?* He knew that post 9/11 eleven, the Postal Service had ramped up security and screened for common mail contaminants by default. *Congress had to have even more stringent security measures, didn't they?*

"What does Wendy have to say about this?"

"Ah, nothing at the moment. Key government staff has been isolated, and the president has been flown to Camp David until they can get a handle on what exactly is going on. It's going to take another hour to get everyone settled and the lines of communication flowing smoothly again," replied Charlie.

Colin knew they were running out of time to act. Things were evolving far faster than they had believed possible. But they were still so blind. There was no way to know if they would stumble their way into a trap from an enemy that was clearly three steps ahead. For all the vagueness surrounding them like the fog of war, Colin knew the best thing to do was to keep moving forward. Inaction killed, especially in war.

Charlie broke Colin's thoughts. "I have a thought on what you should do next. Cartels are somewhat predictable when it comes to their business practices. Especially when it comes to their supply side. Surrounding you within the Lacandon Jungle are three separate cocaine processing sites it looks like the cartel is using. If Descanso is similar to other cartels, those sites will be inspected randomly, every day or every other day at different times. This ensures that if anyone gets any bright ideas about stealing from them, an independent outside observer always shows up at random to catch them. It's usually a lieutenant from the enforcement side of the cartel organization. Given how close these sites are to where we think their headquarters is located, you might get lucky and grab someone of consequence if you can sit on those spots."

Colin thought about this. It was better than what they had been thinking. But they would still need to make it look like it wasn't them. The cartel thought the Special Forces soldiers were dead. And as far as they knew, there wasn't a second team on the ground. If the cartel expected that there was, they would likely ramp up their security and make things far more difficult.

Colin also knew they would likely need to split up to hit at least two of the sites at once. That meant a four-man team and a three-man team with the dog. If the sites had more than twenty guards apiece, they could be in way over their heads very quickly, and with no air support and no EXFIL locations for a chopper to land, they would likely be killed.

"That's good thinking, Charlie."

Sarah chimed in. "I'm having the McRaven launch three predator drones to give us near real-time on the three locations, but I'm warning you they're not authorized to carry ordinance, and the ship only has one more drone onboard. So, if you don't move quickly, we'll need to start replacing one drone at a time, which will leave you blind spots."

"Copy. We'll review the targeting packages and keep you updated on our plan. Please advise when the drones are in place over the targets and route their feed to my tablet as well. And Sarah?"

"Yes, Snowman?" she replied.

"See what you can do about getting that fourth predator

armed. I have a feeling we're going to need some more firepower."

"You got it, Snowman."

"Snowman out," Colin said. He took a sip of cool water from his camel's back. The humidity of this jungle made D.C., where he grew up, seem like Alaska. He was starting to think that he might prefer the dry heat of the Middle East but thought this place had a certain natural beauty that was rare in the world these days. *I'd kill for one of those German Pilsners right now,* he thought. High above him, a monkey screamed. It was an ugly scream that couldn't help but make him feel uncomfortable. Like there was something that they weren't seeing in all of this. And that thought disturbed him. Colin stood up, having enjoyed his break long enough, as Jester walked up.

"Let's go kill some bad guys, Jester."

21

Argentina

Colonel Sigfried Himmler walked through the doors of the non-assuming office building at the base of the village. He wore a suit instead of his uniform this morning; they never wore their uniforms during the light of day, even on the month of Hitler's birthday. Though the SS had vetted every person who lived in the village, they all lived there by choice, and it was nearly impossible to get within ten miles of the Austrian-modeled town; they still didn't like taking chances during the day. The one exception was their highest political holiday of all, which was Hitler's birthday on April 20th.

The town, in fact, was modeled after the ceremonial founding town of the Nazi party, Berchtesgaden. Where Hitler had commanded the SS to wage a guerrilla war in the event of the Nazi defeat in World War Two. The high mountain town was stunning. Sigfried had visited twice before on missions in Europe. A blonde woman at the front desk greeted him and asked for his identification and destination. Sigfried waved his palm over a scanner, and the NFC chip embedded under his skin provided her with his identity.

"I'm here to see Minister Wagner." She looked up at him and smiled, impressed. Most women found it difficult to secure a husband in the New Reich. Licenses for marriage took time, and they could only marry outside citizens if the SS deemed them of pure Arian blood. That left the number of eligible bachelors to be quite small, as most men had compulsory military service between the ages of eighteen and twenty-five and were sent to different military commands to build the bonds of brotherhood within the New Reich. *A ridiculous notion,* thought Himmler. *The idea of creating a pure Arian New Reich was a fantasy and limited their growth.*

Sigfried didn't return the frauline's look, even though he did find her attractive, and she got the message and waved him through to the elevators. He stepped into the elevator a moment later and rode it up to the Finance Minister's office. Different parts of the New Reich's government were broken up and hidden all over the world. Finance was based here in Argentina, leadership in Europe, the military in Africa, and Intelligence in Asia. Only in Argentina, though, where they had fled in the ashes of World War Two, did they have a physical home. In the rest of the world, the New Reich existed in a smattering of outposts and virtually. But every year, their power grew.

The elevator chimed, and he walked out into a well-appointed office lobby that no one would have ever thought would be in the unassuming office building. Two more secretaries, both blonde, sat at the front desk, and they waved him through. He walked to the door at the far side of the wood-paneled lobby, swiped his palm, and proceeded out to what looked like a trading floor. There were somewhere close to fifty men and women behind various sets of monitors, all with trading software or financial information on display.

He walked past them to another door and knocked. "Enter," came the call in return. He opened the door and proceeded inside. Karl Wagner was a large man with dark hair and a round stomach, and he couldn't have been taller than five feet five. Karl rose to shake his hand, and Sigfried noticed with annoyance that the Obergruppenführer was also there.

"Colonel," the leader of the South American district said. Sigfried shook the finance minister's hand and sat down next to the Obergruppenführer.

Once again, this man was meddling in SS business. Of course, he had every right to know what was happening in his area of responsibility, but Sigfried was unused to being questioned by men not in the SS. In fact, most people in the New Reich still greatly feared the organization. *As they should,* he thought. It was the SS that had saved the Reich from death in the final throws of World War Two by establishing rat lines so that key personnel and leaders could escape unhindered.

"How are things coming, Minister?"

"One trillion dollars is in place and at our AI trading algorithms discretion to begin shorting the American market at our say so. This is twice the figure we used in two thousand 2008 and twice that again from our short trades placed around nine-eleven. Organizing this level of capital for deployment was not easy, but with advancements in AI and algorithmic trading, we were able to once again move the money with no one being the wiser. Depending on the size of the crash your operation causes, we can expect to net anywhere from two point five to six trillion dollars. For context, the high end of that is nearly the entire budget of the U.S. government for a year; at the low end, it's more than the U.K.'s budget for last year. Is your operation ready to proceed?"

"Nearly; within one week, possibly less. We're putting the final pieces into place now."

"I remind you, Colonel, the panic must occur on a day the

American markets are open; otherwise, they could refuse to open them for fear of financial disaster," replied Karl.

"How can you be sure they won't pause trading the second the extent of the damage becomes known?" asked the Obergruppenführer.

"We, along with our SS colleagues, have inserted viruses into the major trading index systems and the U.S. government's controls over them. We'll, in essence, be jamming the door open until all our trades occur. Even if they wanted to stop trading, they couldn't. Once we say go, there's no stopping it."

The Obergruppenführer looked slightly uneasy. "What will be the extent of the damage?"

"Truthfully, economic warfare has never been waged at this scale. This is because economic attacks of this magnitude executed on the world's predominant market will have strong ripple effects on the global economy. At the bare minimum, the U.S. economy will be completely crippled on a scale larger than the Great Depression. This will likely sink most Western economies with it and that of all of Asia. The only countries that will be largely unaffected by the downturn will be those so heavily sanctioned by the larger world that their economies are truly separate. Think Russia, Iran, North Korea, etc. From the ashes, the New Reich will rise. This is purely from an economic standpoint, of course. We'll have so much more capital than the rest of the world that we'll be able to do whatever our leaders deem the correct course of action. We could buy back Germany for instance, or any other country thoroughly bankrupted for that matter; we could wage war; we could set up the world's largest corporation. The sky is the proverbial limit unless, of course, they built a rocket."

Everyone in the room was silent as the magnitude of what they were about to do and the possibilities sunk in. There would be devastation, of course, on an unprecedented scale. But a country's abilities to find those responsible would be severely degraded, with national budgets completely crippled. The genius of the plan was using these countries' wealth against them, as they'd done for nearly a hundred years now. It was a miracle to Sigfried that no one had figured out that the Reich still existed. They had so thoroughly deceived the nations of the world that they had won that they were unconcerned with the fantasy that their oldest enemy might still be among them.

"Well done, Minister. I look forward to seeing your results and watching our people prosper by them," said the Obergruppenführer.

"I must return to my operation and align the final pieces," said Sigfried. He stood and snapped off a crisp, straight-armed salute. "Heil Dominance," he said and turned on his heel to walk out of the office, smiling. The Fuhrer would be proud of all they were about to accomplish.

22

Chiapas, Mexico

The two Toyota Hilux pickup trucks were stashed twenty yards off the dirt road with branches covering them. The ten-click trip had taken them the better part of two hours to complete, being sure to avoid civilians and the looming cartel. The team's muti-cam uniforms were gone, having changed into civilian clothes generously packed and provided by Sarah. They had enough to cover the three additional Special Forces operators as well, which was good because they needed to give the cartel the impression that they were dead. They had been staging here, getting ready to take down the drug processing site a click away when Charlie had radioed them that they had gotten lucky and there was definitely a cartel member on the way. They had opted to hit him on the road and then take down the processing site for additional intelligence.

They had taken ten minutes to hide two small signal jamming pods on either side of the road, then had formed into the foliage and behind the trees in a pincer formation. Five hundred yards behind them, Sheriff had been placed in a scouting position to attempt to figure out where everyone was sitting in the vehicles. In case they needed to take out the driver on the run. Witch had climbed halfway up a tree close to the right side of the road with his suppressed M110A3 chambered in 6.5-millimeter Creedmoor. The plan was simple: take out the two thousand nine suburbans' right front tire, and when they stopped to look, kill the guards and take the lieutenant.

Colin itched under his Mithril body armor, which was rubbing against his bare skin. He'd had to place it under his button-up short-sleeve shirt so as not to make it look like he was an American operator. Kitted-out tactical vests tended to give you away as not a cartel soldier. Once they had the lieutenant, he didn't care if he knew the truth. It was about anyone else who may see them. The world, knowing they were here, was bad for business.

"I've got them. Moving approximately thirty miles per hour. Will be at your location momentarily," Sheriff called through the radio. The team acknowledged and the Green Berets next to the team were updated. Their radios couldn't link with the newer encrypted headsets Team Alien was using, and the team didn't have any to spare. Grinch would do the translating once they took the cartel assholes baring down on them. In the distance, through the cacophony of jungle noises, Colin began to hear the unnatural sound of an engine approaching.

A second later, it came around the bend in the road, bumping up and down as it went. From above him, Colin heard the spit of the suppressed Creedmoor round leaving the sniper's perch. It took the driver a second longer to realize than Colin would have liked, and they rolled to a stop right in front of the team.

"Hold," Colin radioed. "On my signal."

Colin brought his MCX Spear to his shoulder and peered through the TANGO6T sight at the driver. He then panned over to the three other men exiting the vehicles. *Fuck, which one's the boss?* he thought. The driver definitely wasn't, and neither was the man who had been sitting behind him. His question was answered when a guy with skeleton bones tattooed on his face lit a cigarette and leaned against the hood, berating the other men to change the tire. Colin had seen a file on this guy. It was Narcisso Martinez. Head of the cartel's enforcement arm, and also the one who reportedly led the assault on the spring break nightclub full of American college kids.

"Okay, everyone, don't kill the guy with the stupid face; everyone else is fair game."

Colin inhaled, held it for a second, and then slowly let out his breath. As he did, his reticle centered on the driver's head, and he pressed the trigger. The suppressed MCX kicked, and a microsecond later, the driver's head snapped back as he fell over. Two other suppressed shots followed from around the woods a second after he killed the two other cartel soldiers. Narcisso whirled around in confusion at his men's sudden fainting spells. The shots, though audible, would have been hard to detect through the dampening effect of the foliage and the near-constant roar of wildlife sounds all around them. Narcisso must have realized something was really wrong when those sounds paused with the shots. The animals knew an unnatural predator was about.

Narcisso went for his gun, but before he could get it out, the Green Beret's dog was on him, grabbing his arm in a fit of snarling teeth. Grinch yelled at the man in Spanish as four rifles were pointed in his face, and he writhed with pain, trying to get away from the growling dog. Slowly, Narcisso stopped, and Panda commanded the dog to release, which he did promptly. Jester grabbed his hands from behind and zip-tied them behind his back. A second later, he pulled the gold-plated Desert Eagle from the ground and handed it to Colin. "Nice piece," he said, examining it for a second.

"You people are fucking dead. Do you have any idea who you're fucking with?"

"By the looks of it, a guy with a stupid fucking face," replied Jester.

"Do you want me to translate that?" Grinch asked.

"Let's get him off the road."

A few moments later, back at the Hilux trucks in the woods, Witch began his work. They didn't have time to waste, so Witch took the medical route immediately. He did a quick workup on Narcisso. Not bothering to ask the standard questions. After taking a pulse and blood pressure, he injected the man with several compounds. One caused extreme anxiety; another accelerated the production of endogenous DMT in the brain, a highly hallucinogenic hormone. He also injected five hundred milligrams of caffeine, a blood thinner, and a drug that made people want to talk.

They then left him alone for ten minutes with a black bag over his head while they waited for the drugs to take full effect.

Narcisso was tearing up by the time Witch removed the black hood from his head. Grinch stepped over, looking surprised at the change that had come over the cartel lieutenant in such a short period of time.

"Translate for me," Witch told Grinch. The team's dog growled at the cartel lieutenant.

Grinch nodded, while Narcisso was bugging out. His eyes were rolling around, and he couldn't stop fidgeting. Tears rolled down his face, and he strained at his bonds as if the extraordinary levels of anxiety he was feeling were going to burst out of him. His arm bled, but the dog, to his credit, hadn't mangled the man too badly. "Narcisso, I'm here to help you, my friend. But the only way I can make all this stop for you is if you give me some information."

The translation finished a few seconds later. "Do you understand what I'm saying?"

It took Narcisso a few moments to collect himself enough to say something. "Fuck you, American," he said in broken English.

Witch waved for Grinch to keep translating. "That's fine, Mr. Martinez. We'll just have to keep upping the dosage until you're more cooperative." Witch grabbed his head and shoved another needle into his neck. This one had nothing in it. The effect of the DMT drug was linear. Meaning it increased in severity for an hour before it wore off and the body was able to restore balance through natural functions. Narcisso would keep thinking things were worse no matter what he did. Narcisso let out an exasperated scream.

"The only way for it to stop is to tell me what I want to know, Mr. Martinez."

Narcisso jumped back in his seat on the truck tailgate as if something was attacking him. But there was no one within five feet of him. Witch had sent him on the equivalent of a bad trip straight from hell.

"You haven't even asked me anything yet," he said. Promptly, he started to beg.

"I'm not sure you're feeling cooperative yet, Mr. Martinez. Let's up the dosage again to see if we can change that." Witch walked up again and shoved the needle back in his neck. Once again, there was nothing in the needle, just the power of suggestion and the drugs already in his system. Witch stepped back. He could tell Narcisso was fighting to maintain his grip on reality. Nothing was scarier to the mind than losing everything it thought was holding it onto this earth.

"Please!" Narcisso yelled at him. "Make it stop!"

"Why?" Witch asked.

Narcisso ducked as if something were attacking him again. He let out a frightened squeal as he did. "I'll tell you anything; just stop them from getting to me."

"Who's getting you?" asked Witch. If he were going to ramp down the hallucinations, he would need to know what to target again if Narcisso became uncooperative.

"The people at the test site, the ones we tested it on."

Witch looked at Colin puzzled, then turned back to Narcisso. "Tested what on?" he asked.

"The virus."

23

Lieutenant Gehring sat in the passenger seat of the 1999 Toyota Landcruiser. It turned right and moved down the potholed street whose name he wasn't sure of. His driver was following GPS but also knew the streets of the border city well. In the back, three more of his men were crammed in together with HK416 assault rifles tucked between their knees. It was dark, and this part of the city was a ghost town at night, but still, he kept a watchful eye on the streets around them.

Juarez was not only one of the most dangerous cities in Mexico; it was one of the most dangerous places on Earth. Fought over by the cartels for generations, there was only one rule here— the oldest rule in nature. The strong survived, and the weak died.

They kept proceeding west toward an overpass, and in the dim light of the streetlights, Gehring could see bodies hanging from its steel frame. All wore the uniform of the Mexican Federal Police. In Mexico, an enormous number of police were on the payroll of the cartels. Those who weren't were in constant danger of being killed. Even the Mexican military, which was typically used by the government to fight the cartels, wasn't immune to compromise. Money and death talked.

"How long?" he asked the driver.

"Three minutes."

Behind them, two more SUVs, all loaded down with men, guns, and cocaine, worked their way toward the staging location for the Descanso Eterno border crossing into the United States. The point had been specially selected to bring the bulk of the drugs across for distribution into the United States into El Paso. Once inside the United States, most cheap cocaine would be cut with additives like Levamisole, Lidocaine, Caffeine, Phenacetin, Starch, or sugar. Cocaine that was cut too much typically received additional additives like fentanyl to bring it back up to snuff. Most precursors came directly from China. Descanso procured theirs directly through a relationship with the MSS, or Chinese Ministry of State Security.

This cocaine, however, needed to remain pure. Several of the additives had anti-viral properties. This would decrease profits for the cartel. Lieutenant Gehring and his men were to ensure that it got to its destination untainted and reached its customers without issue. This would involve crossing the border to ensure that endpoints in the Descanso distribution network didn't monkey with the purity of the product either.

This cocaine's endpoint would be Los Angeles and would be sold through one of the most notorious dealers who dealt directly to many of the town's biggest celebrities and influencers. It was critical that the world saw what happened.

"We're here," the driver said. In unison, the men stepped out of the Landcruiser and walked up to the door of the small warehouse. Two hundred yards behind it was the United States border. The driver knocked on the door and waited a moment for it to open. It did, and the man spoke in hushed Spanish to the guard before waving everyone inside. Several of his men pulled security, while others carried hard plastic cases of drugs inside the warehouse.

Inside was brightly lit with fluorescents and a buzz of activity. Men in forklifts transported crates. Other men packed cases of auto parts into wooden crates. It didn't look like anything illegal was happening if you didn't count the guards roving the warehouse with guns. This wasn't irregular for Juarez. The false bottoms in the crates being filled with kilo-sized bricks of cocaine weren't irregular either.

"Gehring?" asked a man walking up to him. He looked to be in charge. A normal-looking nine-to-five factory foreman.

"That's me," he replied.

"If you'll follow me, your men can place the product into these crates. Fifty kilos each, my men will show them how."

Gehring nodded at his men to proceed, then pressed the foreman. "How does it work?"

"The tunnel we will take you through opens into the basement of an auto parts distributor in El Paso. When packed here, each crate is loaded into their computer systems with a specific weight for automotive parts for distribution around the country. On top are the parts, below is the product. The weight is adjusted by hollowing out the inside of some parts and inflating the weights of others to make sure they match."

"Sophisticated," Gehring replied.

"Mexico is the largest trading partner with the United States. About 64 percent of that trade is machine parts and automotive in nature. A few more crates along legitimate trade lines are hardly noticed."

"If you don't mind me saying, you don't seem like the type to be involved in all this," Gehring said, testing the man.

"In Juarez, it's much safer to be involved than not," he said matter-of-factly.

Gehring nodded. "How does it reach Los Angeles?"

"A semi-truck will take the parts to another automotive warehouse there."

"Why not take the parts over the border closer to Los Angeles?"

The foreman thought about this for a moment. "Mexicali is not a friendly place for Descanso, and traffic gets more scrutiny moving to waypoints directly from the border. If it's just interstate commerce in the U.S., no one cares."

Gehring nodded again. "How long will the crossing take?"

"Two hours. The crates are pushed on carts with rubber tires the few hundred yards underground to the other warehouse. We used to have a machine-driven locomotive, but the border patrol in the U.S. can pick off the engine vibrations through the ground and pinpoint the tunnels."

"What about the rumors of the American military moving to the border?"

The foreman thought about this for a moment. "The American authorities don't know about the warehouse. We know this because in the raids a few days ago after the nightclub incident, they hit every location they knew about. That tells us the location is uncompromised. It should put you far enough past the border that you can move unmolested to your next destination."

Gehring watched as the crates were sealed, and men began shuffling them to a small rope crane that would lower them down into the tunnel. Once the crates were lowered, he nodded with satisfaction and reached for the pistol at the small of his back. The foreman looked on in complete surprise as he pulled the pistol and shot him in the head. Other shots rang out from around the warehouse as his men tied off the loose end. Then he moved to the crane himself; they had a tight schedule to keep to.

24

W itch looked at Colin as if asking where he should take this. They needed information on where the headquarters was, but if this guy had information on the biothreat, they needed to dive deeper. Colin Nodded.

"Tell us more, and I'll make it stop," said Witch. Grinch translated.

"The site up the road," Narcisso said, panting. "We're testing new drugs. It's killing the junkies. I don't think it's the drugs. We don't even have control over the site. We're just supposed to bring more product to them and provide muscle to dispose of the bodies when they ask."

"When who asks?"

Narcisso didn't respond immediately and started looking around wildly. He was sweating unnaturally even in this heat. Witch walked forward and checked his pulse. It was too fast. He went back to his briefcase, got another syringe, injected it into the side of the man's neck, and walked back over to Colin.

"He's close to having a seizure. He needs a break."

"We don't have time to waste. How much more can he take."

"He can't until I stabilize him, or he'll die."

"I don't need him to live. I just need him to tell us enough to keep us going. He's considered expendable by the Director of National Intelligence for his role in the nightclub attack. How much more can you get out of him?" asked Colin.

"I think a lot, judging by what I've seen here. This guy has some serious demons, and I can use that. He's responding well to this technique."

Colin thought for a moment. They needed all they could get out of Narcisso. He was also curious about what was at the cartel's site up the road. He also had orders to dispose of him. Not to mention Colin knew this guy deserved every second of pain they caused him.

"You keep working on him. I'll take Grinch, Jester, and Panda to see what's up the road."

"Sounds good, boss."

They climbed the embankment in a low crawl, carefully disturbing as little of the vegetation as they could. Colin used his rifle to move plants as he listened to the jungle noises and tried to tune in to anything unnatural. Their eyes in the sky didn't see any guards patrolling the perimeter, but that didn't mean there wasn't, or that there weren't any cameras or booby traps around. A claymore would really ruin Colin's day.

Still, though, he was more concerned with snakes at the moment. In his training as a Green Beret, before his untimely fake death, Colin had been given some jungle warfare training, but not to the level the guys who covered South America, Asia, or Africa had. Colin was trained in Arctic and temperate forest warfare, having been focused on Europe and Russia, not to mention all his time spent in the Middle East.

Colin wished he still had his multi-cam ACUs on. At least his arms would have been covered. The short-sleeved cartel costume he wore just wasn't practical for sneaking up on bad guys in a jungle. If that wasn't enough, the fact that a deadly pathogen was likely looming in the structure over the crest of the hill was enough to make a chill permeate down the center of his spine.

Colin had no intention of entering the structure. They had a small ball drone with cameras all over it the guys affectionately called BB-69, due to its resemblance to a Star Wars droid and their childish sense of humor. They arrived at the top, and Colin saw a wood and concrete structure that was a cross between a pillbox and a shanty. It had two windows in the front, a wooden porch that looked like it had been haphazardly added on after it was built, and several blue waste barrels stacked neatly to the side.

The door to the building was open, and something white was sticking out of it. Colin brought up his TANG06T scope and narrowed in on it to see what it was. It looked like an arm. As he did, he scratched his lower back, which was bothering him, and settled in to get more comfortable. He saw the arm and assumed that it must have been attached to a body lying on the ground. From his angle, Colin couldn't see the rest of the body, but Colin couldn't think of another reason besides being dead or knocked out that a person would lay in the middle of a doorway like that.

"Something's not right here," said Jester.

"No shit," replied Grinch. Look over to the right looks like industrial filtration and a generator."

Colin panned over with his scope and saw what Grinch was referring to. He took off his backpack and pulled out what looked like a plastic black ball with shiny circles all over it. He also removed his tablet and placed it next to it on the ground. "Let's take a closer look," he said.

The tablet flashed, indicating the drone had paired, and Colin used on-screen controls to guide it down the hill.

"Cool toy," said Grinch in a low voice next to him before putting his hand on Colin's lower back.

"If you're about to kiss me, don't," said Colin.

"If only you were so lucky, Frost. Blondes aren't my type, though," he said, removing his hand and placing something in front of them. It was a millipede, a foot long, which had been crawling up Colin's back. Grinch crushed it with a rock. Colin looked at it with a mix of horror and fascination, now feeling like he had stuff crawling all over him.

"Don't worry; that was the only one, and I don't think it bit you."

"How do you know?"

"Because if it did, you'd be having a seizure by now."

"I fucking hate the jungle," whispered Colin, looking back down at the tablet. It took him a minute to get back in the zone of controlling the drone. Somewhere in the back of his mind, he now thought every sensation on his skin was a bug. *At least it wasn't a snake;* he hated snakes more.

The drone toppled out of the foliage and into the clearing surrounding the shanty bunker and rolled across it to the open door. In the doorway was a man sprawled out across the ground with full PPE. Colin moved the drone closer to investigate. As he rolled it up to the man's face, he saw what had caused his fall. A gaping hole in his forehead was caused by what looked like a close-range gunshot. Colin maneuvered the drone around and began looking around the three-room compound.

He found three more bodies, all in protective gear, all with bullet wounds. Judging by the lack of collateral damage inside the bunker, Colin thought the hit looked surgical. It didn't seem like the kind of message one cartel would send another. *And why didn't Narcisso know everyone here was dead?*

Colin reached a drone and panned upward. He saw a glass window on an interior wall. *Odd.*

He maneuvered the drone into position next to a desk next to the window and lined it up for its jump feature. This centered the drone and punched a high-speed rod into the floor to help it jump up to five feet. Colin hit the jump command on his tablet and saw everything blur on the screen as it executed the command. When it finished, Colin backed the video up and paused it in terrified disbelief. Inside, the window looked like a morgue.

There must have been a dozen dead bodies, all on cheap beds. There was dried blood from their noses and eyes, and some with foam still coming out of their mouth, completed the macabre look.

"Looks like hemorrhagic fever," said Colin quietly.

"Look at the one with foam coming out of their mouth. They probably just died within the last few hours. That could be an overdose. Maybe they gave him too much of the laced drugs," replied Jester.

"Why would a cartel kill their own customers by going in on bioterrorism? I mean, don't get me wrong—with the insane drug problem America has, it's a great delivery device, but still. Kill all your customers, and you won't have a business anymore," said Grinch.

Colin remembered him telling him in Afghanistan that his sister had been addicted to drugs. "Yeah, doesn't make any sense to me either at the moment. But I'm more worried about something else."

"More worried than a cartel dosing a huge number of addicts in the U.S. with hemorrhagic fever via their coke problem?" asked Jester.

"If they killed everyone here, that means they were done with this site and wanted to clean up. That means they're ready for whatever comes next in their plan. That means we might be out of time. We need to speak with the Director of National Intelligence now."

25

Marine One touched down on the helipad a few hundred yards from the main buildings that made up Camp David. Its rotors began to spool down, and the crew chief told the president he was clear to disembark if he wanted.

"How far behind is Marine Two?" the president asked.

"About five minutes, sir."

The president proceeded out the open door, placing a hand on his Nationals baseball cap as he went so he didn't lose it. He jogged twenty-five yards to the waiting golf cart, his Secret Service detail right on his heels, and jumped in. "Take me to the communications center."

The marine driving the golf cart nodded, and they accelerated toward the heart of the compound.

Officially known as Naval Support Facility Thurmont and nestled into the mountains of Maryland sixty-two miles away from D.C., it was the ultimate isolationist paradise. It featured a golf course, swimming pools, tennis courts, and enough armed guards to make anyone think twice about approaching. It was also beautiful. Enough so that F.D.R. had referred to it as Shangri-La after a novel set in the Himalayas. The tall pine trees surrounding the mountainous retreat brought a sense of calm to anyone who chose to come here. Anyone except a president in the middle of an existential crisis in the United States.

The Presidential Communications Center was a large cabin with what looked like several dozen antennas sticking out of the top of it. Inside was a suite of advanced communications software that let the president conference with and monitor the forces of the United States across the world in real time.

The president heard Marine Two coming in for a landing as they reached it and headed inside. The military members at various stations around the room stood as he entered. "As you were." The president barked, acting every bit the naval captain he had been.

"Mr. President, we've got you set up in a secure sweet in the basement."

They proceeded down a set of stairs in the direction of the commander of the communications center. *This place really is odd,* the president briefly thought to himself as they went. The rustic log cabin and futuristic military command center mix was odd. But he pushed the thought from his head as soon as it entered. He needed to focus on the crisis at hand. The president proceeded through a door into a sitting room with a conference table, fireplace, and a sitting area. The president took a seat. "Coffee, please," he said to the Navy steward, who was laying out snacks and drinks in the corner. *I need to get my head clear if I'm going to figure this out.*

He'd only had half of one beer, but he didn't like the idea of it numbing his senses. He turned to Tom Corrigan, who was now blocking the door into the room. "Tom, I want to be back at the White House the second it's fully cleared. I'm not hiding out here if there's an attack going on."

"Yes, Mr. President. It'll take a few hours, but we'll get you back the second we can."

A few moments later, Bob and Wendy walked through the door in the basement, both on the phone talking over each other in separate conversations. They both lowered their phones and placed the calls on mute.

"Mr. President," they said in unison.

"I'd like answers now," he said, sitting back in an armchair and taking a sip of coffee. It burned his tongue, and he grimaced.

Wendy spoke first. "Mr. President, three representatives have received letters with what we believe to be anthrax in them. It was late in the day, though, so we need to check the entirety of the Capitol office buildings to start. This sweep will extend to all three branches of government in the city. We need to ensure the scope of the attack was limited or understand if we have a much larger problem on our hands."

"The media is already saying it's bio-terrorism and that the government will never be able to contain it after COVID—which is ridiculous because anthrax can be treated with antibiotics," said the president.

"We screen for things like this in the mail, especially in government buildings; how did it happen?" asked Bob.

"We're not sure yet. Mail security has always been more complicated, even with automated screening, due to the volume of correspondence received. We don't know if it was an issue with a screening process or some other vulnerability."

"Something feels off, Wendy. I don't like it," said the president.

"I have the same feeling, sir. The Echo Teams' hunt for Dominick Schmidt feels related to this. He was a key suspect in the Amerithrax case. I have a hard time believing the two are unrelated."

"We should look for links in Capitol building personnel to the Descanso Eterno Cartel," said Bob.

"Agreed, but don't we screen for links like that in the federal hiring process?" asked the president.

"People who work in the mail room, for lack of a better term, are given background checks, but not to the level that an employee with a clearance is. If they had no criminal background and no other record and were born natively, they don't get much of a deeper dive. Since Descanso is so new, it's possible someone skated in, but they would have had to have been clean," answered Wendy.

"Like a sleeper agent?" asked Bob.

"Cartels certainly use criminally unrelated assets in their operations. They function as important cutouts in their business. But they usually have something over them. They are criminal organizations, after all," answered Wendy.

"They're attacking the government of the United States if this was them—which means it's possible the cartel has essentially declared war on us. If that's the case, it's on," said the president.

"I agree, sir, but I'm still unclear on something. Why in the world would a cartel do it? They'd want to fly as under the radar as possible."

The president took another sip of coffee, considering this. It had cooled considerably. He furrowed his brow in thought. There was something here—he just couldn't see it. War had become considerably more complicated in the last twenty years. Adversaries were everywhere, their intentions cloaked behind a wall of cutouts and obscured by the fog of war. The globe was collapsing into spheres of influence and isolating in another Cold War. As always, it seemed like the United States led the coalition of freedom, and a smattering of ex-communist authoritarian powers sought domination.

In this war, however, the very tools that grew because of the prospering of Western life were being used against them. Information was no longer broken into right or wrong but rather into right or wrong based on whoever was providing or consuming it. The truth was harder than ever to uncover. It suddenly became clear to the president that there might not just be two sides anymore. The media was going to scare the American people to no end when this news broke.

Wendy interrupted the president's thoughts. "Mr. President, the Echo Team is making contact."

26

"Ma'am, we have a very serious situation here, and I need to provide you with an update," said Colin. He had moved into the jungle by a few steps to get a few moments of privacy. Typically, Colin wouldn't have conversed so much with any kind of authority figure on a mission. But given the magnitude of the threat to the United States, passing things through the usual channels was time no one could afford. The U.S. government was the largest bureaucracy in the world, and though it had accomplished some of the most incredible feats in human history, its lack of speed was also reaching historical levels.

Team Alien, the Echo Team Colin led, was one of the responses to this bureaucracy. Unfortunately, the only way it could exist was with a black budget and completely outside of the bounds of conventional authority. This had its advantages. Inside a bag they carried were their government badges for nearly every military and law enforcement agency in existence. The names were all fake, but the badges were real.

"Snowman, I'm going to put you on with the president and Chief of Staff. Please relay all the information you have. The president likes details. He has been briefed on your progress up to your last update a day ago."

Colin was taken aback. *The president?* he thought.

He took a breath and steadied himself. Crawling up a nearby vine on a massive tree was an electric blue poison dart frog. Colin remembered it from a book report he'd done as a child. He used the thought to steady himself, even though he felt anything but.

"Yes, Ma'am. Mr. President. We've recovered three surviving members of the ODA you deployed here. They were betrayed by the asset they were supposed to meet with. I've co-opted them for the duration of this mission." Colin paused briefly to ensure there was no communication delay.

"Please inform them I'm sorry for their loss and proceed," came a voice Colin recognized.

"Yes, sir. Upon landing, we engaged in an operation to identify cartel sites and interdict high-ranking personnel on their way to inspect drug operations. In the process, we captured Narcisso Martinez, one of the reported lieutenants who led the attack on the nightclub full of American students." Colin paused. "He's the one with the tattoos on his face, sir. We're still interrogating him for the location of their leadership element. We expect to have it shortly. But in the process, he revealed that one of the sites was being used for testing lethal drugs. He seemed to think that the drugs were laced with some kind of virus. We proceeded to the site and found the personnel dead, which I don't think he knew. Inside were a dozen addicts, all dead of what looks suspiciously like hemorrhagic fever, sir."

"How do you know it wasn't an overdose, Snowman?" asked the Director of National Intelligence.

"Ma'am, overdose victims don't bleed out of their eyes, ears, and nose. And though we could only send in a drone due to our lack of CBRN gear, I spent some time in Africa and have seen

Ebola victims. I am confident that whatever this is along those lines."

A pause ensued. The gravity of the situation was enormous. COVID had a fatality rate of around 1 percent. A virus like Ebola killed approximately 90 percent of the people it infected. Vaccines, though in development and growing in effectiveness, could never be manufactured at a scale to stop something like this in time. Though hemorrhagic fevers could only be spread by bodily contact, they didn't yet know what they were dealing with. If it was airborne, it was evident from the lack of ability to contain something like COVID that the fatality rates would be unprecedented in human history.

"Proceed, Snowman," said the president.

"Yes, sir. We anticipate having the location of the cartel's leadership shortly. However, given that the personnel at the laboratory were eliminated before we arrived, I would guess that the testing phase of their plan is over. I think we need to face the real possibility that there is a biological weapon being prepared for delivery against the United States."

"Do you have any idea how they might deliver the pathogen Snowman?" asked the Director of National Intelligence.

"Ma'am, if the drugs are laced with the pathogen, I would assume they would be transporting the pathogen via that vector into the United States and distributing it to addicts. A huge amount of the people who consume cocaine and whatever else they might use are wealthy. Meaning they can travel at will all over the country. It's a perfect delivery vector. Throw in the fact that addicts are not by nature cautious people and how porous the borders are, and even a shutdown of travel won't necessarily contain the spread. My money's on the drugs."

The president swore under his breath. "Snowman, why would the Descanso do this? It would be like Starbucks killing everyone who liked coffee. No one would ever trust their product again," said the Director of National Intelligence.

Colin thought about this for a moment. "Ma'am. I don't know, but I'll say this—I don't get the impression that Narcisso Martinez knew that everyone at their test site was going to be dead, which tells me that they may not be the only people involved in this."

"What is Narcisso Martinez's state?" asked the president.

"Under active battlefield interrogation," responded Colin.

"When you're finished with him and this is over, Snowman, he will be no longer needed," replied the president.

Colin caught his meaning. "Yes, Mr. President. And sir?" Colin asked.

"Yes, Snowman?"

"This isn't my place, but under Star Set protocols, I would recommend closing all ports of entry into the United States, deploying the military to close the southern border, and stopping all air travel. Even if we get to the cartel's leadership in time, there's a strong chance things are already in motion that we can't stop from here," finished Colin. Some presidents would have been offended at the advice from a lowly intelligence asset. But Colin knew William Joyce's reputation. Sarah had even been aboard his ship with DEVGRU at one point. He was a man who listened to his people.

"I'll take it under advisement, Snowman. Thank you," he replied.

"Please let us know the second you have the location of the leadership element, Snowman," said the Director of National Intelligence.

"Yes, ma'am," replied Colin. He knew the board had been set. He just prayed they weren't too late to take the king.

27

Argentina

"It is ready to proceed?" the man asked in heavily accented English. Dominick was in a heavily darkened room with three large screens in front of him. Oddly, acoustically dampened voices told his ears he was in another office building. An expensive one, he knew. He was once again in plain business clothes, except this time, he was in the SS's home office in Argentina. The building had a long, complicated German name, but most people here in the village called it The Lair.

Dominick nodded at the man on the left screen, "Yes, sir, we are ready to proceed. All assets, both financial and viral, are now in place." The screens were darkened and the voices slightly distorted, such that you could tell a person was there but only see their outline. They were good at cyber security, but the Americans invented hacking, so no chances could be taken.

The man on the right screen replied, "The finance minister's projections are ludicrous."

The other two nodded in agreement.

"I've looked them over, and while I agree they are high, I

don't think they are overly so. I was frankly more surprised at how much we had to put into the operation," said Dominick.

The man in the center now spoke. "Don't be surprised by that. The ratlines smuggled close to a billion dollars' worth of gold, currency, art, and other valuables out of Germany before the fall. That would have been among the largest personal fortunes in the world in the forties. Now imagine that money being invested for eighty years. Even an idiot could have gotten a 6 percent return in the markets over that period of growth. We, of course, with our access to information and"—he paused and scratched his chin—"other opportunities did far better."

Dominick thought this through for a second. It seemed ludicrous for a personal fortune, but a shadow government with an intelligence operation and ties into much of the world's goings-on —maybe not so much. A billion dollars invested at a 6 percent interest rate and compounding over eighty years would have come out to somewhere around 105 billion. At a much higher rate of return, considering what they had done over the years, Dominick now started to get the picture.

"What of the viral projections?" asked the man on the left.

Dominick opened a file on his tablet. "There are roughly one point five million users of cocaine in the United States. Of these, the Descanso operation controls roughly three hundred thousand. The initial delivery, once cut and distributed, will affect roughly half of that within one week—which is far too many for the Americans to handle. There has never been a hemorrhagic fever outbreak on that scale. We judge it highly unlikely that subsequent deliveries of infected cocaine would have any significant effect. This is because the likelihood of users being able to obtain the product, even if we could get it into the locked-down United States, is low. However, the initial spread will be the highest. The virus has an incubation period of eight to ten days. This is the thing our scientists have worked hardest to cut down. The new incubation period is three to five days—"

The man in the center cut him off. "Why have we worked to cut this down?"

Dominick answered, "Due to the scale of this outbreak and our modeling, there was significant concern among our virologists that there would be no stopping the virus from spreading worldwide if the carriers had that long to infect more people. If we die, too, there would have been no point in this whole exercise. The point is to make money, hence our previous discussions. We're not suicide bombers, after all," replied Dominick.

"Very well. Continue."

"Yes, sir. The fatality rate of the strain we obtained is particularly severe. Ebola kills from around 50 to 90 percent of all people it infects. Our strain is the 90 percent variety."

"Can the Americans stop it?" asked the man on the left.

"Stop it?" Dominick asked.

"Through lockdowns or mass vaccinations?" the man on the left pressed.

"There is an effective vaccination just finishing development. But there are only around one thousand doses. Not nearly enough. And there's no way to produce it fast enough to protect the population. That and given the hesitance of the American population toward vaccinations after the botched COVID-19 vaccines, there's no way they could vaccinate their people. But there is no stopping this by any man-made means, sir. It's too many people too fast. It will stop when it burns out."

"Casualty projections?" asked the man in the center.

"If our models hold, which I will caution are all experimental due to their never being an outbreak of hemorrhagic fever at this scale, we estimate nine million people being infected by day five. Of that, around eight million people will be dead five days later. The virus will double again, but with some tailwinds from the first wave, and in the end, before it starts to dip, it will infect around twenty-five million people, with around twenty-two million people dying. At that point, the virus will be beginning to burn itself out in the major cities, and quite frankly, it will run out of bodies. The rest of America is too spread-out to be majorly infected."

The room was silent for a moment. The gravity of what they were discussing would be one of the greatest mass murders in history. Hitler would have possibly even blushed at their methods. *Our job is to win at all costs, to become dominant the world over. We've waited long to fulfill this dream. In the end, history won't remember how we got there because we will write it,* thought Dominick.

"Is there variance in these models?" asked the man on the right.

"We believe with a high percentage of chance the range is from thirty million to fifty million dead at the end in the United States. If there are subsequent outbreaks in other countries, this could swell to closer to one hundred million. However, we expect that other countries could likely contain outbreaks with contact tracing and travel bans," said Dominick. He did not add *we hope* to that statement. There were two models that showed up to a billion dead, but they were statistically unlikely.

"Yes, exceedingly unlikely. All I need now is your permission to proceed, gentleman," Dominick said.

Once again, there was silence. They were about to pass the death sentence of an entire country. One that would fall to ensure their rise. Dominick felt the silence of the acoustic paneling in the room, muting his ears. It weighed heavily.

"Permission granted. Operation AdlerSchlag is a go."

28

"I think we've got it, boss!" said Witch as they walked back up to the trucks where Narcisso was sitting. He was bound, gagged, and there was a black bag over his head, which must have been sweltering in this late afternoon jungle heat. The only time Colin ever saw Witch smile was when he had just pulled some important piece of information from the inner workings of someone's head.

"Seven miles south of here on the beach. Charlie's on; he's looking now."

Colin saw Charlie was on a video conference on a team tablet. He wasn't looking at them; he was furiously typing into his keyboard. Colin took a sip from the camelback in one of the backseats of the Hilux truck they were gathered around. *I'm dehydrated,* he thought. *Or maybe I've just seen something I'll never unsee. Maybe I just saw Hell.* He took another sip from the camelback and leaned against the truck. Thankfully the team was too distracted to see Colin take a minute for himself.

Leadership was by nature solitary, though Colin thought of

himself as more of a ringleader than a boss. He couldn't let his team see that he was shaken. Judging my Jester's lack of jokes, Colin was sure he wasn't their only one. He took another sip from his camelback and came back around the truck.

"Charlie, what have you got?"

"Just one more second, boss. I'm realigning the KH-13 now."

Not wasting time, Colin started relaying orders. "Prep to move back home base. I want everyone kitted out in full gear, with CBRN gear handy. Pass the extras out to our new friends," he said, gesturing to the three Green Berets. You always carried a few extra CBRN suits with you in case something happened to one of them. There was also no real way for them to disinfect the suits if they came into close contact with the virus. So, caution was necessary. Colin knew it would be hot in the suits, but no one complained. The team had seen what they'd seen. No one wanted to die that way.

"I think I've got it!" squealed Charlie in excitement. The hacker seemed to catch his boyish voice and started talking more deeply. "Patching it through now. Oh yeah, this has to be it— unless Bill Gates has a place here, it's huge!"

It is huge, thought Colin, looking at the tablet screen. It had to be at least one thousand acres. He saw one palatial mansion with several outbuildings, including what looked like stables, a pool house, some kind of pyramid with a bunch of military-age males out front, and a guardhouse down a long road. The whole thing sat right on the beach with well-manicured grounds surrounding it. *These cameras are insane,* he thought.

Colin had seen satellite imagery before, but this was the first time he'd seen live footage from one of the new KH-13 spy satellites. What was amazing was the fact that it was in geosynchronous orbit twenty-two thousand miles away. Most spy satellites were typically in low earth orbit. But the Americans were the masters of this game and, as such, unmatched in their capability to gather image intelligence.

"Hitting this is going to be a fucking nightmare. Just look at all the guards," said Jester.

"We'll have to split up, go in quick and quiet, and take out as many as we can before they know we're there," replied Colin.

"Do we have air support?" asked Panda the Green Beret.

"We have three predator drones from the McRaven off the coast, but they're not armed," replied Colin.

"So, we're just going to suicide them into people?" asked Grinch with a sarcastic smile.

"We've requested that they arm one of them with Hellfire's no word back yet," replied Colin.

"I'm realigning the drones now. And we're bringing one back to refuel and hopefully arm it. But we have to be careful. One of the drone's sensor arrays picked up some kind of radar emanating from the tree line of the compound," Charlie chimed in.

"Can we realign the satellite to get a look?" Sheriff asked.

"Doing it now. Woah, momma—"

"Shit," came the collective sigh of several members of the team.

As the satellite cameras panned onto the tree line, they saw clearly a mobile surface-to-air missile rig—more specifically, a Russian-made SA-5 Gammon missile system. It was one of the most advanced and highly lethal surface-to-air systems in production. If the U.S. experience over Iran was any indication, it was more than capable of detecting and downing U.S. Predator drones.

"Well, that rules air support out; there's no way the commander of the McRaven is authorizing Predators over the target with the chance of them being shot down," said Sarah.

"We'll have to take it out," replied Jester.

"Agreed. We'll also never be able to get a Medivac chopper in if that thing's still active," Colin replied.

"Is anyone else wondering how they got an SA-5? I mean, we've seen cartels with handheld SAM's but a full-blown mobile defense rig? That must have cost a fortune. Not to mention the fact that smuggling it into Mexico must have been a chore," said Charlie.

"Could they be getting state funding from Russia to destabilize Mexico?" asked Grinch.

"That would be a pretty amazing way to piss us off. Maybe it's revenge for us dumping all that hardware into Ukraine. As long as they don't use it to down a passenger jet, what's the difference?" said Panda.

"That would be aggressive even for Russia. They're usually more careful than that," replied Charlie.

"Clearly, there's more here than meets the eye," said Colin, putting an end to the speculation, "but let's focus on the problem. Assuming we can get air support, the first thing we need to do is blow that SA-5. We're going to need to split into a few teams. One group needs to get eyes on that pyramid and make sure it doesn't have anything of interest inside; if it doesn't, that should be the target for the Predators. Another team needs to hit the main house, and a third needs to hit the front guard post and block the road so no one can call for or receive help. We've got seven shooters, and we're hitting the house tonight when it's dark. How are we doing this?"

29

An hour later, Team Alien arrived back at their hiding site and gathered the required gear. Thirty minutes after that, they were on the dirt road to a clearing in the jungle four miles away. *It's getting dark fast; good,* Colin thought. The night was when they all operated best and could take maximum advantage of their enemy's disadvantages. As they drove, the last rays of the sun set below the tall jungle canopy, and shadow fell across their fields of view. In another thirty minutes, it would be dark. There was no moon tonight, which meant their enemies would hopefully never see them coming.

Or at least that was what Colin hoped. The truth was this cartel was sophisticated in a way Colin hadn't expected. Taking out an ODA, preparing a bioweapon, and having an SA-5 in what they suspected was their main compound was only the tip of the spear. They ran over a dip in the road that rocked them all from side to side. Colin felt sleep heavy on his eyes. He hadn't slept in a full twenty-four hours at this point. Driving next to him was Jester. Colin reached into a Yeti cooler at his feet and pulled out a

Ready to Drink Black Rifle Coffee Triple Espresso can. He offered it to the four other operators in the car. Three of them took one, and Jester popped another nicotine pouch into his mouth instead.

"You know caffeine makes me jittery, boss. Don't want to accidentally shoot the wrong guy," Jester said.

"Is that a common issue with you?" asked Grinch from the back.

Colin looked over at the two of them from the passenger seat and shrugged his shoulders. "It's only happened five or six times, but every time he shoots the right guy afterward, so at least he's got that going for him."

"I'm a man of many talents and vastly underappreciated for my genius.," said Jester.

"Definitely sounds like you have some deep-seated issues, man," rasped Panda from the other backseat. They all laughed. It was good to break the tension, if only for a few minutes. Laughing about it was sometimes the only way one could stay sane in his line of work.

"Stop," Colin said urgently. Jester hit the brakes, causing the truck to skid to a stop in the mud. The truck behind them stopped less than a foot from the back of theirs. Colin had seen something moving in the woods. In a matter of minutes, the world around him had been transformed from vibrant green to dark, muted indigo, blues, and grays. He rolled down his window and got ready to bring his Sig Spear up.

But it was for nothing. A jaguar walked out of the trees in front of their vehicle and moseyed across the road, not even seeming to care that they were there. It was a weird moment, as if the world seemed to go on all around them as if nothing was happening. As if the world might not end, with millions of people getting sick and dying. "Shit, I've never seen one before. Cool animal," said Panda from the back.

"I heard they eat pandas," Jester shot back as the truck began accelerating forward again.

Twenty minutes later, they had reached the spot Charlie had marked for them to disembark. It was the best place to stage outside of the enemy stronghold before they mounted their attack. Everyone got out and stretched. Colin's lower back was tight. He did a few squats to loosen it up while the team started getting their gear ready. They would each have to hoof it around three miles in the dark in two two-man teams and one three-man team to their objectives. Colin and Grinch would be one of the teams. Jester and Panda, the other. And Sheriff, Witch, and Ford would be the third. Colin and Grinch would be taking out the S-400 and then hitting the house. At the same time, the three-man team would hit the guardhouse in the pyramid, and Jester's element would hit the guardhouse at the end of the road.

Of the three teams, Jester had the shortest walk, and Colin had the longest. Colin's land navigation instructors in the army would have blushed at the task. However, in this case, he had a GPS and not a map, protractor, and compass. Everyone knew the mission, but they circled up anyway. And waited for Colin to speak.

"Listen, guys, we all know what we've got to do. Move fast, move carefully, and, for God's sake, get to your objectives on time. We've got to hit this place in darkness. Keep the radio chatter to a minimum. We have no idea what this group is capable of, and I don't want to find out the hard way that they can hear us. We've got a lot of people counting on us, and no one's coming to help. Let's get it done."

30

The nighttime sounds of the jungle were altogether different than the daytime sounds. Colin felt his neck hair stand up as a guttural growl let off in the distance through the trees. Colin wondered in his head if it was the Jaguar they had seen. Something was having a terrible night if that predator had found them. Colin hoped the predator was more of a foreshadowing of his future than the prey.

Something deeply and instinctually human within him sensed danger as though heightened from his natural surroundings. Instincts evolved over millions of years, deeply on alert from the screams and cries of the nighttime jungle. Colin was viewing the world in shades of blue through his GPNG night vision goggles. The four monocles gave him depth perception—something regular two-monocled versions lacked—and something that helped him navigate the terrain much more quickly. With his Sig Spear, Sig scope, variety of tech, and his trusty M1911A1 at his side, he was the ultimate predator in this jungle, though. He took comfort in that.

Colin knew that the world quite literally rested on his shoulders at this point in time. If he failed, millions could die. He had been on dozens of missions of consequence, but nothing quite to this level. So many had given so much in this never-ending war to protect America. And though former generations had received respites from conflict. The new normal was a constant low-level war to avoid a massive hot one. It was people like Colin and Team Alien here at the bloody tip of the lance who ensured that the massive hot war never came. And they were very good at it.

"Snowman, this is Death Star. I have the Director of National Intelligence for you. Can I patch her through?" Charlie's voice came through his earpiece.

"Roger. Go for Snowman," replied Colin. He held up a closed fist to signal to Grinch they should halt. They both came to a knee and waited. Colin felt the dampness of the jungle floor soaking through his pant leg.

"Snowman, are you en route to hit the compound?"

"Yes, ma'am, our attack will kick off at 0300 local time. Is there any progress on authorizing arming the predators? We're badly outmatched here," Colin asked.

"The president has authorized it, but the drones are only to assist once the air defense system is taken out. The president cannot have the Mexicans knowing we're launching air strikes on their soil."

"Copy, ma'am. That's our first target. We'll provide confirmation once it's taken out." Colin massaged his ribs from where Jester had hit him. It still was extremely painful, even through the painkillers.

"I don't need to tell you what's at stake here, Snowman; we're all counting on you."

"Any update on the situation in Washington, ma'am?"

"The victims are being treated, and no one's died, so that's good. But the whole country is spooked. No one was ready to see people on the news in full pandemic PPE again. People are scared. And there's something else. We're picking up a massive amount of chatter. Something big is going on. And a lot of money is moving around. Enough to set off flags across the U.S. intelligence apparatus. The president is moving the country to DEFCON Three. I can't stress it enough, Snowman, that we are blind. Whatever this is, we didn't see it coming, which is a near impossibility these days."

Colin weighed that for a minute before responding, "Ma'am, I don't know what we're going to run into here or uncover, but whatever it is, we're going to need kinetic resources to handle it."

"You'll have them. The president has multiple warships steaming to the McRaven, including a carrier. They'll be there within eight hours."

"Copy, ma'am."

"Good luck, Snowman."

An hour later, they were within a mile of their objective when they stumbled across the first defenses. A group of two guards stood sentry in the woods next to two ATVs. They stopped and viewed the guards through their night vision. They looked like a patrol and not very well equipped for nighttime fighting. They both carried AK-74s without any optics, and neither had night vision. The ATVs were of the newer electric variety. Colin observed, however, that they both had radios. "Death Star, this is Snowman. How copy over?" Colin asked in a low voice. They were scarcely a hundred feet from the sentries. "Copy, Snowman; ah, what do you need?" replied Charlie.

"Is the jamming up? I've got two sentries with radios here.

"Yes, Snowman, but it's patchy because the drones doing it are sitting low and outside that SA-5's range. Don't let anyone get too close to whoever they're trying to call."

Shit, Colin thought. He motioned to Grinch to take the guy on the right on his shot. They both crawled into position, setting their reticles on either man's body. The sentries seemed thoroughly unconcerned that anyone would be out here deep in the jungle at this hour. Colin took a deep breath and slowly started to breathe out. As he did, his aim steadied, and he pressed the trigger until his weapon snapped, quieted by the suppressor, and the man on the left's head exploded outward from the back. The snap next to him came a second later, but something was wrong. It wasn't loud enough. It was a squib. The round didn't have the necessary amount of gunpowder in it and had gotten stuck in the barrel. Grinch went to try and clear it, but it was too late.

The sentry had just seen his friend's head explode and dove out of the way. Colin stood running down the hill, trying to get a shot at the guy, but couldn't see him. Colin tripped over a route and went spilling down the hill. The guard must have realized what happened because he jumped up, ran to one of the ATVs, and hopped on, trying to escape danger. There was no startup on the electric ATV; it just went. The headlights on it nearly blinded Colin through his night vision goggles as he finally stopped falling.

Colin flipped up his goggles as he got up and ran for the other ATV. He yelled to Grinch, "I'm going for him. Stay here!"

He leaped onto the other ATV and gunned the accelerator. It jolted forward with 100 percent torque, surprising Colin and nearly throwing him off. He tightened his grip and chased after the headlights. There was a narrow dirt trail in the jungle the man was following. Colin switched to his off-hand on the throttle, grabbed his suppressed 1911 from the hip holster at his side, and switched the throttle back to the other hand as he moved his gun to his left hand. He couldn't have hoped to hit the man trying to fire the SIG MCX from his off-hand. The throttle was on the right.

Colin kept pushing the ATV faster. The jungle was whipping

by as he gained on the man, who now knew he had a pursuer. Colin saw ahead of him. The man had something to his lips screaming into it, but it clearly wasn't working, judging by his frustration. Colin tried to fire at the man. He sent two shots, but both missed. Luckily, the sentry dropped his radio when Colin started shooting as he tried to duck toward the handlebars of the ATV. Colin saw a fork in the dirt path coming up; one half veered toward the compound, the other off into the forest. The man looked ready toward the compound. Colin couldn't let that happen. He fired again, this time as close to the left path as he could aim on the bumpy ride with his off-hand.

The man veered right instead. Colin went after him, nearly clipping a tree, trying to steer with one hand in the process. This path to the right was not as clear as the main path they had been on before. The electric engine whined as Colin pushed it harder, as they were coming up a hill. Colin fired again, and this time narrowly missed the guard. Colin grunted in pain as a thick tree branch smacked his shin. But he couldn't stop. If this guy got away, they were screwed.

The ground flattened out at the top of the hill, but the guard sensed it might be an easier place for his pursuer to get a shot and veered right into the jungle. Colin followed and felt himself heading down the side of a hill. Desperately steering now to avoid trees and rocks, the man in front of him had to slow down to avoid hitting the trees, but Colin wouldn't. The world was depending on him. He gunned the throttle again, gaining rapidly on the man. In his head, he prayed that the chase wouldn't kill him before he could kill the man who was about to blow their whole operation.

31

The jungle had other plans for the guard. When he saw Colin catching up, he gunned the throttle again and failed to outmaneuver another tree. He clipped the side of it with the left quarter panel of the ATV and was ejected from the vehicle. Colin nailed the brakes and came screaming to a stop as the man hit another tree with a sickening crunch. He saw he had stopped just short of a brackish swamp, and in the distance, he could hear the waves of the Pacific crashing on the beach.

Amazingly, the man managed to try to stand up in the swamp where he now stood. He managed to reach one leg before a vast shape emerged from the water. In horror, Colin watched as the massive fifteen-foot-long saltwater crocodile grabbed the man's leg. Colin had seen terrible things, but the fear in that man's eyes as he realized the end he was about to come to was up there with the worst. The massive primal beast shook the man. Colin heard the crack of bone like a thick branch snapping underfoot as his leg broke in half. The beast's action, all raw fury and somehow showing no emotion in its black eyes, began to drag him under the water of the dark swamp. Colin brought up his rifle in a show of mercy and shot the man in between the eyes as he started getting dragged down. Colin couldn't let the man live. But he also couldn't bear to see someone get eaten alive.

The crocodile didn't seem to notice or care that the man stopped struggling. Colin turned to his left and vomited, having never seen gore quite at that level. To his right, he heard another one of the beasts moving toward him. He gunned the ATV, making a hard turn. Fighting a crocodile was not on his to-do list today or ever. As a rule, he tried not to pick fights he couldn't win.

Twenty minutes later, Colin finally had the ATV back to Grinch's location in the jungle.

"You get him?" the man asked, stepping out from behind a tree.

Colin swung a leg over the ATV, stepping off of it and rubbing his bruised ribs. The bumps of the dirt road hadn't been good for his injury. Colin gave him a look of wide eyes and an open mouth that said *you won't believe this shit.* "Yeah, I got him."

"Why do I sense I'm not getting the whole story?"

"Well, I caught up to him in a swamp. And was about to shoot him when a fucking crocodile got him," Colin responded.

"You're shitting me."

"I shot him in the head before it dragged him under. No one deserves to go like that. But that was after the thing snapped his leg in half like a twig. I have seen some awful shit, but nothing quite like that."

"Snowmen don't do well in the heat," reflected Grinch. He was trying to defuse the situation with dark humor. It was par for the course in this kind of work, but even he looked uneasy, as if one of the ancient beasts would emerge from the trees and eat him.

Colin gave him a half-hearted grin. "I say we get the fuck out of here and to our objective before we stumble onto another one of those things."

"No arguments from me, Snowman."

"Take point, and don't walk in any fucking swamps."

After another hour of walking, they were getting close to their objective. A few hundred yards in the distance, they could see lights emanating from the massive mansion. They haloed through the trees, casting eerie shadows. They were both careful in their advance to avoid looking directly at the lights, which would obscure their night vision and blind them to potential threats.

They moved more slowly now. Just because they hadn't encountered any more resistance on their way to their target didn't mean it wasn't out here lurking somewhere in the jungle. The jungle noises seemed to recede the closer they came to the mansion, as if the lights had told the natural world that this was not a safe space. Colin agreed. He could feel every inch of his tired muscles. They groaned and jittered with the nerves he felt in the pit of his stomach.

Nerves weren't irregular for him on a mission. But usually, they had more backup, were less outgunned, and didn't have the potential of being infected with a deadly virus. He took a deep breath to calm himself and took a sip of water from his camelback. He swirled it around in his mouth and then swallowed. Even more slowly now, Grinch and Colin crawled toward the objective.

They could see it now—the tips of the missiles dancing next to orange firelight the guards manning it clearly had lit to keep the jungle at bay. *Good, the fire will blind them,* Colin thought. They were scarcely one hundred feet from the guards. There looked to be three of them. One was asleep in a beach chair. The other two looked to be talking over a cheap bottle of rum. *Not very disciplined,* he thought.

The two Team Alien men held their position. They had an hour before they had to hit the target. "In position," Colin radioed to the other teams.

They communicated back that they were in position as well. Once they blew the SA-5, they would need to move quickly to the mansion and begin clearing it. The teams would collapse back to their positions when and if they could. The bulk of the enemy force had to be destroyed first with the drone if they all wanted to make it out of this alive. The drone would help even the odds, but only barely, and only if they could catch most of the guards asleep in the pyramid structure.

Whatever they did, they couldn't allow the mysterious cartel leader to escape. Stopping the biothreat rested on capturing this man alive and making him talk. Jester would block the road. It was Colin's job to ensure he didn't get out any other way. Everything hinged on them.

32

The fact that Gary Wieder was a Nazi would have surprised anyone that knew him from his past life. The former social media executive had spent time leading engineering teams at all of the major social media companies. He was what most people would have described as a *tech bro,* from his chill attitude to his backward hat; he frankly seemed relaxed. But his indoctrination, along with all citizens of the New Reich, came young and hard.

His colleagues at work would have called his politics hard left. That was fine in the tech world. Socialist was fine too, but to think that he was a democratic socialist or Nazi would have been too much for them. That was a title they saved for people on the right. Gary was happy to play into their political agendas. The more they liked him, the more they brought him deeper into the cult and kept moving him up the ladder.

He specialized in gamified engineering, essentially fine-tuning the algorithm underpinning social networks that promoted and amplified some content while not giving other content the time of day. In fact, Gary was responsible for so much of the algorithm's development at all major social networks that a veritable bidding war kicked off every few years when he moved around.

Then he dropped off the face of the earth. The official story was that he had gone on a sabbatical to find himself. In truth, he had placed all of the back doors he was ordered to and brought back the technical teams at the Ministry of Information all the data they needed to accomplish their plans. It didn't hurt that he had made enough money to set himself up for life in the process.

Gary sat back in his chair, letting the extra ten pounds of bulk he'd gained on his lean frame since getting to Argentina hang out. He had been gorging himself on Parrillada since he got here. He loved barbecue, and the Argentinians were in a league all their own in his mind. He pressed shoulder-length blonde hair off his forehead and behind his ear around the blue light-blocking glasses he wore.

"You're ready then?" Sigfried Himmler asked.

Gary gave him an arrogant look. "That's what I told you."

"You understand this part of the operation is the linchpin of the whole plan. The American public must believe that the virus is everywhere and that the government is hopelessly outmatched, and then the division and blame must start. The country must start so viciously tearing itself to pieces that they cannot see their own hands in front of their faces. Ultimately, it can't matter if only one or one million gets infected. We're trying to cause a nationwide panic."

Gary nodded again, more slowly. "I. Get. It," he said, mouthing the words as slowly as possible. He took pleasure in seeing the rage in Sigfried's eyes. Most of his colleagues were terrified of the SS. Not him. He was too valuable to their plans. The truth was he had enjoyed the power he wielded working in Silicon Valley. He alone decided the information that made it to the masses. His bosses tried to give him guidelines, but most couldn't wrap their heads around the complex engineering that went into his work.

The New Reich, though he had been raised in it, was something he began to question in his time there. He believed in socialism at all costs, and killing a few people to get there didn't bother him a lick. But the New Reich had eighty years to get it back into the world. It seemed like they were more interested in profiting off the suffering of others than bringing socialism back. Gary was starting to think they were no better than a global criminal syndicate. Like Specter from James Bond.

But they were more than that—Gary knew. Far larger, far bolder, and with far more resources than a common criminal organization. Some part of him still believed in the core idea of what they were there for. I was the only thing that kept him from leaving.

"Run through the plan again so I know it cold," Sigfried ordered him.

Gary sighed in a bored sort of way, as if what they were doing was the easiest thing ever. "At your go-ahead, our bot networks will begin to flood the major social media networks with content. Content that's been designed in every way to take advantage of the algorithms. It will inspire panic about this new virus and amplify blame from the left and the right, and it will look completely organic. I'm also using back doors I've placed in all the algorithms to ensure the content is boosted out to the masses —which will take the engineers at least a week to figure out what's going on. By that time, it will be too late. The country will have picked up on the narrative from their side and will become our bot network without us having to do anything else. At that point, my job's done."

"Can it be traced back to us?" asked Sigfried.

"Once again, no, it can't. The bot networks for the initial attack are all over the world. It'll seem like basic cyber warfare from Russia and China—nothing they aren't doing every day or didn't do during the last pandemic. But I will need you to tell me when we're doing this because I'm a busy guy. I can't just drop everything at a moment's notice for your plan."

Gary knew the second he said that it was the wrong thing to say. Sigfried gave him a deadly look that told him just how far he'd gone. Gary hadn't noticed how cold those eyes had been until now. He strongly suspected this man was a killer now.

"You'll do what you're told, or you'll die," responded Sigfried matter-of-factly. Gary blushed red like he had told a dirty joke to a room full of people, but no one had laughed. Maybe he wasn't as safe as he'd thought.

"Fortunately, you're in luck. The operation will kick off in twenty-four hours. My men here will ensure you have everything you need." Sigfried snapped his finger, and the door to Gary's office opened. Two very serious-looking men walked in and took up positions on either side of his door. Gary could tell by the all-black business suits they wore that they were SS soldiers like Sigfried.

"What are they supposed to, like, get me coffee or something?" Gary asked.

"No, but they'll be keeping an eye on you for the duration of the operation."

"And how long will that take," asked Gary, already growing uncomfortable with his new babysitters.

"It will all be over by the end of the week." Sigfried laughed, making to leave.

Sigfried walked down the hall of the building. All the pieces were finally in place. Years of planning, all coming to fruition. He wouldn't let this disloyal man ruin it. The SS knew he was wavering. Questioning the cause of the New Reich. In fact, when he was done, the two SS guards watching over him would become his executioners.

33

C olin snuck forward as carefully as he could. The attack would kick off on his signal. He moved one foot in front of the other, probing the ground with each footfall to ensure he didn't make any unnecessary noise. Now, within twenty feet, the flames of the campfire danced in rhythmic patterns off the hanging jungle foliage around him.

He slowed his breathing with no small effort, trying to calm himself for what they were about to do. All three men but one were asleep now in beach chairs surrounding the fire. The third seemed to be muttering to himself in a drunken stupor, the bottle in his left hand and his right gripping the barrel of an AK-74 by his side.

Colin looked over at Grinch and nodded to him, and they pushed the rest of the distance to the edge of the forest, the signal given and received. Colin drew his Special Forces Yarborough knife given to him as a gift from a fellow operator on his first deployment. It wasn't the first time the blade had killed. The familiar hilt in his hand felt safe to Colin, as if this was a weapon he knew well.

He let his MCX rest on its sling, and he drew his custom

M1911A1 from the holster at his hip. Grinch would take the man on the right, and if the far man awoke to his companion's untimely demise before they could get to him, Colin would shoot him. Colin flipped up his night vision goggles and let his eyes adjust to the firelight for a moment.

Then, like a wraith, he proceeded quickly and quietly to the back of the man in front of him. In one swift move, he wrapped his arm around the man's head, closing off his mouth with his elbow, and pulled the blade to the side, opening the skin of the man's neck from ear to ear. The man barely struggled being so drunk, and Colin heard the plastic bottle fall to the soft earth. All the while, he kept his eyes on the man still asleep across from him, waiting for his current prey to die.

A moment later, the man's last spasms stopped. In his peripheral vision, he could see Grinch finishing the guard to his right. But Murphy, it seemed, was not on their side this evening. The man across from him stirred at some unknown sound from the jungle. He opened his eyes in horror, seeing Colin, and went for his weapon. *Too late,* Colin thought. He brought his pistol up in a flash and fired a suppressed .45 round into the man's head. He toppled backward off his seat from the powerful round at less than five feet, invisible blood in the black of night coating his surroundings.

Grinch moved to him as quickly as possible. "You think someone heard that?"

"Not sure. Let's move, though." They ran up to the massive truck hiding in an area to their right that had been hacked out of the trees and ducked under the camouflage netting surrounding it. Colin took one look at it, and all hopes of disabling it quietly evaporated from his mind. He spoke Russian from his Green Beret days, but he could barely read it, which meant the odds of him finding an off button quick enough to avoid detection were non-existent. That and if they were killed, and the enemy turned it back on, the rest of the team could never get the air support they needed to live.

"Grinch, Plan B. Get the C-4. We're blowing this thing."

The man stepped behind him, pulling things out of his backpack while he pulled security. "Got it," he whispered a moment later.

"Wire it up. I'll keep an eye out."

"Copy," replied Grinch.

In the distance, Colin saw a flashlight moving toward them from a hundred yards away. "Get it moving! I think someone heard the shot," he whispered to Grinch.

Behind him, the teammate was strapping bricks of C-4 to the vehicle's fuel tank, launcher section, and one more for good measure on some controls on the side. Colin activated his radio. "Team, fireworks in one mike. Prep for assault on my mark."

He got two copies in return. All was ready. The man with the flashlight was scarcely fifty yards from them now, and Colin thought he could hear him softly calling someone's name over the noise from the jungle.

"Ready," Grinch whispered, coming over next to him. They both moved into the trees to what they judged was a safe distance and hunkered down. Colin nodded at Grinch, and Grinch hit the detonator.

A deafening explosion tore through the night, silencing the jungle and reflecting orange light onto everything. Colin felt hot air rush over him as the heat wave pushed outward before collapsing back in on itself. The massive trailer momentarily lifted in the air before flipping onto its side with a metallic clang. The missiles in their armored carriers did not explode, but judging by the fact the trailer was on fire, Colin made a mental note to stay well clear of them.

"Execute," Colin said into his radio. He stood from his knee and began running back to the clearing around the house. The guard who had been moving toward them was just getting back up from being knocked over by the blast. He looked shell-shocked. Colin put two rounds from his Spear center mass into the man as he raced past the trees toward the house.

"Drone on the pyramid in one minute," Charlie said in his ear.

Colin hit the wall of the house, using it to stop his momentum from his all-out sprint like a hockey board. A moment later, Grinch arrived next to him. Lights were starting to turn on in the windows over their heads. Colin followed the wall to its end and turned into a driveway in front of the house. He counted three Ferraris, two G Wagons, and three sleepy-looking guards emerging from the front door looking confused.

Everything was bathed in luminescent green and blue as he moved, and the guards seemed to be having a hard time finding the lights in the confusion. Colin painted one of them with the infrared laser on his MCX calling his shot and saw Grinch's laser settling on the other. His rifle spit twice, and the guard going for the lights crumpled to the ground. A second later, the other collapsed next to him. Colin sighted the third guard preparing to fire, but Grinch got him first, dropping him with two more shots.

They bounded not for the front door the guards had come out of, but a side door to the house ten yards to the left. They stayed low as they ran. The lights were still out, at least out here, but they didn't know who was watching upstairs.

A moment later, they reached the side door, stepping from earth onto manicured bluestone, and prepared to make entry.

"Ready?" Colin asked Grinch.

"Let's breach."

34

Chiapas, Mexico

Witch, Sheriff, and Panda poured fire onto the entrance of the pyramid structure. They could see everyone emerging from the structure from their perch in the trees due to its well-lit opening.

"Snowman really kicked over a hornet's nest!" Sheriff yelled to Witch. Panda let out a burst from his XM250, the Army's newest replacement to the beloved SAW. Two guards threw themselves back into the entrance of the pyramid as the .277 Fury rounds slammed into the structure around them, sending bits of grayish-yellow rock flying through the air.

Sheriff painted one of the bad guys with his infrared laser and hit him three times center mass as he tried to make a run for the trees. The only advantage they had was that it was dark, and none of the cartel soldiers they were firing at could see them.

"Charlie, where's that drone?" he said into his radio. As if in answer to his question, a familiar high-pitched ripping sound emerged from the heavens above, and Sheriff closed his eyes knowingly.

A second later, a fantastic explosion turned the pyramid into a tomb as its hellfire missile closed its entrance forever. The hellfire, which could take out a modern battle tank, was more than enough for the crumbling structure, and the overpressure that hit the inside of the structure must have done catastrophic damage to the men inside. For a moment, they stood there as the light from the explosion faded, waiting to see if anyone made it out. They didn't.

Colin heard the blast in the distance as they kicked in the side door to the house and proceeded inside. It was empty where they entered the mansion, and it looked like a mud room. To the left was a door to the garage, and to the right was a kitchen down a hallway. "Hold," said Colin. He turned left into the garage, hoping the place had no basement. As he opened the door, he saw it was empty and searched for a second. A moment later, he found it. The fuse panel to the house. He ran to it and flipped off the master breaker to the house. *Now no one will have lights,* he said in his head.

"Lights out. Let's go," he said to Grinch a second later. They proceeded in a stack into the kitchen. It was massive with double islands. They split, and both took a side, heading toward the family room. In the distance, Colin saw a guard running through the family room and shot him twice. The suppressed rounds echoed in the house, but that didn't matter. The cartel knew they were here now. They just couldn't see where.

Grinch split right through a butler's pantry and dining room, and Colin took the family room and office. It almost looked like a normal family home, a wealthy one, but oddly normal for a cartel headquarters. Although Colin wasn't sure what he expected. He cleared the office and family room in another thirty seconds and made his way toward the front hall, where the front door had been.

Grinch emerged to his right and fired three times, killing another guard who was emerging from another room off the front hall. The foyer was an open two-story area with a crystal chandelier overhead. Colin and Grinch proceeded to it together, and a cacophony of unmistakable AK-74 fire greeted them through the door. Colin looked at Grinch and nodded, and then they both pivoted away from the door as Colin tossed a flashbang grenade inside.

Normally, he would have tossed a fragmentation grenade during a hostile assault like this, but they needed answers, not indiscriminate dead bodies. They both stepped inside the extremely well-decorated room and fired several times. Two more guards went down from the quick spits of their rifles.

"Snowman, this is Sheriff. Proceeding to your location. Pyramid is toast."

"Copy, Sheriff. Secure the grounds closest to the beach; stay frosty over."

He got an acknowledgment as they stepped back to the front hall and started moving up the stairs. Colin heard yelling in Spanish. They moved as fast as they could, pressing to the top of the wrap-around staircase. At the top, they paused, using the right wall as cover. There were two hallways: one went left, and one went right. Colin was just motioning for Grinch to take the right when more gunfire ripped down the hallway toward them.

It was blind-fired but effective enough in the controlled space of the house. Something heavy slammed into the Mithril body armor Colin wore right on top of the bruise from where Jester had slammed into him. He grunted in pain, doubling over involuntarily.

"You hit?" Grinch yelled, returning fire down the hallway. Colin felt himself for blood, but his hands were dry. He felt the pancaked round sitting between his camouflage jacket and the vest.

He grunted. "I'm fine. Let's go that way," Colin said, motioning toward the gunfire.

He righted himself, and Grinch took point. It felt like he had cracked a rib, but he could at least move for the moment without the agonizing shooting pain of a full break. Colin took a deep breath in, which hurt like hell, and did his best to steady himself. They moved down the hallway. There were six doors on either side, three left and three right. They cleared a series of bedrooms in succession, but it was a dry hole. There was no one there. They turned back the other way and went down the other wing.

This hall had matching doors on either side but also one door at the end of the corridor. They cleared the first two before arriving at the third set of doors. Colin was about to kick them down when gunfire shredded the door. Colin grabbed Grinch by the vest and pulled him back just in time to avoid being hit. The gunfire continued shredding the white door in front of them. Colin grabbed another flashbang off his vest and tossed it inside.

The gunfire stopped, and he and Grinch hit the room together. Two guards had been shooting at them from behind a dresser they had moved for cover. They shot both with several more spits from the suppressed Sig's. They proceeded out into the hallway, checked the last room, and prepared to make entry into what must have been the master bedroom. Colin did a tactical reload, placing the other magazine with a few rounds left in his pocket. It was a double set of doors. Colin kicked them open. Then rolled back away while Grinch tossed yet another flashbang in.

The grenade had landed in a hallway and had stunned no one but the walls. They followed it in regardless. And cleared a palatial walk-in closet and a small sitting room before getting to the bedroom. There in front of them was the man who must have been the boss. To his credit, he wasn't cowering. He was attempting to control the situation by holding a pistol to a beautiful Hispanic woman's head, who was half naked, covered in seductive black lingerie.

"Put the gun down and let the girl go," said Colin. Grinch translated.

"I speak English. Now get out or I kill the girl. My men will be here soon, and you'll die for this!"

"Your men are dead, and you're coming with us."

The cartel boss grabbed the woman hard by her large breast and pulled her closer to the wall. "No, it can't be!" the man said exasperatedly.

Weird, this cartel guy seemed weirdly upset about being captured. Wasn't it a badge of honor to stay stoic around the authorities? He put the thought aside.

"You're coming with us. Now drop the girl and put the gun down slowly."

The cartel boss seemed to struggle with this internally. Colin saw a grainy tear running down his cheek in the night vision. He reflected that the man might just not be used to having dark shapes in the night pointing guns at him. The man's reply shocked him.

"Only if you help me get my daughter back."

35

Washington, D.C.

Wendy Simons stepped out of the black Suburban and breathed in the scent of flowers. D.C., or more specifically Old Town, Alexandria, right across the river, was quite literally a breath of fresh air this time of year. She took in the delicious smell of white wine, butter, and garlic that permeated the lower block of King Street even at this late hour and saw it was crowded this evening despite all that had gone on across the river. *People don't want to waste the nice night, especially after the winter they had this year,* she thought.

She turned right, walking toward the river rather than toward the restaurants she loved so much, and took off at a brisk pace. It was 10 p.m., and forty minutes earlier, the president had granted her permission to leave Camp David and whisked her by helicopter to Joint Base Anacostia Bolling, right across the river. An FBI counter-espionage agent she trusted had requested to meet with her in person with information on the attack.

She'd agreed and had planned to meet with him at FBI headquarters, but he'd requested to meet outside the building somewhere more inconspicuous. That's why she'd wound up here. She hit the water and saw the shining lights of D.C. shimmering across it. She turned left past Black Wall Hitch and the Chart House and walked past the tall ship toward the park that skirted the river line.

After walking for five minutes, she saw him sitting on a bench staring at the river and approached. "Nice night for a stroll," she said.

"If you didn't get your hands covered in anthrax today," he responded gruffly.

"Fair but true. Why did you want to meet Agent Savarese?" she asked.

He was short and skinny with big, bushy eyebrows. He looked around for a moment, checking that no one else was present. "I think I know who got your Green Beret team killed in Mexico."

Wendy looked at him seriously. "I'm listening."

"You remember John Fischer?"

She did. He was one of the agents working the Amerithrax case with her after Nine Eleven. He worked for the Defense Intelligence Agency now as a director, focusing on countering left-wing governments in South America. She had helped get him a job a few years back when he wanted to do something new but not retire. They were friends in a casual sort of way, as good coworkers were. But she couldn't claim to know him well.

"Of course. I've known him for many years."

She had a bad feeling about where this was going. Savarese worked counterintelligence for the FBI. He'd even been involved in the high-profile takedown and indictment of Senator Rand last year in a Chinese conspiracy. The takedown had helped bring the new administration to power in the last election cycle.

"Well, then, you know he left the Bureau under a cloud of suspicion."

"I did not," she said outraged.

Savarese held up a hand. "It wasn't known. In fact, there wasn't even an investigation. There were just suspicions from counterespionage that could never be proved. Believe me, they tried a few times, but nothing ever came to fruition."

"What gave them that idea?"

"Odd details in several cases. Misplaced pieces of evidence. Various agents reported it to internal affairs. They couldn't get anything on him either. They sent it to us and said they couldn't prove anything, but he seemed off. Then he jumped to DIA. And frankly, we were too buried to follow up on pure smoke."

Wendy frowned and crossed her arms. She didn't like hearing this about anyone working in her field. But she especially didn't like hearing it about someone she was friendly with in a professional capacity. "Why do you think he's involved here?"

"Well, I may have done some extracurricular activities to keep an eye on him. Flagged a few credit cards, gone through some trash, broke into his house once or twice—"

"You did what?" Wendy asked, cutting him off.

He held up a hand in response to quiet her. She wasn't used to anyone speaking to her like this anymore, but having come from the field and still deeply respecting that pressure, she conceded.

"I found something. Well, two things to be exact. One file was shoved under a floorboard. A background report on Mr. Dominick Schmidt's parents from the Amerithrax investigation, and an armband, black with a red swastika on it. The file showed that his parents were German refugees after World War Two. The armband I'm not sure about. It didn't show up in any of the other cases he worked. And it's not a symbol for any Nazi-like groups."

Wendy had been over every bit of that case. She'd never seen anything about Dominick's parents being refugees. She also wasn't sure why it mattered. That case was about Islamic terrorism, not right-wing extremism. She made a mental note to investigate that file. "Could the armband be some kind of family heirloom from before the Nazi fall?"

"Not that I could tell. The colors are also always the other way around. With a red background and a black swastika. But even so. Hard to imagine anyone making it into the FBI with leanings like that. The background checks, psych evals, and polygraphs screen most of the nut jobs out."

"We've gotten it wrong before. Think about Robert Philip Hanssen. He was an agent and wound up being one of the most damaging spies in U.S. history."

"Still, it's unlikely," Savarese said, slowing the last word down for emphasis. Wendy stared out at the Potomac. The temperature was starting to drop. Spring hadn't quite fully erased winter's breath yet. She felt uneasy. Like some new player had emerged that hadn't seen before or even thought to look for.

"Outside of the file and the armband, what's telling you he's guilty of something?"

"Well, not to bury the lead, but he didn't show up to work today at the DIA. And he bought a plane ticket out of the country on a credit card he doesn't know we know about. Pair that up with the anthrax attack today, and things start to look pretty suspicious. Oh yeah, as the DIA chief for Central and South America, he would have known about the Special Forces team being sent in. Seems convenient, don't you think?"

Wendy's eyes widened. Something was happening here. "When does the flight leave?"

"In thirty minutes. From Reagan," he said, pointing at the airport in the distance.

36

Colin's gun was still trained on the cartel boss's forehead. The woman in the black lingerie squirmed against him and let out a string of muffled sobs. Grinch advanced slowly on his right, pressing the gap between them and the man, letting him know that there was no way out of this. "What are you talking about?" Colin demanded.

"They took my daughter! That's the only reason I'm doing any of this. She's sick, and they said they could help her, but only if I helped them!"

"Who took your daughter?" Colin pressed.

"That deranged Doctor Dominick Schmidt and his gang of Nazi thugs."

"The fuck are you talking about?" asked Grinch.

Colin knew the name. It was why they were here in the first place, *but Nazis?* This guy had lost him. He pressed for more information. "Tell us where the tainted drugs are first, and we'll help with your daughter. But only if you put the girl down."

"Give me your word," the cartel leader said.

"I give you my word," replied Colin. The man took a second sizing him up, but in the end, he sensed something rock solid and dependable there. The gun dropped to the floor. The girl went running to Colin and wrapped her arms around him. Colin peeled her arms back and passed her to Grinch. Not that he didn't enjoy the attention, but he had work to do.

The drug dealer dropped his hands from the air behind his back as Colin zip-tied him. "What's your name?" he asked.

"Ernesto Gomez," the cartel leader replied.

"Okay, Ernesto. Why don't you tell me what's going on here? And listen to me very carefully. I need you to tell me everything, or I'm not going to be able to help you. My government designated your organization a terrorist group. Meaning we have different rules for how we can treat you. If you don't want to be subjected to"—Colin weighed the words for a moment trying to decide what would have the most effect—"battlefield interrogation, then I need you to be very forthcoming."

Ernesto looked like he wanted to protest. Like every fiber of his cartel thug being wanted to tell him to piss off. But he was a father first and foremost, and that fact seemed to be winning out. Colin saw this in his eyes, which was why Witch wasn't on his way up to the bedroom right now with his bag of tricks. Colin also had to remember that this man was all that stood in between his country and a biological attack. His niceness was a facade, and he wasn't afraid to break it if he had to.

Colin set Ernesto in a chair and set up a mobile phone across from him to record the interrogation. As he did so he got the all clear in his earpiece from his team. They were safe. For now. A helicopter would be on its way from the McRaven to take them and their prisoner to safety when they were ready. Grinch went to confer with the team and was replaced by Panda and his Belgian Malinois. The dog growled when it saw Ernesto, then settled into a down stay next to his master by the door.

Ernesto gave the dog a nervous look. "I never liked dogs," he said to break the tension. "Too many wild ones on the streets where I grew up. Been bitten too many times. Not the same as your pets in America. Though I sense this one could give the wild ones, I grew up with a good scare."

Colin nodded at him. "Please begin." He wasn't about to small talk with this guy. He could be nice enough to him to talk, but they weren't friends.

"About five years ago, I ran operations for a Sinaloa-based cartel. In short, this meant everything from procuring the product to transporting it and seeing that payment was delivered and processed. But my daughter began to become sick. I had made enough money and wanted to spend more time with her. So, I tried to get out. Funny thing about what we do—there really is no way out. Once you're in, you're committed for life. Luckily for me, the head of our enforcement arm decided he wanted more from life, too. Meaning he wanted to take over the whole operation. A civil war ensued, and the cartel fractured into two, three pieces at first. But no side could get control of the others. During this time, my daughter's condition began to worsen." Ernesto paused for a minute, wiping an eye, as if this brought him deep emotion.

"Please continue," Colin said after a moment. "No one could figure out what was wrong with her. She was dying, and it wasn't any of the usual culprits. During that time, a man approached me. They said he represented a series of backers who were interested in starting a new organization. Well-funded and fully backed by their might. I said no at first. This civil war was my opportunity to slip away. But they found out about my daughter Louisa. Said they could help. That they had many leading doctors on their payroll. They said while I thought about it, they would have someone take a look at her if I liked. I agreed."

"What was the organization called?" Colin asked.

"I didn't find that out until years later. They are called the New Reich. Or at least I think that's what they are called.

Anyway, one of their doctors saw her and said he had seen this before and that he could treat her with an experimental medicine that could cure her. I knew what would come next. The organization agreed to treat her under the condition that I stand up and lead their new cartel. I had little choice but to agree. Louisa was dying. So, I began setting up their organization. It was quick work. I'd done it before for Sinaloa. And with the backers hundreds of millions, they committed we were soon growing into one of the largest in the business."

Ernesto looked proud when he said this. Like it was his life's labor to be a scumbag. He seemed to think of himself in the same light as Warren Buffet or Elon Musk.

"And your daughter?" Colin asked.

"She recovered with treatment. And was doing better. For a time. Her health seemed to grow with Descanso Eterno's. The name we chose for our organization. But she required regular checkups and doses of an experimental medicine they were giving her. But the deal came with certain conditions. Any time the organization asked me to do something, I had to do it without question. Every time I didn't, treatment would be delayed, and she would get worse."

Colin interrupted, "You built one of the most powerful cartels in the hemisphere. It seems like you were gaining enough power to push back on an arrangement like that."

"I tried. That's when things got worse. Louisa took a turn for the worse, and it became clear the only option for her health was to comply with their requests—which became more ludicrous by the week starting a few months ago."

"The nightclub massacre?" Colin asked. Ernesto nodded in reply.

"And the drugs. They began requesting shipments to experiment on. For months, we shipped them large batches of cocaine. Then they made a new request. We were to round up several customers and take them to a forest bunker they had constructed. We did this several times. And were never allowed to see what they were doing. But I snuck a man in the jungle to take a look. What we found—" He shuddered.

"Well, was shocking, to say the least. They were clearly running some kind of viral experiment with the drugs. Then, a few days ago, they stopped their experiments altogether. And requested one final batch from us. Several hundred kilos. Around the same amount, your country consumes in a day. That was two days ago."

Two days ago, Colin thought. *Not good.*

"Where's your daughter?" Colin asked.

"They took her for treatment. Said they had a new treatment that might cure her. We've only communicated via video chat for a month. It was heavily implied that I would get her back when they were finished with what they were doing."

No wonder this guy had capitulated to this New Reich. His balls were in a vice. Parents would do anything for their children. Especially to keep them alive. Colin had never come even close to having kids. But he remembered how his sister cared for him when he was young. That was about as close to a mother's love as he thought he might ever experience. It was powerful. He could only imagine what he might do for his own kid someday.

"Where are they holding her?"

"I'm not sure. But I think I know a way for you to find out."

37

The president had opted to stay the night at Camp David to give his people a breather. The past few days had been long, and truthfully, a fresh cup of coffee in the cool morning mountain air sounded useful to his strained mind. He needed to think things through and order his thoughts on all that had happened. He knew his people were working in overdrive to find out everything they could about this shadowy New Reich.

The Echo Team they'd sent in had done good work getting so far in such a short period of time. But now they were faced with more questions than answers and a clock that wouldn't stop ticking toward oblivion. The president took a sip of steaming hot coffee and stared up at the mountain. *Well, mountain is a bit generous,* he thought. As with any mountain on the east coast of the United States, it was more of a very tall, steep hill. But he appreciated the quiet of it all away from the buzz of the White House and D.C.

"Morning, Mack," the president said to Mack Tomlin as he walked up in his Army PT's. Mack was avid about maintaining his shape even though he was a member of the General Staff.

"Mr. President. Any chance there's any more java?"

"Of course," said the president, motioning toward a carafe and another mug next to him. "Run clear out the cobwebs?"

Mack frowned. "If you're asking if I've accepted the loss of most of a Special Forces ODA at the direction of this New Reich and the cartel, then no, I'm not sure I'm going to be able to shake that off for a while. But a good run always helps to cut through the clutter."

"Good. We're going to need to be clutter-free today if we're going to stop this. We're going to need to temporarily close all ports of entry into the United States and seal the southern border. And when I say sealed, I mean *sealed*. Not like it is now where things still make it across. The ports are easy. We can put a temporary hold on ships and aircraft coming in internationally. We have plans in place for just that contingency. The southern border will require executive action. We can federalize the Texas National Guard and deploy forces from Fort Bliss. The 1st Armored Division is doing a work up there now and is fully geared up to be deployed. I think we can plug the border with that to start and some support from the Air Force."

"You think?" asked the president.

"Nothing certain, Mr. President, but this gives us the best chance."

"Do it. What are our containment options if this thing makes it over the border?"

"Well, Mr. President, hemorrhagic fevers are inherently not easy to spread. Unless this is a genetically modified variant that's airborne, which is unlikely if they're attaching it to cocaine. I would say containment would be a fairly simple exercise if it were a limited outbreak. But if the drugs break containment and are distributed across the U.S. to hundreds of locations, we're going to have a very hard time."

"We need options, Mack."

"We have them, sir. They're just not good. All the operational plans for this fit under Operation Hydra, a plan that was heavily modified during COVID-19. The first step in a scenario like this with a truly deadly pathogen—which would be anything upward of twenty percent—would be a total shutdown of interstate travel enforced by the National Guard and a declaration of martial law. The authorization allows for the suspension of Posse Comitatus with an emergency two-thirds Congressional vote. You have the numbers for that, sir."

Posse Comitatus was the law that prevented the military from operating within U.S. borders.

"That's a bad option, Mack. Half the country would rebel after the COVID lockdowns. They'd think it's some kind of government takeover."

Mack's frown got even deeper, which was saying something. "It would be, sir. At least for a short period of time. It's the only plan that gives us the best chance at stopping the spread. We've put the virology teams on alert at Fort Deitrick to begin receiving samples from the cartel bunker in Mexico. From there, they can get a read on whether our experimental Ebola vaccinations will be effective against the pathogen. If so, we need to take pharmaceutical manufacturing facilities under the Emergency Defense Production Act to begin producing as much of the vaccine as we can.

"In conjunction with that, our stockpiles of PPE are full to bursting from COVID. We'll begin airlifting massive quantities of supplies to military bases across the country to be distributed to hospitals at the correct time."

The president grew more concerned with every word Mack said. "Mack, half the country's not going to take a vaccine after COVID. And we're going to have an open rebellion on our hands if we try to mandate it. What kind of casualties are we looking at if this thing breaks containment?"

"The problem is the major cities, sir. We can concentrate our response around those areas. The country's rural areas are spread out enough for spread not to be an issue if people keep to themselves. But most of the U.S. is concentrated in the major cities. If this virus averages what other Ebola strains can do, we're looking at losing roughly twenty to thirty percent of the American population within two months."

"Mack, that's almost a hundred million people."

The silence hung in the air, as if the dire consequences of failure were sucking all the oxygen from the space they were in.

"What about if it's a contained outbreak in one major city?"

Mack thought for a second about this as if scrubbing his mind for details. "If it's a small city closer to the border, say Dallas or Austin, we could cordon it off and not let anyone in or out until the outbreaks stopped. We have plans for this under Operation Hydra. If it breaks loose somewhere like Los Angeles, the response will have to be somewhat more acute, Mr. President. The roads in and out would have to be sealed with military units and possibly airstrikes to get them sealed rapidly enough, but there are too many people there to help. Not that we wouldn't try. But if they tried to break free or there was an uprising to leave the city, which we've anticipated in our war games on the operation, the only way to effectively put it down and stop the spread would be massive bombing."

"You want me to bomb my own people?" the president asked in horror. "If it comes to it, we will request it, yes, sir. And there's one other thing. If we're about to lose containment of a major metro area, say New York City, the only option available to us will be a tactical nuclear strike. Like cutting off our gangrenous arm to save our body."

"I'd never authorize a nuclear strike anywhere, let alone on American soil."

"You would if it meant sacrificing a million people to save 350 million more."

"Even then... we have to stop this from happening, Mack. The country won't survive something like this. And if the world sees America doing this to its own people to save itself, I can't imagine the chaos that will ensue."

William Joyce stood up and drained the last of his coffee. It was going to be a busy day. "Hopefully, our Echo Team can stop things before it's too late."

38

The MH-60S Knighthawk came in low over the water to avoid radar before landing just off the beach. It wasn't quite dawn yet, but the stars were slowly disappearing, and the sky was lightening. The rotor wash whipped sand everywhere, instantly reminding Colin of his time in the Middle East. He took one last look at the palatial estate before grabbing Ernesto Gomez by the arm and dragging him to the waiting helicopter. The rest of the team followed, loading bags of equipment filled with electronics and paper files from the house.

Another team was on its way to collect samples from the virology lab, and a third Ground Branch team was heading in to blow up the equipment they'd left in the woods. Resources were starting to pop up everywhere as the gravity of the threat emerged. Colin sat Ernesto between him and Jester so he couldn't go anywhere, and a second later, he felt the helicopter begin to lift off.

He kept his eyes out the door of the Knighthawk, scanning for threats, but none materialized, and eventually, they were far enough away from land that a lucky shot with a shoulder-fired missile wouldn't hit them. Colin relaxed for a second, taking a deep breath and closing his eyes. The quick opportunity for sleep was one of the few he would get before this thing was over, and he was desperately tired.

Thirty minutes later, they touched down on the McRaven, and Colin woke up. He yawned and stood up, grabbing Ernesto with him. A familiar face greeted him on the flight deck.

"Follow me!" Sarah Gonzalez shouted over the powering down rotors.

Colin did so, following her into a second, smaller hangar bay where a familiar setup was waiting for them. Several computers were set on a bunch of folding tables and a litany of other supplies, including coffee and snacks. Colin reached for the coffee and grabbed a sandwich as well. He identified it as turkey only after taking a bite. He was too hungry to care.

"Hey boss, long time no see," said Charlie Allen.

"Good to see you guys too."

Team Alien was its own little family. Made extra close by the fact that none of them had families of their own. It was a prerequisite of being a part of one. So, when Colin said it was good to see them, he meant it. He placed Ernesto in a chair. "Charlie, we've got a job for you," he said, handing him a phone. "This is Ernesto's phone. He was FaceTiming with Dominick Schmidt; can you figure out where the call came from?"

Charlie had clearly been waiting for this. The interrogation video had been sent to them as soon as Colin was finished, two hours ago.

"No problem, boss," Charlie said eagerly, taking the phone and plugging it into his computer.

"How long?" asked Colin.

"An hour. Maybe two," replied Charlie.

"All right, everyone. Get some sleep, food, and a shower if you can. We don't know where this is going to take us next," Colin said to all the operators in the room. He grabbed another sandwich himself, this time roast beef, avoiding the tuna salad. The military never did fish well, and he sat down next to Charlie.

He was clicking away at a loud mechanical keyboard at an unbelievable speed, locked in a world only he understood. Colin watched for a minute in muted fascination. He was trying to process everything he'd been through in the last two days, but nothing was making sense at the moment. He was too tired.

39

John Fischer had been sitting with a stunned look on his face for hours. The bland interrogation room inside FBI headquarters in downtown D.C. looked like any primetime cop drama. A table, three chairs, and a mirror on one wall. John, as a former FBI agent, had probably seen rooms like this hundreds of times. Yet he still looked stunned into disbelief, Wendy thought. He didn't even seem indignant at his capture. An innocent man would have been going on and on about how he was a high-ranking government official. But John wasn't.

He looked like a man who had been caught red-handed. "Tell us why you were running, John," Agent Savarese said from her left.

John looked pained, like he was agonizing over what to do. "I was just going on a trip. Taking some time off to refresh myself."

"Without informing your direct superiors. During Star Set protocols with interdiction operations happening in an area of the world you're responsible for?" asked Wendy, not believing a word of his lies.

"It must have been an error; I submitted for the time off before I left."

"No, you didn't. Stop lying. It's you're only way out of this," said Agent Savarese. John very much looked like he wanted a way out of this. She could see it in the look that flicked across his face when Agent Savarese spoke. Like he didn't know there was a way out of this. Wendy was starting to put something together in her mind. As if a couple of pieces of this complex puzzle just started to fit together.

"We found the armband, John. And the missing file from Amerithrax. Tell me, how long have you been a member of the New Reich?"

John went from looking stunned and unsure about his situation to fearful. "Where did you hear that name?" he whispered, like someone was going to hear him if he didn't keep his voice low.

Savarese shot Wendy the slightest look, telling her to keep moving in this direction.

"They're behind this somehow, aren't they, John? Behind Amerithrax as well, and you've been working for them all along," she prodded.

"You need to stop. You don't know what you're getting yourself into. You should walk away and forget you ever had this thought."

"You know we can't do that," Agent Savarese responded.

"Now tell us how it all fits together and how we can stop it, and we'll see what we can do to take the death penalty off the tables," Wendy pushed.

John looked exasperated, like his only choices were between getting eaten by a lion or throwing himself off a cliff.

"You're leaving the country because you're scared of what they're about to do. That's the only reason you're running. What do you think's going to happen when we announce to the world that we've caught a high-profile traitor right next to your name and face? Do you think you'll ever make it to trial? I don't like your chances judging by how scared you are of these guys. Or maybe we're out of space here, and our only option will be to take you down to a hospital, handcuff you to a chair in the emergency room, and let you reap what you've sown. We'll see how quiet you are when your organs start liquifying, and your eyes are bleeding," Savarese bellowed, his mouth spitting venom with every word.

"You can't do that," John said, his lip quivering in fear.

"Then tell us how it all fits together," said Wendy, "or so help me God, I'll let Agent Savarese make good on his threats."

John sighed, clearly shaking out of nervousness as he did. "Okay. But can I please have some water and something to eat? I've been sitting here for hours, and I'm diabetic. I need to keep my blood sugar steady."

"Start talking, and we'll get you something," replied Wendy. She nodded at the mirror. Someone behind the glass would go to the kitchenette and get the man something. She had observed the insulin pump clipped to his belt when he walked in. And having this guy die on her wouldn't help them with anything.

"I've been a citizen since I was born—"

"So have all of us. What the fuck does that mean?" Savarese shot back, looking annoyed.

"Not of the United States. But not of the New Reich as well. I was born in Argentina. My family, though, was originally from Germany. They made it out in the ratlines set up by the Vatican after the fall of the Third Reich toward the end of World War Two. My father was important. He was a high-ranking Gestapo officer and had helped architect some of the ways people got out when it became clear the war was lost. And a lot of people got out," John said, looking Wendy dead in the eye.

"How many?" she asked.

"Thousands. I don't know the exact number. Secrecy is a part of life in the New Reich. But enough to start over. And vast amounts of capital. Keep in mind we controlled essentially all of Europe at our height. And the resources we managed to gather. Well, let's just say the Allies didn't recover as much as they thought they did after the war. We've been careful over the years. No one knew we were there. We've been growing in numbers. Gathering resources, and our planning."

Savarese looked at Wendy, stunned.

"I've heard of the ratlines. We've investigated them many times. Nothing ever comes up besides some German-looking villages in Argentina and a lot of speculation," stated Wendy.

"We are well hidden and frankly everywhere. You'd need more than half-hearted investigations and an unquenchable desire to believe you defeated us so absolutely we could never come back. But if America has failed to learn any lesson in the past eighty years, it's that wars are never truly won. Your enemies may disappear for a while, but they always seem to pop up somewhere else."

"Why should I believe you?" Wendy asked.

"Just look at Amerithrax. Our handprints were all over it. Look at that file you found on Dominick Schmidt's parents. Oddly, same story as me. Parents emigrated from Argentina with a German background. And do you remember the money that moved during 9/11? Nearly one and a half trillion dollars were wiped off the market in a day. Seven hundred billion dollars were traded in and out of the dark pools before the markets closed. Five hundred billion, gone forever, with no explanation when the market opened again. Financial crimes chalked it up to people being scared, pulling money from the market. Convenient," he said.

Wendy stared at him in silence, thinking through the facts. His statistics were correct on the day, and she remembered them well as part of the Amerithrax case. A knock on the door interrupted her thoughts. A blonde female agent walked in and put a Styrofoam cup and a protein bar in front of John. "Eat," she said. "We'll be back in a moment."

Wendy and Savarese walked into the room behind the mirror and closed the door behind them. "One minute, please," she said to the blonde agent who'd brought the cup. The agent nodded, stood up, and left.

"What do you think of all this?" Savarese asked.

"I can't argue with anything he said. I honestly don't know. If he's right, he—" She stopped talking in alarm, staring through the mirror before running to the door and bursting back into the room with John Fischer. He was foaming at the mouth, choking as he gripped his throat, trying to make the agony stop. Wendy ran to him. "Tell me where they are!" she pleaded as she watched him slip away. He began to slump in his chair but managed to choke out one word—*blonde*—before he died.

"Who was that agent?" she said, whipping around toward Savarese.

"I don't know," he shot back.

"Go after her and lock the building down!"

40

Mexico, Pacific Coast, The McRaven

Colin awoke with a start as Sarah shook him awake. For a second, he didn't know where he was. Then it clicked that he was lying flat on his back on the hangar deck with a jacket underneath his head as a pillow. "How long have I been out?"

"About three hours. It took Charlie longer than he thought to get something." She replied. She offered him a strong hand to help him to his feet. He took it, standing up and stretching for a moment. She brushed off his back while he yawned, then handed him a coffee. Some days Colin swore he could drink nearly unlimited cups. The large amount of muscle tacked onto his frame, though, required more fuel than most people.

"What do you have, Charlie?"

"Well, first, I want to say this. The encryption I just broke to get us this information was advanced. Some of the best I've seen. We're talking somewhere between us and the Israelis, which is impressive. I broke it with our Lockpick tool, but even then, it took an uncomfortable amount of time."

Colin knew Lockpick was a quantum computer-based encryption breaker that the NSA had developed. While most computers used the binary language of only ones and zeroes and thought in bits, quantum computers could think in ones, zeros, ones and zeros, and essentially all combinations of those numbers at the same time, or what were called qubits. Charlie got excited when he explained qubits to Colin. The NSA was one of the first to figure out how to use the technology for espionage. As such, Lockpick was tightly controlled as an offensive cyber weapon that could snap any country's encryption, protecting their governments in the opening salvo of a war.

"I thought that Lockpick could break anything in seconds; isn't that kind of the point?"

Charlie got more excited but also looked concerned. "In most cases, yes. Most of the world's cryptography is based on RSA, ECC, and DH protocols. These systems rely on computationally difficult problems for current computers to solve. Generally, standard computers would take so long to break some of the more advanced encryption that most solutions rely on stealing the key to decrypt things rather than solving the problem. Whatever this was a form of post-quantum cryptography, most likely Lattice-based or Multivariate Polynomial. I sent it to the quantum guys at the NSA to work out. The only reason we know about them is because we've been testing several forms of post-quantum cryptography that the Lockpick system helped us develop. This is the first time we've seen it in the wild. The fact that this New Reich group has this is concerning."

"Everything about this is concerning Charlie. What else did you find?"

"I can tell you they're in Argentina. Most likely the Mendoza Province somewhere within the vicinity of Aconcagua—which is the highest peak in the Americas."

"They're in the Andes Mountains?" Colin asked. He'd heard

of the mountain before. He knew some guys in the Green Berets who had gone to climb it at one point.

"Well, they're at least somewhere close enough to see it. I'm still working on exact coordinates."

"Let me know when you have something."

As he finished talking to Charlie, the captain of the McRaven walked into the hangar. "Snowman?" he asked, walking over to Colin.

"Yes, sir."

"I'm Captain Gentry. I'm to tell you that samples of the suspected virus have been secured and are on their way to the United States for analysis." Captain Gentry was a tall man, easily two inches taller than Colin's six foot two and lanky. But his posture was rigid. He must have been competent to get command of the McRaven, Colin thought. The weapons systems on this ship were the most advanced in the fleet.

"Thank you, Captain. It looks like my men, and I will need to get to Argentina next," Colin said, motioning toward a computer where Charlie was busy tracing the location the video calls had come from. On a map, a red circle was narrowing over the presumed location.

"I can steam the ship in that direction, but our helicopters can't make it over the Andes. At a range that will get you there in a reasonable amount of time. They'll burn too much fuel in the thin air getting you around that mountain. We do have a carrier forming up. They could put you on one of their Ospreys. That would roughly work, but I think you need to get there faster. The best bet is to get you to a private airstrip on the ground and on a fast plane, which will get you there in around six hours, not two days."

Colin nodded. "Sarah," he said.

"On it, boss," she replied.

"Oh shit!" Charlie sighed.

The hacker rarely, if ever, swore. Colin knew it wouldn't be good. "What's up?" he asked.

"That call was only routed through the data center in Argentina. The call came from Belarus."

"You're telling me they're in Belarus?" Colin asked.

"I think Ernesto Gomez's daughter might be. I've got an exact fix on where that signal came from. But there's definitely something going on in Argentina. I'm in their system now. There's something massive there. The network node in Belarus is labeled; damn, it's in Cyrillic. Hang on."

Colin walked over to the computer. He learned Russian during his time in the Special Forces. But Charlie was faster, saving Colin from trying to decipher the strange letters of the Russian language. "The network node is labeled 'laboratory.'" They all looked at each other in the dim light of the hangar, the door to the outside being closed because of the cold Pacific weather. "That can't be a coincidence, can it?" Colin asked.

"You think they worked on the virus there?" Captain Gentry asked.

"I don't have that information here. Their IT footprint is just very neatly labeled now that I'm in."

"It could be nothing. But we can't take the risk that it is. Ernesto's still spilling his guts on their distribution network but refuses to give us the endpoints until we have his daughter. We can't be in two places at once. We need someone else to hit that lab."

"You know Belarus is a close Russian ally, right? With everything going on in the Ukraine, that's a very risky maneuver and could easily be seen as an act of war by the Russians if we're found out," Gentry added.

"Not sure we have much of a choice, Captain. We either do it, or tens of millions of Americans could die."

Five minutes later, they were being patched through to the

president. *Odd that Wendy is currently unavailable, but then again, she sees to a great number of things,* Colin thought.

"What's the situation, Snowman?" the president asked. Colin saw the look of surprise from Captain Gentry at the way the president addressed him. But then again, the captain had been the same rank the president was when he'd left the service. Perhaps they knew each other.

"Sir, we believe Ernesto Gomez's daughter is being held in a laboratory in Belarus. We need another team to hit that location while we proceed to Argentina. Ernesto won't give up any more information unless we retrieve his daughter safe and sound."

The president coughed. "Did you just say Belarus, Snowman?"

"Are you trying to start fucking World War Three?" another man asked. Colin recognized the voice as the president's Chief of Staff. "I know it's risky, sir, but it greatly increases our chances of stopping this attack from happening. I think we need to do it." Colin replied.

Silence followed for a moment. Colin could tell the president was thinking through his options. A third voice spoke. "Sir, we have a Delta Force team at Rammstein Air Force Base we could send in. They'd be perfect for this, and they're close by."

Colin knew Delta Force as the world's most elite Special Forces unit. He'd once had aspirations to join it before his fake death. More silence followed. As the president thought. "This needs to be full black, Mack. No one can ever know we were there or we'll be at war with Russia within a week."

"You got it, Mr. President."

"All right, spin 'em up."

41

Brest, Belarus

Master Sergeant Jake Lewis sat in the dark front seat of an old GM van that reeked of stale cigarettes. The team had been flown from Rammstein air base in Germany to a private airfield outside Lublin, Poland, then smuggled over the border by Arcady, their driver, who was on his second pack of cigarettes, since their journey had started two hours before.

Part of his exorbitant smuggling fee the CIA was gracious enough to pay to get them in and out of the country was several cartons of American Lucky Strikes, which apparently were a hot commodity inside sanctioned Russia. Jake would have been surprised if any of those cigarettes made it out of this car, let alone to Russia. In fact, he didn't trust this guy at all. The CIA said he could be trusted—something about them getting one of his relatives out of Ukraine. But Jake had been burned before. In front of him was a quiet neighborhood with homes and businesses interspersed throughout. It was a mix of Soviet-style ghoulish architecture and more classic European looks. Their target was fifty yards in front of them. A three-story building that looked like it could have been an apartment complex at some point but was now some kind of medical building.

It looked dark, but it was late—well past working hours local time. The proximity to Ukraine ensured that most businesses and homes turned off their lights as early as possible at night. It wasn't unheard of for a stray missile to land in Belarus these days, and no one wanted to add to their risk profile.

Behind him sat the five other members of his team, all kitted out in black with a variety of suppressed weapons, ranging from HK416 to MP7 submachine guns. On most of their laps sat Ops Core helmets with four monocled GPNVG night vision goggles. The helmets were on their laps because the van's ceiling was too low for the goggles in their flipped-up positions.

Another van sat on the opposite side of the building, carrying another assault team. He didn't know why this lab was so important, but he was betting it had to do with the Star Set protocols in effect. Worse yet, they were looking for a little girl. He didn't like the sound of a little girl being situated next to some kind of WMD. He missed his little girl back home in North Carolina. They were scheduled to rotate back home in another three weeks, and he didn't intend for anyone to mess that up.

"Bravo, this is Overwatch. The janitor just locked the front door and is on his way out. You're clear to proceed," came the call in his earpiece.

They couldn't use drones in Belarus, so the call came from a sniper from Alpha Team who was on a roof across the street.

"Alpha, this is Bravo 1. Execute," Jake said. Like clockwork, his men dismounted the vehicle, strapping their helmets on and stacking up to move the fifty yards to the front door. It was a black-out. Even the streetlights had been extinguished here, and the team moved with speed to the front door of the building while Alpha moved to the back.

The glass front doors to the building looked like they needed to be replaced, and the old lock keeping them closed took his breacher Ramirez all of twenty seconds to pick. "Breaching in ten seconds," he whispered.

"On your count, Bravo," came the reply from Alpha Team. "Making entry," Jake whispered. The team moved swiftly into the lobby, fanning out as they did so. The world was lit in pale shades of green with wraith-like lasers tracing the air as the IR beams from their rifles showed where their weapons were pointed. The plan from here was simple. Alpha Team would clear floor two while Bravo team cleared Floor three. They began moving to the lobby when an armed guard stepped out of a door to their right. He couldn't see them in the dark. Jake held up a fist, telling his team not to fire. The door behind him closed automatically. When he began walking, Jake fired a suppressed subsonic round into his head, killing him instantly. He'd wanted the door to close before in case there were more men in that room.

He motioned two of his men to check while the other covered the two elevator doors and a third that led to a staircase upstairs. Luckily, the man had come from a bathroom. "Guys, not feeling too well, judging by the smell," Ramirez said.

"He's also fucking dead," replied Regutti, grabbing the body and dragging it back into the bathroom.

"Can it. Alpha, first-floor lobby clear, proceeding to the third floor," Jake said, motioning his men to move to the stairs—elevators were death traps.

They moved with speed to the stairwell and proceeded carefully but swiftly up the three flights of stairs to the third floor. When they reached the door, they stacked up and prepared to make entry. Just as they were about to make entry, Jake's earpiece squawked, "Bravo, hold. You've got a tango right on the other side of that door. Make entry on my signal."

"Acknowledged," Jake told the sniper from Alpha Team. A second later, he heard glass break on the other side of the door and a thud as a man lost the top of his head to a suppressed 7.62 round fired from an HK417 across the street. The team pushed through the door, the threat having been removed, and were greeted by nothing. Outside of a few roughly framed offices, the entire third floor was a blank canvas that looked to be under construction. They fanned out and looked around regardless, but it was empty.

"Alpha, this is Bravo; third floor's a dry hole. Any luck?"

"Bravo, we got three bad guys, but this floor is empty."

"Copy. Let's get—"Jake stopped short as he turned back toward the staircase and saw a map of the building on the wall. "Alpha, looks like there's a basement. Pull security on the lobby while we proceed down and search it," Jake said.

"Copy."

There wasn't a basement on the plans, Jake thought as they went down the stairs. But the plans they had dated back to the nineties, and judging by the construction they'd seen on the third floor, things had changed a lot since then. "Bravo, there's another staircase at the back of the building we made entry at that goes down. It's a good bet you can get to the basement from there."

"Copy, coming out the lobby staircase in three seconds," Jake said. He didn't want to get shot, especially not by his own guys. They crossed the lobby, and he fist-bumped Alpha Team's leader as he proceeded to the back of the building toward the other set of stairs. They reached it twenty seconds later and moved down a flight of stairs. When Jake got to the bottom, he saw fluorescent lights through a window in a metal door. He flipped up his night vision goggles and peered through. It looked like the wing of any modern hospital back in the U.S. It was the fact that it was in the basement of a Belorussian office building that surprised him.

He motioned to his men that there were two more guards on the other side of the door. The lack of security was surprising but not concerning. The bad guys didn't think anyone knew this was here. *Knew what was here, though,* Jake thought before swinging the door open, and two of his men spun into the room. Two suppressed shots with subsonic ammunition followed, and two more dead guards lay on the white tile floor, blood spreading from their heads in neat pools.

There was what looked to be a nursing station set up, but the night nurse must have been doing rounds. Past, it looked to be four hospital rooms with charts hanging outside their doors. The team cleared the first two rooms at the same time. In one, they found the night nurse administering drugs to an elderly man. The man looked to be in a coma. The nurse, they zip-tied and gagged, leaving her on a floor. Jake didn't like the idea of killing nurses, and she couldn't identify them. His team took photos of both of their faces for good measure. They then moved to the next two rooms. One was empty, but the other had a sick-looking little girl in a bed. And the oddest-looking doctor Jake had ever seen.

Odd because he was holding a gun to his patient's head. Jake knew his team's first reaction would be to shoot the man before he could react. But he grunted "Hold" to them. He knew the girl was important, but this doctor might be involved somehow. He needed to make a quick determination here.

"Who are you?" he asked the doctor.

"I'm Doctor Dominick Schmidt," the man said with too much enthusiasm.

Red flag.

"Why are you holding this girl hostage?"

"Because—" the doctor started.

But Jake had already pressed the trigger.

42

"You're telling me we lost her?" Wendy Simons asked. "I'm telling you we can't currently find her," the head of security for the building responded. "What kind of nonsense response is that?" she shot back. "Find her now or find a new job."

Wendy was pissed. Not only had she lost a valuable lead in the hunt for the people responsible for the impending attack, but the person who had lost her that lead, in an FBI office in Washington, D.C. no less, was now gone. She regretted snapping at the uniformed security officer almost immediately, but she needed results, or her country was in trouble. Not to mention the fact that being that close to death tended to heighten one's awareness of their own mortality. She took a deep breath. Three FBI agents armed with submachine guns now stood guard by her while they determined the threat and searched for the assassin.

They were losing, and Wendy couldn't seem to do anything about it. America's vast intelligence apparatus, which she was responsible for, couldn't seem to keep up with its adversaries anymore. Every time they flipped over a rock looking for the snake, more scorpions skittered out. Something needed to change. They needed a win and a big one to put their enemies on their heels and regain the initiative. Being the king was hard.

One of the protective agents near her put his hand to his earpiece and listened intently for a moment. "The cameras in the building are on a loop, ma'am," he said.

"How the hell did they manage that?" she asked, not hiding her frustration. The cheap fluorescents in the corner office they sat in flickered annoyingly.

"Unclear, ma'am," the agent said back in a monotone voice that frustrated her more. This guy had no idea what was at stake here. *But then again, how could he*, she reflected. She'd been awake all night, and the lack of sleep was getting to her. She tried to compartmentalize it like when she was first coming up at the FBI. She could live on far less sleep back then. At fifty-five now, nothing seemed to work as well as it used to. But she had a certain mental toughness that seemed to grow with age. Something she had on her younger self. Something that had brought her to the highest ranks of the intelligence community.

She sat quietly, reflecting that everything now rested on two special operations teams across the globe, which held the fate of millions in their hands. Her phone chimed. It was from Mack Tomlin. It said one word:

"Bingo."

Brest, Belarus

"How's she doing?" Master Sergeant Jake Lewis asked his medic. "Not good. I'm not sure what's wrong with her, but her vitals are weak. I'm not even sure moving her is advisable in her current state."

Jake looked his medic in the eye, gauging the seriousness of the situation. Sometimes, a look was worth more than a thousand words. His medic's look was dire.

"We don't have a choice. She can't stay here. Can you stabilize her for transport?" It hurt him to make the request. The innocents always suffered the most needlessly in war. But Jake wouldn't be here if millions of American lives didn't depend on this little girl.

"Let me check her chart." The medic walked over to the little girl's bed and sat down next to her, picking up the clipboard. It was an odd contrast seeing the Delta Operator looking so menacing in his black battle gear and cooing at the young girl.

She looked at Jake, seeming to sense he was in charge. "Will... will you take me to see... my father?" she asked in a tired voice that reminded Jake of his daughter.

"Soon, sweetheart," Jake replied in the softest voice he could. He saw his medic snapping a picture of the chart on his phone. He was running it through translation software so he could read it. Jake's eyes flicked to the blood stains on the tile floor. Remnants of the dead Doctor Schmidt, who'd looked too menacingly at this small child. Jake had made a split-second calculation that the micro-expressions on the man's face spoke to his intent to kill. He'd been right. As the doctor had toppled out of his chair, the gun in his hand fired as he had fallen to the floor.

One of his men had dragged the body out of the room to send pictures back to command to ascertain the true identity of the doctor and, mercifully, to get it away from the child. His medic stood, motioning for him to follow into the hallway. He did, and they stepped away from the door so the little girl couldn't hear them.

"What's going on?" Jake asked.

"She's due for some kind of treatment—which is supposed to be arriving here in the next twelve hours."

"How do you know that?"

"The dosage schedule is on the chart. It looks like she receives a dose of two different medicines, each alternating every twenty-four hours. It could be some kind of autoimmune treatment or something. I don't know; it's above my head. But there's some kind of tracking information here for the next dose." His medic clicked the string of letters and numbers on the photo he'd taken of the chart. The tablet had converted the handwritten letters and numbers into text and, when clicked, instantly took him to an international shipping company's website. The point of origin was Argentina, and the online portal marked the shipment as indefinitely delayed.

"Do you have any idea what's wrong with her?"

"No, but my guess is if she misses that dose, she's not gonna make it."

Jake frowned. "If we can get her back to Rammstein, the doctors there might be able to help. But this facility looks experimental and off the books. So, my guess is we're dealing with something experimental and not available to the general public. I'm going to get an IV in her and get her ready to move. But we need to take it easy, and Arcady needs to not smoke any fucking cigarettes. She's too weak to take even that."

"How long?"

"I'll have her ready in fifteen minutes. But I need someone at command to try and figure out what kind of medicine they were shipping her. Or this girl's going to run out of time before someone can help her."

43

Brest, Belarus

Both vans had been pulled around the rear of the underground hospital building. Jake and his team carried the girl on her mattress up the concrete steps from the basement. She had an IV sticking out of her arm, which their team medic held above her as they went. They paused for a moment at the top of the stairs. Jake listened to his earpiece for a second before nodding at them that they were clear to proceed outside.

They did, bursting out into the cool night air. It was still as black out as when they had entered the building over an hour ago. Stabilizing the little girl enough for transport had taken time, and moving with her slow enough so as to not exacerbate whatever was wrong with her took careful doing. She seemed to be sleeping again. Restlessly, though, like even sleep couldn't hold back the pain she was in. Her raven hair matted to her forehead in tiny beads of sweat. It reminded Jake so much of his daughter he had to go to great lengths to try and keep his focus.

Both vans had their rear doors open, and Jake could see Alpha Team pulling security all around the dark parking lot looking for trouble. In the distance, Jake heard the unmistakable roar of fighter jet engines racing through the dark sky. This reminded him immediately that they were not far from a war zone—he never seemed to be far from a war zone.

He walked up to the team leader of Alpha and fist-bumped him. The bearded man kept his night vision on and whispered to Jake, "Vans are ready to go, and there's a plane waiting for us at the airstrip in Lublin, ready to take off. Poles say there's no unusual activity at the border. Doesn't look like anyone knows we're here. How's the girl?"

"Not good. But we've got no idea what's wrong with her. We need to move fast, or she's not going to make it."

"Command says she has to make it."

"I know, so let's get moving."

They both looked at each other as a radio call came in. "Everyone, hold tight. We've got company. Looks like one police cruiser coming in on patrol. Don't think he knows we're here."

"Copy. Everyone, stay out of sight," Jake responded. The girl was already in the back of the van, so they closed the door, and everyone stepped into the darkest patch of night they could find. Jake watched as the late-nineties model police cruiser pulled into the parking lot, moving slowly and clearly looking out for trouble. Jake had a bad feeling about it. The dozen or so infrared lasers trained on the cruiser's windshield didn't help.

Come on, come on, just go away, he thought as the car inched closer. In the distance, Jake heard more fighter jets racing back and forth. The deepthroated roar of their engines pulsating through the night sky. The cruiser was almost level with them now. Suddenly, the cruiser flipped on its searchlight and began panning over the vans. The cop never finished. Two dozen snapping sounds from multiple directions broke windshield glass and killed him instantly.

"Let's go, now!" he said into his radio. Jake ran to the front seat of Bravo's van. Watching one of the operators pulling security check the cop car as he ran toward the van. The operator fired two more shots into the car. *Not good,* he thought.

"There were two of them. One was radioing for help. We need to get the fuck out of here now!" said the man, frantically sprinting back to the vans.

A moment later, they were off, moving out of the parking lot and into the dark streets of Brest. The second van stopped for a moment behind them and picked up the sniper who had been providing overwatch, then accelerated to catch back up with them. Jake partially rolled down his window and listened. In the distance, he heard sirens start.

"Baseplate, this is Bravo. We've been compromised by Belarussian police and are proceeding to the primary extraction route. We need local communication monitoring to see if they know where we are. Over."

As if in answer to his question, Belarussian police cruisers came out of nowhere, with blue lights flashing and sirens, the European variant blaring. "Contact rear," came the radio call.

"Alpha, this is Bravo. Take those two cruisers out and go dark," Jake said. He looked behind him to try and see what was happening, but the rear window was so fogged up he could barely see through it. A moment later, the two cruisers started dropping back, their occupants certainly dead. "Put these on," Jake said to Arcady, pulling a spare set of night vision goggles out of his bag and shoving them over the top of his head. Arcady protested for a moment but then accepted them, and Jake flipped off the lights to the van.

"I'm never working for you Americans again. Winding up in a Russian prison wasn't part of my deal," he said in thickly accented English.

"A little testy without the nicotine, 'ey Arcady?" Jake asked sarcastically.

"A little testy about winding up in a gulag," the man shot back.

"You never know. The Belarussians might want to keep us, seeing as we just shot up a few cop cars."

"This country is Russia, and you're American CIA. We get sent to Russia if we get caught."

"Woah, woah, I'm just a Polish businessman here to pick up my niece from a doctor's appointment."

"You double my rate or this is over," Arcady said back, looking over at him. Jake looked back seriously.

"You know I could just waste you right here if you want, Arcady. Seeing as we just did all those cops, what's one more?" As if in answer, a pistol cocked from behind Arcady and was pressed into the base of his skull by one of the other Deltas. Jake looked at his face, gauging his reaction. Hard to tell with the eyes obscured by the night vision goggles, but he could tell the man was scared and clearly in for way more than he bargained for. He waved at the other Delta, and the man pulled the pistol back from Arcady's head.

"But okay, Arcady, you've earned some extra pay. We'll double the cash. Can't do anything about the cigarettes, though. Still, if you betray me, Arcady, I'll shoot you myself."

Arcady looked relieved but happy and sighed. "God bless America."

44

There were slightly faster planes than Gulfstream G450, but with a cruising speed of Mach 0.85, or 561 miles per hour, it was one of the faster commercial private jets available in the world and the only one the CIA could charter for them on such short notice in such a remote location. In fact, the plane was chartered out through a subsidiary owned by Ernesto Gomez, which meant they were taking a free ride because the CIA was in the process of seizing all of his assets across the globe.

Argentina being a major non-NATO U.S. ally meant that the team had a relatively clear road to operate on after a call from the president explaining the situation. No country wanted any major attack to be launched from their soil against the most powerful nation in the world. Especially not one they were friendly with.

Argentina was sensitive about the Nazi undertones to its history. Following the fall of the Third Reich at the end of World War Two, thousands of former Nazis fled to the country through ratlines set up by the SS and other private organizations, including the Vatican. In fact, the country had entire villages that looked and sounded like they were in Bavaria. Many Argentinians even spoke German. The country had worked hard to distance itself from this narrative, but Nazi lore was popular in pop culture the world over. And somehow, it kept getting dredged up. There was even a show on the History Channel investigating whether Hitler had faked his death and escaped to the country on a U-boat.

Although there were odd pieces of evidence scattered throughout the country, including bunkers, German war rations, Nazi schools, and photographs, nothing compelling had ever been discovered to point to some sinister organization attempting to reconstitute the Reich. Colin's guess was this New Reich was some kind of criminal organization.

But the more info that flowed onto Colin's tablet from Charlie, the more he grew confused. There were billions of dollars that went missing after World War Two. Where did it go? And this money trail during the 9/11 attacks; how did that fit into all of this? It hurt Colin's head to think about it. He rubbed his eyes. He'd slept for the first hour of the flight while Charlie and Sarah had worked away, attempting to piece together everything they could on what was going on.

Colin stood and stretched his back, walking to the galley at the front of the plane to get a snack. This being Ernesto Gomez's plane, it was loaded down with the most high-end snacks and drinks imaginable. Colin opted for an expensive-looking bag of walnuts and a chocolate bar. He also grabbed a mineral water. He was tempted to grab a beer or one of the expensive bottles of liquor, but he decided to save that for the plane ride home. He could have used the pain relief, though. His body ached. At only thirty-one, he was still young and in excellent shape, but their operational tempo was soul-crushing.

Most people only lasted five years in the Echo Teams. Colin

was nearing that mark. He'd done well. But inside, he yearned for a life. Something he hadn't had since joining. Most people spoke of work-life balance. For Colin, work was life. In fact, technically, he didn't exist at all outside of work. His identity and any history of him was locked in a vault somewhere until he retired from the teams or was killed in action. If the latter happened, any trace of him would disappear forever.

Still, the teams had given him a lifetime of experience in a short period of time. And Colin had quite a bit of money put away. Besides the fact that he had inherited money from his parents and then his siblings, the Echo Teams paid extremely well and were completely tax-free. It amounted to a GS-15 step 10 on the pay scale, but it was also better because everything they did was completely paid for. All that money sat in an account waiting for him when he wanted to resume his life. He also had an accelerated pension, which kicked in five years from joining the Echo Teams at the top government salary level.

Colin could never work again if he wanted to after only a few more months. But he knew he would. Getting out of the Echo Teams would mean having a life and not stopping doing what he loved—which was protecting his country. But he wanted a family. His had been taken from him. He knew it was through no fault of their own, at least in the case of his parents. But he had made himself into one of the best killers on the planet to make sure he could be there for his. To make sure he was hard to kill and stood the best chance of being there for the long haul.

I should probably focus on finding a girlfriend before all this family talk, he told himself. He'd been out of the game for almost five years. *No, you should focus on the mission, or you'll never make it to that point,* he reminded himself.

He walked back to his seat and stretched a bit more before sitting down. Jester was sitting across from him, his head lolling back and forth with the steady rhythm of the plane as he slept. Colin popped the top on his mineral water and took a sip. "If that's a beer, march your ass back to the galley and get me seven," Jester said, not even opening his eyes.

Colin smiled. "Sorry. Last one."

Jester's eyes snapped open. "You're shitting me on this ride? What a piece of junk."

"I think I've got them!" Charlie interrupted excitedly.

Colin leaned to his left to look at Charlie's computer screen and rubbed his eyes. "I might be tired, but all I'm seeing is a blurry screen."

"Exactly! Check this out," Charlie said. He zoomed out, making a pinching motion on his trackpad. The satellite picture of the area widened. The rest of the picture was clear except for about two square miles, which remained blurry.

"What the hell?" Colin asked to no one in particular.

"That blur isn't on the photo itself—it's in the software. Like what the government does to sensitive locations on Google Maps."

"I take it that blur is not coming from us, given our clearance level?" Colin asked.

"Nope, someone inserted this into the software. It's in such an uninteresting part of the world that it's not surprising no one's ever noticed. We're not usually using spy satellites to scan wine country in Argentina. Usually, military sites, conflict zones, or hostile countries. Why scan such an innocuous area inside an allied nation? It's a gross misallocation of resources. Of course, it's justified now," Charlie said, shooting Colin a mischievous look.

"Can you unblur it so we can see what we're dealing with?"

"I don't think so. It's already corrupted the image from the satellite we just got, and I don't have access to the raw files. The

Geospatial Intelligence Agency which manages these things is very sensitive about their raw data."

"Well, get on the horn to them now and tell them they got hacked." Colin shook his head. "Years ago, probably. And I'll let Command know we've found them."

45

Mendoza, Argentina

The Gulfstream touched down in Mendoza as the morning light was just cresting the eastern horizon. It was a beautiful morning, made doubly so by the sleep everyone had managed to get on the plane. Colin unplugged his tablet from the USB-C charger and shoved it into his Osprey backpack as the plane taxied to a nearby hangar. Out front, he could see three Land Rover Defender 130's.

"Nice trucks," Jester said, peeking out the window.

"Yeah, if you want to break down while looking pretty," replied Sheriff.

"I just care about looking good for the ladies. Not impressing other dudes," Jester shot back.

Witch let out a rare laugh from the back of the plane, which made everyone else laugh.

"What about you, Snowman? What's your ride of choice?" Panda the Green Beret asked.

Everyone looked at him like he had five heads, then waved him in unison.

"What the hell is that supposed to mean?" asked Panda, his dog's ears perking up.

"Jeep wave, man! Come on!" Sheriff replied.

"I kind of have a thing for Jeep Wranglers," Colin said.

"I feel like we just walked into the middle of something," Grinch added.

"You certainly fucking did. Jester here likes Broncos, Bossman likes Wranglers, Witch likes Landcruisers. And the debate over which is better has been running non-stop for four fucking weeks now. And you reignited it by asking, which means you need to get the hell off my plane," Sarah fired off. Her Latina accent came out far more when she was annoyed.

"Technically, it's that asshole drug lord's plane we just took down—" Panda began, but Sarah's glare stopped him short.

The door to the plane opened, and the stairs extended down. Colin moved toward the door but paused. "Just so we're clear, it's not a debate. Wranglers are an American classic. Landcruisers are Japanese. Broncos are a poor knockoff of Jeeps, and I'm the boss. So, debate over, I win."

"Snowman?" a man with dark, curly hair asked as they approached.

"That's me," Colin responded. The man handed him a manilla envelope and a large duffle bag. Colin opened them, finding a map with the location of a safe house and a million dollars in cash. Colin had no idea what they were going to run into, and his experience operating in this part of the world was non-existent. But in his experience, money was typically a universal language, and if they had to bribe their way to the bioweapons, they would.

"Are these vehicles a bit flashy?" he asked their escort. "Nope. This area of the country is big on high-end wine tourism. The Malbec's here are becoming some of the most popular in the world. It's like a South American Nappa Valley. Tons of rich tourists are all over Mendoza. The nicer you look, the less anyone's going to notice."

"How far is the safehouse from the coordinates we sent you?" Colin asked.

The man laughed. "Safehouse? Nope, it's an Airbnb for tourists here to drink wine. Closest we could get you on such short notice. Our nearest safehouse is a hundred miles away."

Great, Colin thought. Not that they had planned on being there long. They were running out of time. Their only option was to build the plane as they flew it and hope they could get it started before it crashed. Or, in this case, before it killed millions of Americans.

The team piled into the Land Rovers with all of their gear and took off into the mountains for the roughly thirty-minute ride to the Airbnb safe house. Mendoza was frankly beautiful. It reminded Colin of Bavaria in Germany, and he could see why fleeing Nazis might have set up shop here, a world away from their home. Their escort, who was now calling himself Hector, had been right. Colin saw high-end vehicles everywhere, whisking tourists off to vineyards that pockmarked the low valleys and mountain slopes.

Colin saw no large resorts, which told him the area was popular for only part of the year or hadn't yet become popular enough for large-scale development. The country was rugged, insurmountable, and wild, but with a beauty that couldn't be denied. In short, it was a perfect place to hide something. And in the distance, looming like a giant over the terrain, was Aconcagua, snow still dusting its peak.

The safe house was roughly five miles away from the blurred zone on the satellite photos, on what looked to be an abandoned farm. It was like HGTV and the popular show Yellowstone had a baby together as they finally pulled up to it. They might as well have painted rustic on the walls of the house in bright red paint, the owners were trying so hard. The only thing that helped it fit into the larger area was that it was set back so far off the road that no one could see it.

Colin didn't mind the country. It was just the foreign setting that was throwing him off. And he supposed if he squinted hard enough, the place kind of looked like Montana. A few minutes later, they were inside the log and glass structure masquerading as a farmhouse. Colin briefly thought the CIA must have spent a fortune renting this place, but then he was holding a duffle bag with a million dollars in cash in it. What was a couple grand a night?

"It looks like Chip and Joanna Gaines threw up in here," Jester said, walking in the door.

"Let's get everyone in the kitchen and get a plan together; we don't have time to lollygag around," Colin said, dropping his gear by the door.

"Shit, all this square footage, and everyone still just hangs in the kitchen," Jester said with a laugh. Colin gave him a "dude, what the fuck is wrong with you" look before shaking his head and walking away. He had an idea. A very stupid, dangerous idea.

46

Mendoza, Argentina

C olin took his first few steps into the mountains' woods and immediately felt the altitude. The change from operating in the low jungles of the Lacandon Jungle to the mountains of Argentina in such a short period of time was bound to impact anyone. Colin knew he just needed a mile or two to get used to the change and steady his breath.

The plan was relatively simple and incredibly stupid. But it was the best option they could come up with short on time. Colin had geared himself up in jeans and a t-shirt and planned to wander his way into the heart of the enemy, looking more like a back-packer than the ex-Special Forces black operative he was. Jester and the two green berets would stay a half mile behind him, ready to support at short notice if needed. In the meantime, Witch and Sherriff would head to the address of this mystery medicine that Louisa Gomez was supposed to have been receiving in Germany back in town.

Colin's earpiece, shoved deep in his ear canal, buzzed with Charlie Allen's squeaky voice. "I've got you on ISR, boss. Just another four and a half miles to go, and you should start seeing something interesting."

Colin looked up at the sky, trying to catch a glimpse of the drone that Charlie had up. It was the latest in stealth quadcopters and coated with a similar paint to the F-22 Raptor, making it nearly invisible to radar detection. Because of the color of the paint, it was also nearly impossible to see on a clear day like this.

"Copy that," Colin replied, stepping over a fallen tree. According to the map they had looked at before hatching this brilliant plan, Colin had to proceed uphill for two miles before the terrain leveled out. According to the old maps Charlie had been able to dig up from the Geospatial Intelligence Agency, the area should be idyllic, with farmland and clean mountain streams. *Should be,* Colin thought.

The truth was that he had no idea what he was going to run into when he got there. And if he was caught, there was no telling what would happen either. The Nazis of World War Two hadn't exactly had the most stellar reputation for the treatment of prisoners. But then again, getting caught might be the fastest way to get to the bottom of what was happening here.

Colin had stashed his Colt M1911A1 in his backpack. Guns weren't uncommon here, but tourists carrying them were. He realized that if someone wanted to start taking shots at him, the odds of him getting it out in time to save himself were very low. He'd buried it under a sleeping bag in his Osprey hiker's pack. The one thing Colin did have going for him, though, was the weather. It was a beautiful breezy seventy degrees with a cool breeze coming down from the snow-covered mountain peaks above. The trees were just beginning to bloom, and the birds were singing cheerfully as if nothing was wrong.

That was a good thing for now. If the birds stopped singing, it likely meant Colin was being watched. He walked for another mile before pausing and taking a sip from a water bottle in his pack. His breathing had settled down now, and the cool breeze helped to keep his heart rate low.

"Boss, I'm getting some interference on the ISR," Charlie said.

Colin looked up like he could see it. He couldn't. "Copy. Keep me updated if it gets any worse."

Colin kept walking for another mile before the lightly forested hillside finally started to level out.

"Death Star, sitrep on the interference?" Colin asked. Nothing. He repeated the call for information, but still got nothing back. "Jester, can you get Death Star?"

Colin was greeted with nothing. He repeated his call to Jester again and still received nothing. He looked up. He could still hear the birds chirping. That was good. The radio silence was not. He paused again and pulled a mobile phone out of his pocket. It was a burner Charlie had set up for him—an old model iPhone that functioned only to contact the team on their net. The rest of its capabilities were scrubbed for security reasons. There was no signal.

Colin's only explanation was that he had just entered some kind of bubble of electronic jamming. Although it was likely more subtle than that. Electronic jamming was usually very loud and noticeable by military equipment such as radars. It usually required powerful equipment to burn through. This was something different. Charlie could probably explain it to him. But he couldn't talk to Charlie right now. His only choice was to keep going. All their advanced tech was blinded by whoever or whatever had also managed to blind the Geospatial Intelligence Agency. Colin's feeling of foreboding grew with a shiver down his spine, even though his lower back was drenched in sweat from his steep ascent.

Colin finally reached the top of the hill he had been climbing for miles and was greeted with exactly what the old maps had shown: idyllic mountainside charm. A high elevated plane filled with farms, from what Colin could tell, growing some kind of wheat. In the distance, Colin could see something where the plane began to climb again. It looked like it might be buildings, possibly a small town, but Colin was too far away to tell.

He decided to keep going, as if it was a choice and not some kind of internal moral compass that kept pulling him forward. Colin descended through a maze of trees before stopping at the edge of a wheat field. In the distance, Colin could see what looked like a worn-down wooden barn. Well-kept, but weathered with age. He looked to his left and right, gauging if he could skirt the edge of the field, but it was miles across. It would take too much time. Time was something he didn't have. He took a step forward and stopped short, his blood running cold. The racking of the shotgun behind him had caught him completely by surprise. The birds had never stopped chirping.

"May I ask what you're doing on my farm?"

47

The White House, Washington, D.C.

T he president nervously paced the hallway outside the press room. Talking to the press was his least favorite part of the job. But feeding them a big nothingburger after the attacks yesterday was going to make them ravenous for his head. Worse yet, he was about to make a series of incredibly unpopular moves for the country's safety, with little to no information to give on why he was doing it. *This is going to be a blood bath,* he thought.

"Mr. President, you're on," his aid said.

"Wish me luck." He smiled back, walking to his fate.

As he entered the room, the press core remained mostly silent and respectful. He was well-liked by both sides of the aisle as far as presidents go, which meant the press was usually nice to him for about a minute as he came into the room. He could tell from their faces they were itching to interrogate him.

The president settled in at the podium, shuffled his notes, and began, "Thank you, everyone, for being here today. I know the last day has been chaotic. We've been in the middle of an evolving national security situation, and I wanted to wait to speak with you all until I had some more information. As you all know, yesterday there was a series of anthrax attacks at the Capitol building. You'll be happy to know that no one has been killed, and the victims are currently recovering at an undisclosed location. I ask you to please respect their privacy as they regain their health." He looked up as he said this, trying to impress the seriousness of his request on those in front of him.

"Mr. President, what can—" a reporter from CNN started, but William held up a hand, cutting her off.

"No questions at this time, please. Now, the attackers are still, unfortunately, at large. Our law enforcement and intelligence communities believe they have a handle on the terrorists responsible and are pursuing every avenue at this time. But until such time as we have a fuller understanding of who perpetrated this attack and can ensure the safety of the American people, we are implementing a few emergency measures. First, all ports of entry into the United States are being closed, and all domestic air travel is suspended for the next two days." At this, the press core exploded into furious, quiet conversation.

The president held up a hand and waited a moment for them to quiet down. "Second, due to the ongoing issues of our porous southern border and our need for no one to enter the United States until we can ensure it is safe for all with Congress's authorization, I have federalized and deployed the national guards of Texas, New Mexico, Arizona, and California to help our law enforcement community in shutting down the border and ensuring nothing gets in. These troops began deploying last night and are authorized to use deadly force by order of the Congress on anyone trying to illegally enter the country."

The press positively exploded at this. All of this had happened without anyone catching a whiff of it, which made them even more rowdy because they were unprepared with questions. *This is going to be a feeding frenzy,* he lamented internally. He held up a hand again, trying to project calm through the room and to the American people. It took longer this time, but the press did eventually get the hint and quiet down.

"This situation is evolving, and as such, until we can get a handle on it and apprehend those responsible, I request, not order, but request that all Americans stay home unless their work is essential. I leave it up to you personally to determine that. This is for your own safety. And one last thing before I take any questions. We are doing this all as a precaution to ensure everyone is safe. I ask that everyone remain calm. Personal responsibility and selflessness are what being an American is all about. Sacrificing for these two days will ensure that everyone is safe. Thank you, and good afternoon," the president said, leaving the podium without taking any questions. By not answering questions, he was attempting to control the narrative and not let the press spin any of his off-the-cuff answers.

A firestorm of shouted questions followed him as he left the room. And he was sure that he'd heard the word Hydra yelled as well, which was not good. Operation Hydra was as secret as secret could be, but it was only a matter of time before the press learned what it was. Sealed within the Congressional authorization to deploy troops to the border was also authorization for Hydra. Already federal troops were staging and prepositioning equipment to prepare to close interstate travel in an interconnected web of major highways and small back roads.

Though it was nearly impossible to do this completely, America was just too big with too many roads. The plans were extremely thorough. Already, naval warships and Coast Guard vessels were moving in between the United States and Cuba and deploying in a grid pattern to defeat common drug underwater submarine routes used by smugglers. The small carbon fiber submarines had become ubiquitous in the last twenty years and were extremely hard to find and kill. It wasn't that they were too stealthy. It was just that the ocean was too big. In fact, that was the problem with securing the country in general from small threats. It was just so big that there were never enough resources to go around, even with the vast wealth of the United States.

William Joyce was hoping that that same size would work to their advantage. If the huge military and law enforcement resources of the United States couldn't stop the virus from getting in, maybe the size of the country could keep it isolated long enough to be eliminated. That was as long as they could kill the source before they struck again.

48

Mendoza, Argentina

Sheriff stared at Global Shippings Solutions' shabby front office from the passenger seat of the Land Rover Defender 130. Witch sat to his left in the driver's seat, watching the meandering morning crowd move through the small downtown. It was near lunch, and the crowds seemed perfectly content to leave their office jobs early and head out to an early meal. Sheriff noted that most of them were locals and assumed most tourists stayed outside the main town to enjoy the beautiful countryside.

"Ten bucks says we have to shoot our way out of this post office," said Sheriff, staring at the entrance.

"You might be the most negative person I've ever met," Witch replied.

"I'm just pragmatic. I've been on this team for what two years now? In that time, have we ever managed not to need to shoot our way out of a situation?"

"Yeah, you're right that things were much better run before you joined," Witch replied.

"So, you're not going to take the action?"

"No, I'll take it. But only because we're not going to get into a gunfight in a knockoff UPS store."

"Okay, you're on. Just so you know, there are two armed guards right inside the door." Sheriff laughed.

Witch shook his head. "Asshole. So, what's your genius plan to get this package?"

"Well, you're going to go blindside one of those guards and run, and I'm going to walk in the front door."

"You're joking?"

"You got a better plan?"

"I just don't get why I always have to be the asshole. It seems like you guys always need me to torture someone, punch some dude in the face, or off some poor guy," Witch said, looking hurt.

"You just have that psychopath look about you. Me, I'm likable. You look like you're going to kidnap me and wear my skin."

Witch rolled his eyes and keyed his communicator. "Death Star, this is Witch. We've got eyes on the storefront with two armed hostiles inside. We are preparing to make entry."

"Death Star copies all," Charlie replied in a squeaky voice.

In unison, Witch and Sheriff stepped out of the vehicle and made their way casually up the street. Each wore civilian clothes, jeans, flannels, baseball caps, dark Oakley sunglasses, and concealed Sig P320 X Carry's beneath their shirts in the appendix position. Sheriff walked ten feet to the right of the door and leaned against the wall, pretending to text on his phone. Witch walked with purpose into the front door of the store.

Sheriff stood by and waited. Within seconds a loud commotion ensued, and Witch booked it out of the store, one of the guards hot on his heals, his weapon thankfully aimed at the ground. Sheriff waited a moment, and the other guard followed, albeit slower, holding his face from where the big man had clocked him.

"Nice work, Witch. Making entry now," he said, placing his phone in his pocket and walking into the store.

"We're closed," the disheveled-looking man behind the counter said. The place was plastered with Western Union signs and cheap cell phone burners. Sheriff also noted with satisfaction that he could purchase an array of pills that could make him perform for hours in the bedroom. *Nice place,* he thought.

"No, you're not," he said, advancing on the man and pulling his Sig P320. He centered the Romeo Pro sight on the man's head with one hand and fished a piece of paper out of his pocket with the other. The man looked at him bored, as if he had been held up a hundred times before. *Hence the armed guards,* Sheriff thought. "I'm here to pick up my package," he said, casually placing the piece of paper on the counter.

He watched the man go for the piece of paper.

"Slowly," he said. He was sure the man probably had a gun behind the counter and wanted to make sure he didn't go for it suddenly. His Spanish wasn't good, and shooting this guy and then trying to locate the package in the computer would complicate things. Mendoza, in general, was safe, but the South American Gangs were ruthless and had serious sway in most of the major cities, resulting in large no-go zones for the police. Judging by the state of the neighborhood, he thought this might be one of them.

The store clerk lazily entered a few numbers from the piece of paper into his computer and waited for a second. "The package was canceled a day ago," the man said. Sheriff looked at him skeptically. In his head, he knew this wasn't good. The New Reich canceling this shipment meant they were almost done and were starting to clean house of everyone involved. The little girl was collateral damage, and so was everyone else who had been involved.

"Do you still have it?"

"I do," the man said back lazily.

"Then get it."

The clerk stared at him a moment more, then moved through some red beads that were covering the entrance to the back of the store. Sheriff moved to it, parting the beads and keeping an eye on the man who was rifling through a mail cart full of boxes. A moment later, he pulled a brown cardboard package up, inspected the label, then walked back over to Sheriff and handed it to him. "Will that be all?" he asked sarcastically.

"One more thing; when was this scheduled to arrive?"

The man walked back to his computer and looked for a moment. "Next day, sir. So today. But it was canceled shortly after it was delivered here, so it was never sent to the plane."

Ten minutes later, Sheriff picked Witch up in the Land Rover and drove east toward the private airstrip they had landed at. "Death Star, this is Sheriff. We have the package and are heading toward the plane."

"Copy, inspect it to make sure it's intact," replied Sarah in a cool voice. Sheriff passed it to Witch, who tore open the cardboard box and extracted a black pelican case from the interior. He undid the latches and opened the case. Inside were two vials and several dry ice packets. Witch closed it quickly, trying not to let more of the chill out than he had to. "Death Star, package is intact. We have the treatment. Just hope we're in time."

49

"She's dying. I can't tell you why. At least not in time to save her. She's got twelve to eighteen hours at most. All I can do is keep her comfortable," Dr. Lynette Correnti said. She looked grave—in the way only a pediatric ICU doctor could when delivering terrible news. Jake was devastated. The team of doctors had been running test after test on Louisa Gomez for over two hours. Her brown eyes reminded Jake of his daughters, and this whole mission was hitting far too close to home.

"Doc, there was some treatment slated to be delivered to her today. Do you think it would make a difference if we could get it to her?"

Lynette thought about this. He could tell she was weighing her options, refusing to give any kind of answer that could deliver false hope. She looked him in the eyes, gauging the type of metal within his soul. Hardened steel met her.

"Look, I'll tell you something my colleagues wouldn't want me to. I think whatever is going on with her is the result of some kind of genetic experimentation. We ran a quick DNA screen to try and see if there was anything obvious wrong with her. I say quick because the larger screen takes weeks. But we can see some things quickly. We're not seeing anything in particular, but her DNA looks… wonky."

"What do you mean, *wonky*, Doc? I'm just a grunt. I need a bit more," Jake said.

"The test got flagged as not human in origin—"

"Hold on a second, Doc—"

She cut him off in return and continued, "It's not what you think. It means the computer flagged one of the base pairs as animal, not human. Most genetic treatments use gene pairs from animals and interject them into humans to get certain results. The technologies are still new and extremely experimental, but say you wanted to be invisible."

Jake looked at her, bewildered, but she continued, "We could take DNA from a chameleon and inject it into yours. Provided we knew the right segment to cut out and inject into you, it would alter the way your body reads the strands and provide you with an adaption. Of course, it's far more complicated than that, but it's essentially the way it works. Somewhere in this little girl's DNA, an extraneous sequence has been added for some kind of effect. It's either part of a treatment or part of what's killing her."

Jake weighed this information for a second. He'd heard of CRISPR and other such things on the news, but he had no idea anyone was seriously using the technology in humans. He rubbed his face, thinking. It had been a long night, and the bright fluorescents of the hospital were straining the muscles in his eyes. He had to get this little girl united with the cure to whatever was killing her.

He had no idea what this was all about. He strongly suspected it had something to do with the attacks at the U.S. Capitol today and the heightened military alert status. "Can she be moved, Doc?"

"You want to get her closer to whatever this treatment is?" Lynette asked.

"I do."

Jake saw her thinking this through. The conflict on her face was apparent. On the one hand, moving her could put a strain on her system and kill her faster. On the other hand, if they didn't cut the time it took to get her treatment, it might not matter at all. "Yes, carefully. And I'm coming with you."

The White House, Washington, D.C.

Things aren't going well, President William Joyce thought as Wendy continued briefing them.

"The interrogators aboard the McRaven have been unable to ascertain the location of the tainted drugs from Ernesto Gomez. He's refusing to talk until his daughter's safe and healthy. We've secured her, but until she receives the treatment this New Reich promised her, she won't be healthy; in fact, the doctors tell us she has about twelve hours left before she expires. Ernesto holds all the cards.," she said, frowning. "He knows his distribution network backward and forward, and until he provides us with the location of all the drug pathways into the United States, we run a huge risk of not being able to contain this pathogen."

"Good and bad news on that front. The Echo Team in Argentina has secured what they think is the treatment that was bound for the girl. The bad news is they're 7,500 miles apart. The average cruising speed of jets is 500 miles an hour. That's a fifteen-hour trip minimum," Mack Tomlin said.

"Every second we waste, this girl comes closer to dying, and we come closer to losing millions of American lives. Work the problem here, people. What's the solution," the president said with such obvious irritation that it took everyone back a second in the situation room.

"With your permission, sir?" General Courtney Granger said to Mack Tomlin.

Mack nodded at the man.

"Speak, General," the president told the Air Force chief.

"Yes, sir. We can cut this trip down a bit. With some help from our friends in the Navy," he said, nodding at the admiral seated across from him. "I suggest the Echo Team puts that package onto the Gulfstream G450 they flew down on. Have them fly the package to Northern Brazil. Ah—" He looked back at the Air Force aid.

"Natal, Brazil should do, sir," the man said curtly.

"From there, they can gas up and transit the Atlantic to Naval Station Rota in southern Spain. In conjunction, we can fly Louisa Gomez from Ramstein down to Rota on a C-17 Globemaster and have her there and settled into a Naval hospital by the time the treatment arrives. I'd say total time will be about 8 hours if everything goes according to plan."

"That's cutting it awfully close," Wendy said.

"True, but it's the best option we have on such short notice," Mack said.

"Mr. President, if we're going to do this, we need to get them moving now. There is no time to waste."

"Do it," the president said, praying they would make it before it was too late.

50

Mendoza, Argentina

"I don't want any trouble," Colin said, raising his hands above his head. The exertion of his hike had evaporated from his mind the second the attractive female voice from behind him spoke up. It was beautiful yet chilling in a way Colin couldn't quite describe—deep but feminine in a classic sort of way.

"If you don't want trouble, then why are you on my family's land?" she asked. Colin kept his eyes on the farm in front of him. A soft breeze ruffled the waves of grain growing in the field.

"I didn't know it was your family's land. I was just on a hike and got a little lost. I'm not from around here."

"Americans," the girl said in a playful sort of way. The man in Colin wanted to turn and see what the attractive female voice looked like for himself, but the operator in Colin told him to play it cool and not make any sudden movements. People inexperienced with aiming guns at people had a tendency to twitch when those people made sudden moves.

"Listen, I'm a little tired from the hike. Would you mind if I put my hands down?"

"Very well, but do it slowly." Colin caught the slight German edge to her accent. He moved his hands slowly down and scratched his ear on the way, pushing the earpiece a bit deeper into his ear canal as he went. Then he turned toward the woman holding him captive. Her looks matched her voice. She had medium-length, slightly curly blonde hair with a pale face and red lips. Her form was petite yet fit in a way her looser fitter farm clothes couldn't quite hide. In short, she was a perfect ten, and Colin was slightly dumbstruck at finding something like her in such an odd place.

"My name is Colin," he said. Noticing she still hadn't lowered her shotgun. She raised an eyebrow and gave him an up-down as if appraising his six-foot-two frame for her own internal monologue.

"Alina," she said back, still looking him over.

"Look, I'm no threat; I just got a little lost. I can head back the way I came if it's okay with you. But—" he said, pausing. He needed to think on his feet quickly. This girl might be his only way into whatever lay ahead, and walking back the way he came wasn't a realistic option. If he managed to get the gun away from her and detain her, he still had no idea who would come looking. "I'm out of water. Any chance I could trouble you for some before I head back?"

Slowly, her eyes eased a bit, and her lips curled into a soft smile, revealing perfectly white teeth. The shotgun lowered back toward the ground. "It'll be dark soon. The hills can be dangerous at night, especially to outsiders."

"I'm sure I can take care of myself," he said with a playful smile, trying his best not to come off as creepy in any way. He was a bit out of practice with the ladies, but he was still sure there was a fine line between an attractive stranger in the woods and a creepy hillbilly.

"Still, why risk it? Come with me. Let me get you some water and something to eat," she said and began walking straight past Colin. He turned to follow her, watching the attractive sway of her hips as she stepped confidently over the rough terrain back toward the well-manicured farm.

"So where are you from?" she asked.

"Virginia, out in wine country. Here to check out the local wineries," Colin said. He'd learned through his training that the best lies were often wrapped in truth. He'd grown up in D.C., not Virginia, but it was close enough.

"Wine country in Virginia." She snorted. "Not exactly what comes to mind when I think of wine country. What brings you to Mendoza?" Colin had drawn even with her now on their walk. Her eyes flashed green as she looked into his, waiting for his answer.

"Well, I'm a bit of an outdoorsy kind of guy. Like taking in the sights. But I was hoping to learn more about the local vintners. I'd like to open a winery of my own someday, and some of my favorites come from here."

"Really? Which ones?" she asked. Her accent had an Argentinian edge, but the German was hard to miss.

"Well, malbecs, obviously. But my favorites are Catena Zapata and El Enemigo Cabernet Franc," Colin replied. Those were the two names he remembered from the local culture knowledge section of the brief Sarah and Charlie had put together. If she asked for any more, he was screwed. He liked wine, but his knowledge was limited to general types and places. Enough to get by at a restaurant, but not here.

"I've never had either," she replied nicely.

Swing and a miss, Colin thought. He smiled back at her.

"I'm just a humble farm girl," she replied. "We're very isolated up here, but if you'd like, my family does make our own wine. We have some vines on the mountain. Would you care to try some?"

"I'd be delighted," Colin replied, not taking his eyes off her. It wasn't hard.

They walked for ten more minutes before reaching the barn and the small farmhouse that lay beyond. She went inside to get water and wine, and Colin dropped his pack sitting down on a small picnic bench beneath a tree. He had cooled off considerably from the hike. He made a show of inspecting the tree while quietly whispering to see if anyone on his team could hear him. There was no response to his hails.

A few moments later, he saw Alina walking back toward him with a glass jug of water, a bottle of wine, and two glasses. "I can't thank you enough," he said as she placed the water in front of him and uncorked the wine. He noticed the shotgun was no longer with her. He made a show of drinking the water eagerly. It was cool and refreshing.

"Now you must try the wine and tell me what you think," she said.

Colin eyed her suspiciously. "It's not poison, right?"

Alina laughed. "And why would I poison you?"

"Well, I don't know. You hear stories about meeting strange people in the woods," he said with a playful grin.

"You should talk," she said with a small giggle.

"Fair point," Colin said, taking a sip. The wine was delicious. It had the earthy taste of a malbec but the sweetness of fresh berries from a farm.

"It's fantastic," Colin said, savoring the taste. She drank with him. "I'd love to know how you grow it. Is it something you do with your family?"

"It used to be. My father and my mother were killed a few years back in an automobile accident. It's just me these days."

"I'm sorry. I'm shocked a woman such as yourself doesn't have the boys pounding down her door. No husband?" Colin replied.

"Well, they try, but it's very remote up here, so most of them don't know where to find me." She played back. They were flirting now in a more than casual sort of way. Only an idiot could have missed that Colin knew, but how he was going to get her to let him head closer to town, he wasn't sure yet. He decided on a different track. "Do you have a phone by chance? I haven't gotten any signal since I started up the mountain."

"Only satellite phones work up here. Mine died last week. But there's a phone in town that you could use. They never ran the landlines out to the broader village."

"There's a town up here?" Colin asked, doing his best to look bewildered. "I didn't see anything on GPS before I left the house."

"It's very remote, and you'll find most of this area is a bit incomplete on Google Maps," she said. "We didn't become very well known until a few years ago for our wine, and even so, we're a bit of a backwater compared to broader Mendoza. I wouldn't be surprised if you ran into a bunch of villages that didn't show up on your map."

This was the first lie Colin was sure she told him. His phone was a satellite phone, and the fact that he didn't have cell reception meant she was lying through her perfectly white teeth.

"Fair point," Colin said, letting nothing on. "Is there any chance I could make it up to the village to make a call to get someone to come pick me up?"

She thought about this for a moment, and then an idea sparked in her eyes. "I'm heading up there in an hour for a yearly celebration we have. You could come with me and use the phone and even talk to some of the local vintners while you're there if you'd like."

Colin was sure something deeper was happening here now. Everything was just a bit too convenient. But he was in the belly of the beast now and had no choice but to let things play out.

51

45,000 Feet Above the Atlantic Ocean

Jack Connelly had some weird missions in his twenty years as a pilot for the Central Intelligence Agency, but this one was chalking up to be one of the strangest. He'd been in Brazil only five hours ago transporting the head of station and two members of the U.S. Intelligence committee on a routine diplomatic partner mission when he and his co-pilot had suddenly been reassigned.

"Heading to the head for a bit, Jim. Take over, would you?" he asked his co-pilot Jim Dorset. Both were former Air Force pilots; both were feeling severe gastrointestinal distress after their meal out last night.

"Hey, light a candle back there, would you?" Jim joked back. They'd flown together for over ten years now, and their repour was second nature. Jack proceeded to the back of the plane and checked on their passenger as he went. The Pelican case was seat belted into a single leather chair, looking undisturbed in the otherwise empty cabin.

Very strange someone was spending all this money to send

such a small package on a Gulfstream across the Atlantic he knew. Even stranger, the original pilots were nowhere to be found when he had arrived at the plane with Jim six hours ago. The CIA typically liked to leave pilots with the planes they flew on. No one liked the idea of such an expensive government asset being in an unfriendly country with no one to babysit it. But Jack was also pretty sure this wasn't an agency plane either, judging by the high-end bar in the galley. Even private government planes had a way of being starker than their civilian variants.

Jack was just settling into the toilet when he felt an odd shutter. He chalked it up to turbulence and went about releasing what was causing him so much distress. Another shutter rocked the aircraft, making him brace his arm against the wall of the bathroom. This time he noticed a pitch change in the sound of the engines. *What the heck is that,* he thought to himself. His typical plane was a Bombardier 6000, and he only rarely flew Gulfstreams. He strained against the turbulence and against the difficult time he was having on the toilet.

A moment later, he decided to cut his time short in the bathroom and head back to the cockpit to get an update. The sounds coming from the aircraft now seemed lopsided, as if one of the engines was straining. Even for an inexperienced passenger, the noise would have been hard to miss.

"What's going on, Jim?" he asked, entering the cockpit. "Losing fuel pressure in Engine Two. Trying to diagnose the issue now. He saw Jim flipping switches and checking for lights. Across the expansive control boards. Jack took his seat and put his headset on. He could hear an even odder sound now, as if the starboard engine was stuttering.

"How's the pressure in One?"

"Looks fine. I can hear it coming from the right. Pressures are good in One. Check the fuel pump for Two,"

Jack leaned over the control board and let his eyes adjust for a moment from the bright, clear sky over the Atlantic. "Some kind of fault in Fuel Pump Two. Getting a light here. It's fuel-starving on Two."

"That would explain the noise."

Jack knew that the G450 had an engine-driven primary fuel pump and an auxiliary electrical-driven pump for emergencies. "Let's switch to the auxiliary," he said.

"Agreed."

Jack flipped a series of switches to move to the auxiliary pump. A moment later, the sputtering got worse. "That doesn't sound good. Try the switch again." Jack flipped the controls again, attempting to toggle to the auxiliary pump. A feeling of nervousness and worsening gastrointestinal distress grew in his gut—which was worse, he couldn't tell. He knew the plane could make it on one engine, but they were in the middle of the Atlantic. And their only real option was to keep flying toward Spain and look for an alternate location to land. Typically, pilots would opt to land immediately if something happened like this mid-flight over land. The backup was there to keep them safe; if that was all that was left and it failed, they would be heading toward the ground fast. Jack prayed it worked.

A moment later, the engine sputtered worse than ever, and they could tell it was heading toward a stall. "All right, both pumps are out on number two, so let's shut it down."

"Agreed," Jim responded.

"Adjusting throttle," Jack replied. While Jim shut down the engine, Jack adjusted the power to the other engine to compensate.

"Let's make a Mayday call to Mother and look for an alternate," Jim said in a strained voice. Their orders were to keep communications to a minimum with outside air traffic control. They needed to call the CIA for instructions before picking a site. Their cargo, whatever it was, could get them in trouble otherwise or compromise a sensitive U.S. Intelligence asset. Jack grabbed a satellite phone rather than a radio and made a call to their controller. Moments later, he was stunned when he was connected directly through to Wendy Simons.

He looked over at Jim, covering the receiver with eyes wide. "It's the Director of National Intelligence," he mouthed. Jim held up both palms in a who-freaking-knows motion.

"Jack, this is Wendy Simons, Director of National Intelligence. Report, please."

"Ah, hello, ma'am," he said, taking a moment to recover his composure. This was roughly his boss's boss times a hundred. *What the hell have we stumbled into?* he thought. He flipped the phone to speaker mode so Jim could hear the conversation. "Ma'am, we have one complete engine failure. The second is holding. We judge it imperative that we find a place to land."

A short pause followed. "Jack, the cargo you carry is extremely time-sensitive in two ways. If it doesn't arrive at its destination on time, a little girl is going to die, and tens of millions of Americans might lose their lives as a result. I need to know. Can you make it to Rota or not?"

Jack looked at the lights aboard the aircraft and thought as hard as he could. He knew whatever they stumbled into here must have been extraordinarily serious if he was on the phone with the Director of National Intelligence. He also knew that if this plane crashed into the ocean, whatever they were carrying would likely be lost forever and definitely wouldn't get where it needed to on time. He looked at Jim, who shook his head no in response. The aircraft was too unfamiliar to them to make this kind of guarantee. They had no idea what the maintenance status was on the other engine. He frowned. "Ma'am, in our judgment, we're more likely to crash than make it all the way to Rota. We need an alternate, or this cargo might never make it at all."

The plane shook again as the number one engine struggled to

stabilize the plane against the turbulent Atlantic air. The silence on the other end of the phone was deafening. Jack couldn't help but feel like he was letting his country down, but there was nothing he could do. "What's the farthest you can make it, Jack?"

Jim was scrolling an iPad next to him, looking for an alternate. He mouthed at Jack. "Cabo Verde."

Jack entered it in his flight computer to get a distance and baring. They could make it to the West African Island. "Cabo Verde, ma'am. Will that work?" More silence followed.

"It'll have to. Make it there, Captain, or we're in big trouble."

52

The old Ford F-150 bounced its way out of the farmhouse drive and turned right toward the small town scarcely a mile distant. Alina drove the old truck and chattered with Colin about their small town's history. Colin did his best to listen to the beautiful blonde while also trying to memorize his surroundings. He might be getting out of here in a hurry, and he was also looking for any signs of Jester or the Green Berets following him. The lack of contact with them was worrying. And the spikey ball of uneasiness in his stomach was getting worse the further they went.

Somewhere in this town was the key to stopping this attack. He didn't know what it was, but he had a feeling he would know it when he saw it. There was also the unmistakable feeling that he was driving toward a cliff, and if he couldn't stop in time, there would be no coming back. If he couldn't stop this attack, there wouldn't be much of a country to return to anyway. It was this knowledge that kept him pressing forward into the unknown.

"Are you listening?" she asked him, taking her eyes off the

road and staring at him. She had changed for the party in town into a white linen shirt and tan pants. Everything about her was casual and disarming in a way that Colin couldn't help liking but also be suspicious of. Something was off. But then again, he wasn't quite sure what was off.

"Yeah, sorry. Just a little tired from the hike today. Honestly, I was a bit taken aback by how beautiful this place is. I can't believe more people don't come here." Colin motioned around to the blue mountains imposing themselves on the orange light of early evening. The fields of grain surrounding them waved lazily in a soft breeze, and in the distance, he could see grape vines climbing the hills. It was idyllic in a way that was familiar to many Americans but was like a bunch of different pieces of North America all jammed into one.

"Well, that's why my grandfather and his people bought it all, although when they got here, it was a bit of a dump. But they knew it had potential."

"Can I ask where he was from?"

"Switzerland," she responded without missing a beat.

"Is that where your accent's from? I noticed it's a bit different from the locals'," Colin asked.

"Yes, I still have a bit of it, though. Don't ask me to speak it—I'm terrible." She giggled. Colin laughed playfully. "Well, your English is so good one could scarcely notice."

She frowned. "Everyone's English is good outside of America. It's the Americans who can't speak anyone else's language."

Interesting, Colin thought. "Well, you've got me there. I can barely speak English on a good day. Especially not after a few glasses of wine." He smiled. She snorted at his joke. *She's good,* Colin thought. *Always laughs at just the right time.*

The town loomed before them, now past a thicket of tall pine trees, which looked very much intentional to hide it from the valley of farms below. It was hard to miss the neat rows they were planted in. They continued uphill through the trees before emerging onto a scene that took Colin's breath away. He wasn't sure if he'd been transported to Bavaria or if he had crossed into some kind of simulation. In front of him, built into the mountainous hillside, was a picturesque German village that looked right out of a snow globe.

"Woah," Colin said, not hiding his surprise. "Welcome to Neues Berchtesgaden," she said, admiring the mountainside village with him. A sign to their right as they entered in neat lettering spelled it out for him. He didn't speak German, but he knew Berchtesgaden as the location of Hitler's Eagle's Nest during World War Two and the ceremonial home of the Nazi party. It was said the SS was supposed to wage guerilla warfare from its mountainous peaks until the Reich could be reestablished. *Maybe they just moved it somewhere else,* Colin thought in a horrified type of awe.

He decided to continue playing the dumb tourist, even though he was now fairly sure how this was going to play out. "Berchtesgaden, is that Swiss?" Colin asked. He continued to scan the area for everything he could possibly pick out as he went. He was looking for security measures, guards, escape routes, and anything out of the ordinary. The issue he was running into was that everything here was out of the ordinary.

"It is," she replied. "The town has about a thousand people and is close to ninety years old. Though it is made to look older. All the buildings are nearly exact replicas of the founders' original favorites from the region they are from."

"How do you keep something like this so well hidden? I could imagine if tourists knew, this place would be absolutely crawling."

"Well, that's a bit of a trick on the town leadership's part. The whole area is technically held as one private piece of land, so on the map, it would just show up as private land that's not accessible to the general public, except for the occasional lone hiker like you." She smiled.

"I promise I won't tell. I just might never want to leave," Colin said, staring around at the incredible stone buildings around him.

"You're not the first person to say that," she said. "Though it can be a bit boring being in such a small, secluded town."

Through the rolled-down windows, Colin could smell the crisp mountain air mingling with wood fires and what he thought was cooking sausage. It was intoxicating. Further up the hill, he could see people moving upward toward some kind of commotion. He assumed this to be the festival she spoke of. He didn't think he would ever make it there. Alina rolled up the windows and stopped several hundred yards short of the crowd next to a closed store.

She looked at him very seriously now, all traces of the bubbly, beautiful blonde now hidden behind a new look. One of intense focus. The silence in the cab of the truck was heavy in a way that hurt Colin's ears. Finally, she spoke. "You're American Special Forces or CIA, yes?"

Colin raised his eyebrows in surprise. "No, I'm not sure what you're—"

She cut him off. "Answer the question, or we're both going to die."

Her accent had suddenly shifted into something far more familiar in a way Colin hadn't expected. "I really don't—"

She cut him off again. "Fine, I guess I'll show you mine, and maybe you'll show me yours. I'm Alina Chapman, MI6, and I'm going to need you to cooperate if we're going to stop the bioweapon that's about to hit America."

53

Mendoza Airport, Argentina

Charlie was starting to feel like he spent most of his life in airport hangars. He would have given anything for his comfortable X-Chair. He craved the lumbar support and the heated massager at his lower back. Instead, he was stuck in a crappy metal folding chair with his butt aching. Worse yet, he didn't even have anyone to bitch to about it. Sarah was as hard as they came, and she had no patience for complainers. It wasn't that Charlie was one. It was just that passing the time bitching about things seemed to make things go faster.

Half of the team was currently completely dark to them. Something that, unfortunately, was becoming increasingly common in their line of work. For years, it had seemed like the fog of war was being peeled back more and more by technology. But now the bad guys had caught up, and sophisticated cyber countermeasures were making his job harder than it had ever been before. During the Global War on Terror, Charlie had cut his teeth as an NSA cyber warrior. Hunting down terrorists and hacking state sponsors and financial backers.

That had been easy, and he'd been one of the best in the world at it.

He'd moved from cyber warrior to building offensive cyber weapons for the NSA and Cyber Command, then had been recruited to the Echo Teams. Everyone always needed a competent geek. Especially one that could work alone and had no issues blurring the lines between white hat and black.

With the Snowman, Jester, and the Green Berets completely dark to him and Witch and Sheriff racing to catch up to them, there was nothing he could do but try to make himself busy helping the NSA. There was a lot to do. According to Wendy Simons, there were thousands of short trades arrayed across legit institutions, dark pools, quant funds, and shell companies, all ready to be triggered when the second news of the pathogen broke. In addition, Charlie strongly suspected there was a massive cyber propaganda campaign ready and waiting across millions of bots to inspire panic across the American populace.

Charlie has seen some of this during the COVID-19 pandemic. In fact, he'd worked with the NSA to try and fight some of it. But it was a losing battle, and the tools they had at their disposal were nowhere near comprehensive enough to stop the state actors drumming up despair and misinformation. In the end, the enemy's greatest weapon against a democracy was helping its citizens to lose faith in its founding principles.

This was all still fresh in everyone's mind. The healing had come slow, if at all, and the political divisions had grown starker. The country would tear itself apart through fear and mistrust if they couldn't either stop the pathogen in its tracks or kill the short trades and bots the enemy had pre-positioned. And that was before people started dying or losing their life savings to the crashing economy. Charlie knew the equation was a simple one. They won, or they would die.

Charlie took a sip of black coffee as he tapped away at the

keys of his mechanical keyboard. The satisfying clicky switches helped him to think more clearly. Switching to coffee from energy drinks made him less jittery, and it helped him keep the pounds off. That also helped him to think more clearly. And it was this thinking clearly that made him think he had found something. *Just because you guys came up with some new cool shit doesn't mean we didn't, too,* he thought to himself.

"People always seem to forget that we invented the fucking internet," Charlie said, hoping the stoic Sarah would finally engage with him.

"What is it now, Charlie?" she asked.

"What makes you think it's anything? Maybe I'm just talking to myself."

"Because every time you make some declarative statement to thin air and I'm nearby, I can always tell you want to explain something super nerdy to me that I'm only going to half-understand."

"Oh," he replied, looking hurt. He quickly glanced at her out of the corner of his eye. Finally, she rolled her eyes in response, "Okay, go ahead if you feel like you have to."

Charlie smiled, knowing that she was just humoring him but also really wanting to explain. "Well, you see, everyone always wants to talk about Russia and China when they talk about people doing shady shit online. Hacking, stealing, quantum computing, AI, you name it. When in reality, they should probably be worrying more about what we're doing. I mean, we invented the internet. We even destroyed an entire country's nuclear program with a simple computer virus before it could even get off the ground. No shots fired."

"You're referring to the Stuxnet thingy we hit Iran with?" she interrupted.

"You're learning so much," Charlie said sarcastically, but still excited. "In fact, we're the OGs at all this stuff. Broadly, all major developments in these domains are made in the West and copied by our adversaries. They're just way less subtle about using them than we are. Some people think it's just them being assholes, but honestly, they're less competent in general than we give them credit for. Having said all that, take a look at this code," Charlie said, gesturing to his screen.

Sarah leaned over him to examine his screen. "I have no idea what I'm looking at."

"I didn't think you would. Now take a look at this piece of code," he said, leaning back from the screen.

"Is there a point to this?"

"Humor me," he replied.

She leaned over the screen again and stared for a moment. "They look the same. Or close to the same," she said, standing back up.

"Exactly!" Charlie yelled a bit too loudly. Sarah looked at him, bewildered.

"The first one is the code for Stuxnet directly out of the NSA's Arsenal code repository. The second one is some piece of code I just found by analyzing traffic hitting the data center that led us down here in the first place. I found it by back-tracing encrypted packets being sent, then using backdoors the NSA has at the financial institutions they are coming from. Once I knew what I was looking for, it was easy to find the malware."

"Hang on," Sarah said with dawning comprehension. "You said financial institutions. How many?"

Charlie suddenly looked uncomfortable and felt fear growing in the pit of his stomach. "Well, that's the thing. I checked three of the biggest banks in the U.S. Every one of them had it. But in the hour or so I've been looking, the data center has received packets from almost a million endpoints. That's a million different computers at who knows how many different banks, hedge funds, and day traders across the U.S."

"What does it do?"

"I'm not sure. I need to pull it apart, but I'd say it's a good bet it's designed to make trades without anyone noticing. If a million small trades come from everywhere, it just looks like noise, not a pattern. I'd bet we'll find something similar on all of the social media platforms, although in that case, it would probably be bots or individuals' phones or computers."

"Can you stop it?"

Charlie looked grave. "It's on too many devices for us to stop at this point. It's been spreading from system to system for God knows how long. The only way to stop it is to ensure it never gets the go command. It's in some kind of dormant state. All it does is spread. We'd have to issue some nationwide patch to eliminate it, but it would never get done in time. But when that data center fires off the go command, it's going to crash the whole market and spread fear and chaos on a level we've never seen before."

"So, we need to destroy the data center?"

"First, we need Snowman to find it. And we've lost all contact with him."

54

Neues Berchtesgaden, Argentina

Colin watched as two guards in black uniforms moved toward the truck in the distance. He was still silent, trying to decide whether to believe this beautiful blonde woman next to him. On the one hand, if she was British intelligence, she could help him find a way to stop the attack. On the other hand, she could just as easily be a Nazi trying to get him to reveal himself.

"I need you to give me your choice before those guards get here, or we're both in trouble," she replied, gesturing at the black-uniformed guards who were definitely now heading their way.

"Why didn't you tell me this back at the farm?" Colin asked.

"Because I wasn't sure if I could trust you yet, and I needed to be sure."

In the end, Colin's choice was simple. In the absence of figuring out what was going on, getting caught was his best way in. He'd just have to hope Jester and the Green Berets weren't far behind.

"Fine. What do we do, and how do we stop this?"

"First, follow my lead. Then we'll talk about stopping this."

"Okay, what do you need me—" Before he could say anything else, she leaned over and kissed him. Colin was stunned into inaction, but only momentarily. It wasn't long before instinct took over, and he kissed her back. Her lips were soft, and he felt her eyelashes softly brushing his cheek. If it were any other situation, he would have been deeply enjoying himself. For now, he settled for only kind of enjoying himself. She broke contact with his lips hovering centimeters from his face. Her breath smelled like the sweet wine they'd drunk at her farm. They looked into each other's eyes.

"Are they walking the other way?" she whispered. Colin's eyes lingered on hers for a moment before peering over her blonde hair. The guards had turned and were heading in the other direction.

"They're heading the other way," Colin whispered back. Slowly, Alina turned back and unbuckled her seatbelt, keeping her eyes on Colin's for a moment longer than she probably should have.

"Follow me," she said, exiting the truck. Colin hopped out behind her and followed her up a winding staircase that led to the street above their own. The whole town was built like a giant terrace on the mountainside. When they got to the street above, it was less crowded than the one below, and she ducked into a small alley with him.

"The guards are here to keep people out, not bother the inhabitants. But be careful of them. They're not your average fighters. Most are SS. New Reich Special Forces. They'll be easy to spot tonight in uniform, but beware of any in plain clothes."

Colin felt like he'd walked through a time warp to 1940s Germany with modern accents. "Who are you, and why are you here?" Colin asked, cutting around everything she was telling him.

"My family has been here for generations. When I went to

school in London for university, I was approached by MI6 and recruited. I've been a double agent ever since. Stopping this is my ticket out of here to a new life free of this insanity."

"How'd you know who I was?"

"I was warned by my government to be on the lookout for Americans. It was obvious who you are from the second I saw you, even with the blond hair and blue eyes."

"Do you have a way of communicating with them? I've lost all comms."

"No. We use dead drops; electronic communication is too risky here. And we're deeply compromised as well. There's a jammer in the center of town on that roof," she said, pointing to a three-story building in the distance. Colin could see an antenna on top, even in the fading light.

"Why didn't your government warn mine if they knew there was going to be an attack?"

"For the same reason yours didn't give us a heads-up. There are too many compromised endpoints in the system, and we don't know how deep this goes. I was the only asset able to get inside this, and we don't even really understand what this is yet."

"I need to make contact with my team—which means we need to shut that thing down," Colin said.

"How big is your team?"

"I've got six shooters, not including me. They were supposed to be close behind, but I lost comms with them the second I met you."

"You brought seven men to deal with this!" she shout-whispered harshly. She looked fearful now. Like she knew she was going to die.

"What is this? How do we stop the attack?"

She took a deep breath, looking frustrated. It's all been very hush hush. But whatever operation they have going, it's moved to the mountain command bunker now. If we're going to stop whatever it is, we'll need your team, and we need to get up there," she said, pointing now at the mountain in the distance.

"Where?" Colin asked, looking.

"Do you see the copse of trees there on the left that look slightly taller than the rest of the trees in its area?"

Colin squinted. It did look slightly odd, but if he hadn't been told to look at it, he never would have noticed. "There is a hangar cut into the side of the mountain there. That is where the command bunker is. It should be lightly staffed tonight if we can get there. Everyone will be here at the celebration."

Colin looked at her, wide-eyed. "What celebration? The harvest festival?"

"That was a lie. Tonight is the Fuhrer's birthday. The highest of all celebrations for the New Reich. Hence, all the guards are in ceremonial uniforms."

Colin's eyes opened wider. "When will the attack occur? Why do we have to hit it tonight? If we can wait, I can get more men."

"It will occur tomorrow. All the preparations have been made. Assets who have laid the groundwork for the bio and cyber strikes have all returned. That means the attack is imminent. I work in personnel management for the SS. We're out of time. We must stop this tonight."

Colin's mind was moving a million miles a minute. He had no choice but to comply and hope Alina knew what the hell she was talking about and that she wasn't going to betray him. Colin resigned himself to the fact he probably wouldn't live long enough to find out.

"Okay, what do we have to do?"

She smiled devilishly at him. "First things first, the party should start picking up soon. It will be utter drunken chaos. We can use that as coverage to get to the building and shut off the jammer to make contact with your team. We'll also need to steal an officer's credentials to get into the bunker. A few uniforms wouldn't hurt either. Also, try not to speak to anyone—your English will be a dead giveaway.

"Got it. Be a mute and follow your lead."

"Look cute and follow my lead. You're my date tonight. And if we have a chance of pulling this off, we need to blend in."

"Okay then. Where do we start?"

"We start by getting a stein of beer."

55

C olin followed Alina into the street and toward the crowd in the distance. Already, he could hear music and drunken Germanic yells. The smells of fire and cooking food permeated the cool spring night. Colin stole the occasional glance at Alina's swaying hips as she walked. He wasn't being creepy. He was just trying to determine if she was carrying a concealed weapon. They had kissed, but they hadn't gone all the way, and Colin wasn't sure he trusted her yet.

The crowd looked relatively normal as they approached. And Colin thought it wouldn't have looked out of place at Octoberfest. Most people wore normal clothes people in the mountains in any country wore. The exception was the few in lederhosen and the menacing-looking guards in black uniforms. Literal jackbooted thugs. Colin avoided any of these men. He was careful not to look at them. A killer could tell a killer by looking in their eyes, or at least Colin thought they could.

His senses were on overdrive, probing the crowd for threats and taking in every aspect of the town he could in case he needed to try and escape. Alina said hello to the occasional passerby weaving them through the crowd toward the center of the event.

Small wooden stalls sold various wares and food on the sides of the square. Colin had the brief thought that this place might look pretty picturesque during Christmas, except for the Nazis.

Alina proceeded to one of the stalls and purchased two steins of beer. Colin looked at her, subtly letting her know he wasn't sure if this was a good idea. She raised her eyebrows in response, telling him to just go with it. Colin took a sip of the Pilsner and was surprised at how good it tasted. Crisp and refreshing with no hoppy aftertaste. He might buy this himself if he were anywhere else in the world. She cheers'd him and smiled. "Someone's about to come up behind you. Follow my lead, and don't do anything stupid, or you'll get us both killed."

Colin nodded subtly, making it look like he was taking another sip of the beer. The ceramic stein felt heavy and looked to be hand-painted.

"Ms. Chapman, how are you this evening?" a man asked sternly. Colin turned around to step out of the man's way. She smiled warmly at the man in the black uniform. He was tall and intimidating, with a severe face, pasted-on smile, and graying eyebrows.

"Captain, it's so good to see you," she replied before turning to her date. "Colin, this is Captain Fritz. Commander of the local guard. Captain, this is Colin. He's a friend from the United States. Here on orders to lie low after participating in our latest operation in the country."

The man's smile evaporated instantly, and he seemed to straighten up a little. "Pleasure to have you," the captain said respectfully. "It's fortuitous you're here on such a special occasion. You get to see Neues Berchtesgaden in all of its intended glory. Have you been before?"

Colin could tell the man was unsure about him. Maybe even a little bit fearful. He thought this might mean that working for Alina meant he wasn't someone to be trifled with. Colin did his best to play into this but also tried to say as little as possible. "Unfortunately, I don't get to leave the U.S. much. Business."

"Ah, so you haven't been here before?" the captain asked. Colin stared back coldly, doing his best to keep his face impassable as if he weren't interested in talking. Colin saw suspicion in the captain's cold eyes. He wanted to ask more, but he was also hesitant for some unknown reason.

Alina spoke up. "Captain, you know how it is in our line of work. The less said, the better. Besides, you wouldn't want it to get around to Colonel Sigfried that you were asking his men questions."

The captain's face darkened, as if this was a threat he wasn't interested in coming to fruition. He maintained eye contact with Colin, though, for a second longer than he would have liked.

"Of course not. It's a celebration, after all. Enjoy your evening and pray we one day don't have to hide our true selves from the world." He snapped his heels together, and his arm shot out straight; then he turned on the balls of his shiny boots and walked away into the crowd. Colin waited a moment, faking like he was taking another sip from his stein before asking Alina if they were in trouble.

"He thinks you're an SS operative in the Intelligence Directorate. Or at least I alluded to it. Hopefully, he won't ask us any more questions," Alina said, watching the captain as he moved through the throng of people. Colin suspected she wasn't sure if her plan had worked either.

"What does he do?" Colin asked in a low voice.

"He's in the Security Directorate. They're considered low-level muscle and beneath the other SS. But they function as security for the town, the bunker, and other sites across the world.

"Do they always wear uniforms?"

"No. In fact, usually they're dressed like police, at least here. But this is our highest of holidays. The Fuhrer's birthday. During today, all rules about maintaining secrecy are thrown to the wind."

"This all seems a little much. How could we not have known about it?" Colin asked in a low voice.

"Well, the collective West somehow didn't wake up to China being a threat until COVID happened. And they're a global super-power. Hiding all this seems trivial in comparison."

It was a good point, but Colin still felt uneasy and unsure about everything he was seeing.

"Does it function as a country or some kind of criminal syndicate?"

"Both, and neither. Like many countries these days."

Colin couldn't argue with that. "How—"

She cut him off. "Follow me, and don't rescue me for at least five minutes." Alina surged forward toward another man in a black uniform, leaving Colin standing there dumbstruck and feeling very exposed. This one was younger. He had darker hair, and his cap was tucked neatly under his arm. He held an equally large stein of beer in his hand. "Lieutenant?" Alina said seduc-tively to the man in front of her. He turned toward her, and his eyes lit up.

Colin moved closer but stayed back far enough not to arouse suspicion. It wasn't hard in the rowdy crowd.

"Alina, my darling!" He grabbed her, picked her up, and spun her around, kissing her on both cheeks. She kissed him in return and blushed heavily.

"What a perfect evening. Made even more perfect by you," he said shamelessly. Colin thought it was a dumb opening line. But then, some cultures were more forward than others. She reached up and whispered something in his ear. His eyes went wide, and he nodded excitedly. He grabbed her by the hand and pulled her through the crowd toward a building on the far end of the square.

Colin followed, trying to blend into the crowd. He made a

show of drinking from his stein and had to watch his footing on several loose cobblestones beneath his feet. This had the effect of making him look like he had been drinking like the rest of the people surrounding him. He kept his eyes low and moved parallel to Alina and the Lieutenant. They moved past the building they were walking toward, and Colin saw Alina pull the man into an alley between a seven-foot-tall brick wall and the rear of the building.

Colin walked toward the building, put his back to it, and had another sip of beer. The party in front of him was really picking up. With each drink he saw people take, they seemed to get louder and more rambunctious. *People were the same everywhere,* he thought. He checked the Stirling Durrant watch on his wrist. It was a gift from a friend who had started the company in the British SAS. He'd had to throw out his Garmin smartwatch years ago when the watches had been hacked by an adversary on a deployment with the Green Berets. He still had four minutes to kill. In the back of his mind, he knew this whole thing could still be a trap, but he was out of options and out of time.

Suddenly something caught his eye in the crowd, and his stomach dropped.

The captain was watching him.

56

Neues Berchtesgaden, Argentina

Colin took another sip from his stein, trying hard to blend into the wall he was leaning against. The severe-looking captain was lingering at the edge of the swelling crowd. Somewhere in the distance, a band had begun playing. Colin kept his gaze low and only looked in the captain's direction again when he took another sip from his drink. He was sure now that the man was watching him. He made no effort to hide it.

Colin ran through scenarios in his head. He had another two minutes before he needed to follow Alina into the alley. In that time, he needed this man to either lose interest in him or he'd likely follow the second Colin moved. This situation was already out of control. If he introduced any more variables, he wasn't sure he could keep the train on its tracks. Colin made a show of reaching down to tie his Origin hiking boot, placing the stein carefully on the ground next to it. He finished and stood back up, looking at the captain as he did, but the man was now out of site.

Colin sighed with relief and moved toward the alley. He'd done enough sitting around. He saw darkness was beginning to fall across the town as he approached the rear of the building. People's moods seemed to rise with the coming of night. An ominous sign, Colin judged. He turned left into the alley and saw the lieutenant with his back to him, kissing Alina. The smallest hint of jealousy flashed through Colin's animal brain before he stowed it, reminding himself it was an insane emotion to feel.

He moved quietly now, watching his footfalls as he went so as not to make any sounds. It was darker here in the shadows of the alley than in the surrounding area. His hand instinctively went to go for his gun when he realized it wasn't there. It was still sitting in the bottom of his backpack in Alina's pickup truck. There was the knife at the small of his back, but the hefty stein in Colin's hand would do fine.

As he reached the back of the lieutenant, he brought it down with a crunch onto the base of the man's skull. Beer sprayed everywhere, and the ceramic didn't break. Colin suspected that sound had been the lieutenant's skull. As the man crumpled to the ground, Alina held up a key card she'd taken from the man's uniform.

"Let's stash the body and get out of here now!" she said.

"You don't have to tell me twice," Colin responded. He grabbed the man's legs and dragged him into the shadows behind a set of trashcans. He placed the stein into the man's fingers, hoping that if anyone did catch a glance of him, they'd think he'd just passed out drunk. If they turned him over, they'd understand the truth of the situation immediately. The back of the man's head was covered in blood from where his skull had been fractured.

Alina motioned him forward, and they moved to a gap in the brick wall. They followed this into a small cemetery and ran at a low crouch parallel to the main road away from the party. The rising moon cast shadows across the tombstones. When they reached the far side, Alina undid the latch on a wrought iron gate and led him out onto a side street. Colin tried to remember the maze they were moving through as he went. He might need it if he needed to get out of here in a hurry.

There was no one on this side street, and Alina slowed to a walk and grabbed Colin's hand. "For appearances," she said to him in a low voice.

"Are you armed?"

"No, are you?" he asked.

"Yes," she said, reaching to her ankle and yanking up her pant leg to show a 9mm compact. It looked to Colin like a P365, but he couldn't tell.

"Do you have a suppressor?" he asked.

"No, but the rounds are subsonic."

"That's not going to help us. That shot will echo like crazy off these stone buildings."

"You try fitting a suppressor in pants this tight," she replied crossly.

Colin raised his eyebrows at her. "Okay, the guns are a last resort. How do we kill the jammer without bringing this whole town down on top of us?"

"It's three hundred meters away on the top of that building. If we can get there, I can set it to standby mode. With everyone at the party, no one should notice tonight, and there should only be a few guards present."

"A few?" Colin asked.

"Two or three. We'll be fine," Alina replied.

"Fuck it. The only plan's the best plan. Let's go."

A few minutes later, they arrived close to the building with the jammer on top. It was made of white stone and wood and was iridescent in the moonlight. It almost looked like a church, and the steeple on top would have given that appearance to anyone viewing the building from the air. But the jamming antenna it hid was obvious when viewed from the side.

"Let's go around back. We should be able to use this to get in from there without attracting attention," she said, holding up the keycard. Colin nodded and followed her around the side of the building. It smelled like trash cans from a cafe were nearby. The smell of rotting coffee permeated the air. When they arrived at the rear of the building, Colin saw a steel door barring their entry. To its right was a keycard scanner with a faint red light glowing from it.

Alina approached it cautiously, observing her surroundings for signs of a camera or surveillance. None were apparent to Colin. She moved the card toward the scanner and froze. A voice from behind them had spoken in a commanding tone, followed by the racking of half a dozen guns. It was the captain.

"It appears your new friend must have led you astray, Alina."

57

El Paso, Texas

Drug Enforcement Agent Mick Aldridge was more than a little surprised when the president of the United States entered the briefing via teleconference to speak to them directly. By him, he meant the five other DEA Special Response Team Units now gearing up for action in different cities close to the Mexican border. The briefing they were receiving was also unique due to the presence of the military, the CDC, and a smattering of three letter agencies who had joined the Hydra task force.

Their mission, if Mick understood it correctly, was to interdict the viral drugs if they made it to this side of the border and contain them. If the drugs were located on the far side of the border, military special operations forces from across the Army and Navy would be responsible for interdiction. One member of the CDC's fast response and containment team would accompany each of the strike teams in an advisory capacity.

Mick was grateful for the new CBRN suits they had provided his team, even if they weren't a new thing. During drug raids, more and more often than not his team found themselves wearing the old, uncomfortable things. As the prevalence of fentanyl grew, and more DEA deaths had accompanied it the Agency had wised up and started requiring the wearing of suits on raids. Even a microgram of fentanyl breathed in or touched through the skin could kill a human. Mick thought he would have preferred that to dying of hemorrhagic fever.

"Shit, Mick, we haven't done something this high speed since the FAST teams," his second in command Alan Swick whispered to him, referring to the Foreign Deployed Advisory and Support teams they'd worked on burning poppy fields in Afghanistan.

"I'd rather that to this. This stuff gives me the willies, especially after COVID."

"COVID wasn't shit compared to this man," Alan replied. They both quieted down as the president continued speaking.

"I know it might be a bit of a shock, but I asked to be a part of this to stress the gravity of the situation. We're here with teams from across the military and law enforcement communities. All working together to protect our country. A few days ago, we moved into Star Set Protocols when we discovered the nature of the biological threat against us. For those of you who don't know, Star Set protocols move into effect when there is an immediate existential threat to the United States. And this threat is existential. In short, it clears the board and brings to bear every resource available. Through this investigation, we've discovered an unknown terrorist organization plans to move an unknown amount of cocaine laced with hemorrhagic fever into the United States. If the drugs break containment and get out into the broader population, we'll face casualty rates potentially into the hundreds of millions of Americans." The president paused, letting the information sink in. It was deadly quiet in the briefing room. A mix of nerves and eagerness to deal death and judgment to those responsible mingled in the air.

"Your CDC counterparts will brief you all on the nature of the biological threat. But I'm here to let you know you have my full support. The fate of the country rests on your shoulders. Get it done."

The president finished speaking, and there was a lull in the briefing as the speakers changed. "He didn't say where the drugs are. How do we stop them if we don't know where they are?" Alan said to him. "Fuck, if I should know, why don't you shut up, and we'll find out."

As if in answer to his statement, a Navy captain came onto the screen, "As to the location of the viral narcotics, we have captured a high-level source in the cartel whose network is being used to distribute them. To protect his anonymity, we won't use his name. This information does not leave this briefing room, but the organization is Descanso Eterno."

"Shit, those guys are bad news. I bet the SEALS grabbed his ass," Alan whispered. Mick's eyes opened wide, telling him to shut up. He talked a lot when he was nervous.

"Once we have satisfied the terms of our agreement, he will give us the distribution points that are likely to be used. We'll then hit all of them simultaneously. Whoever finds the drugs wins. Under Star Set protocols, all bad guys are to be considered enemy combatants. This includes domestically. You may shoot first and ask questions later. If you get the opportunity to take someone alive, do it. But if anyone breaks containment, the game starts all over again until we eventually lose and potentially millions of Americans die."

Mick was surprised by this. He'd been on a hundred no-knock warrants. He'd been in a lot of gunfights, too. But actively being told to shoot first and ask questions later wasn't something he'd ever been a part of.

The briefers cycled again, and this time, someone from the CDC came on the screen. "Samples of the virus are currently en route to Fort Dietrich in Maryland. There the virus will be analyzed for deadliness and contagiousness. Until we have those answers, here are the assumptions. Hemorrhagic fever kills roughly eighty percent of those it infects. The symptoms are severe. It will essentially dissolve your insides and force you to bleed out of every hole in your body until death comes one to three days after symptoms set in. There is only one known vaccine, and it's experimental. We also don't have enough of it for even all the people on this task force, and it won't save you from getting it after infection. Keep your gear on at all times, and do not touch anyone who's been infected. Hemorrhagic fever typically isn't airborne, but that's not to say this one isn't. If it's been placed on the drugs, it's likely been nebulized, so if the powder gets into the air, it will infect you and kill you. Once you've secured the drugs, keep your gear on until follow-on CDC teams arrive and decontaminate you. After you've been decontaminated, you'll enter quarantine for two weeks to ensure you haven't contracted anything. Your individual CDC liaisons will answer any additional questions and make sure your gear is on correctly."

Someone piped up across the table. "What happens if our gear is compromised? Like we get shot?"

"Get away from those around you. And pray you're in the lucky 20 percent."

58

White House, Washington, D.C.

"Mr. President, we now have one suspected case of hemorrhagic fever in El Paso, Texas. A man checked into the ER an hour ago with a severe fever and is now exhibiting symptoms consistent with the disease. Mainly bleeding from the eyes and the nose," Bob Mylod said. They were sitting in the situation room watching briefings occur across various military branches and law enforcement agencies.

"How is that possible? Narcisso assured us the drugs hadn't entered the United States yet, and the virus has a three- to five-day incubation period," the president responded.

"We just don't know, sir. But that could mean the virus has already been released and we're too late."

"Mr. President, if these reports are confirmed, we need to proceed with the rest of Operation Hydra and quarantine El Paso immediately. There's no time to waste."

"I just don't understand it. How could it have gone this far this fast? I thought we were ahead of this. I—"

The door to the situation room opened, and his press secretary walked in with an iPad in hand. "Mr. President, the stories are already breaking on the internet. It's now trending on Facebook and X. The major news outlets are already calling for comment."

A frazzled-looking assistant followed her into the room with a cell phone to each ear. The president sat back in his chair. But scarcely anyone noticed. His entire cabinet was now arguing and discussing how this could have happened.

William knew this was all too convenient. There was just no way this information could have gotten out so fast when they were only just finding out about it. The hospitals were under strict orders from the CDC to report cases directly up the chain of command and not to make public comment.

"Mr. President, with your permission, sir, we need to get Operation Hydra moving. Supplies need to be airlifted to hospitals, and we need to get the city quarantined. If the virus is already out, we need to be prepared to quarantine other areas as well as soon as the CDC can complete contact tracing," Mack Tomlin said over the noise. The president didn't respond. He was deep in thought. Before he was a Navy captain, he was an intelligence officer, and everything about this smelled.

"Another case has just been reported in Los Angeles," the press secretary blurted out urgently. "This one hasn't been confirmed by the hospital yet. It's starting to pick up traffic on social media."

More arguing and shouting now ensued from the cabinet. Still, William sat silently thinking, ignoring the panic his advisors were spewing. Blame would help no one at this point. Neither would panic. Finally, he held up his hand, calling for quiet. It took a few moments for everyone to notice and get the message. Slowly, the room calmed down.

"Now I know we're all scared right now. But we can't fall apart. Failure of leadership right now could result in the deaths of millions. Mack, begin operation Hydra. Quarantine El Paso and be ready to quarantine anywhere else the contact tracers say the virus could have spread. Wendy, how long until the sample of the virus arrives at Fort Deitrick for analysis?" he asked.

Mack picked up a phone and began barking orders into it.

Wendy spoke next. "It should be landing in the next twenty minutes or so. They're standing by to do their analysis."

"Tell them to work fast. We need to know what we're dealing with. Rob, how is this getting out so fast? Even with social media, this feels staged. Can we stop it?" the president asked the head of the NSA.

"Sir, it's emanating from a huge number of bots, from what we can tell. Our teams discovered them when we uncovered the net preparing all the short trades. We can't stop them all in time for market opening tomorrow, and the fastest way to get them all closed down short of shutting off the social media sites is to kill them at the source, which would be the data center in Argentina. Can our team there handle that?"

"They'll have to. Wendy, pass word. Jason, we need to suspend trading for the day tomorrow at least, and I'm not sure we're going to be able to stop this in time. Please have SEC execute that. If we can stop the misinformation and financial warfare here, people, and contain the virus, we'll be just fine—" The president stopped dead in his tracks. The look on the head of the SEC's face was dire. "What is it, Jason?"

"Mr. President, our systems have been affected. I told my people to prepare for this eventuality, and I've just been informed that we can't seem to flip the switches to halt trading. I've got teams working on it, but we're not even sure what's wrong at this point. Several years ago, we created direct integrations with various exchanges, like the NYSE, NASDAQ, etc., to automate our circuit breakers in the event of an attack or unusual trading activity. The market stops automatically at certain thresholds, typically severe drops of 7%, 13%, or 20%. A 20% drop in the market would trigger a suspension of trading for the day. We can do this preemptively in a case just like this, but it's just not working, and the exchanges are now reporting some kind of incursion in their servers as well. We're already seeing unusual activity on MIDAS in after-hours trading. We could use some help." The man finished referring to the Market Information Data Analytics Solution.

"You're kidding me?" the president asked with a deadly serious look on his face.

"No, sir," the man replied sheepishly.

The president sighed. "Wendy, give Jason everything we have to try and sort this out. I don't care if it comes from CIA, the Army, FBI, NSA, or some other classified programs—just get it done."

"Yes, Mr. President," Wendy replied, standing and motioning Jason out of the room with her.

The lead Secret Service agent now entered the room and whispered in the president's ear, "Sir, we are beginning protocols to lock down the White House. We'd like to move you to the bunker to quarantine you and maintain continuity of government. We're already relocating the Vice President, and we need to separate and isolate the cabinet."

The president nodded, processing this, "Vice President fine, White House fine, but the Cabinet and I stay put here. We need to sort this mess out."

"Mr. President, I strongly recommend we—"

The president cut him off. "No. Now if you'll excuse me, we've got work to do. What's the status of our teams in Argentina and El Paso?"

59

USS Gerald R. Ford, Mediterranean Ocean

"Tower, this is Blackjack 26, ready for taxi to EMALS Catapult One."

"Blackjack 26, taxi to EMALS Catapult One."

Lieutenant Webster acknowledged the communication from the tower and advanced the F/A-18F Super Hornet toward the electromagnetic catapult of the Gerald R. Ford supercarrier. A yellow-shirted catapult officer directed him into position with hand signals. And he followed with hand signals of his own to lower the launch bar into position. A moment later, a Greenshirt confirmed to him the launch bar was in position, and Lieutenant Webster gave him a thumbs-up to acknowledge the connection. He saw on the horizon the low orange sun dripping into the Mediterranean Sea.

Lieutenant Webster gave his aircraft a final systems check for the last-minute mission of mercy. He watched as the Greenshirt signaled the shooter, who in turn signaled for him to advance to the afterburner for his shot off the carrier. Lieutenant Webster saluted, and the shooter signaled him to launch.

Instantly, the electromagnetic catapult ripped his aircraft from the spot and pulled him from zero to 165 knots in 3 seconds. He felt the pressure sandwiching him into his seat begin to release as his aircraft left the deck, and his relative acceleration eased. He climbed away from the carrier into the low morning sun and oriented his aircraft southwest for his trip to Cabo Verde off the coast of Africa.

What he was retrieving was a mystery to him, but he knew he was to land in Cabo Verde, pick up a package, refuel, and transit directly to Rota, Spain. As such, he ensured the tail hook and catapult bar were retracted as he continued to climb.

"Tower Blackjack 26 is airborne."

"Roger Blackjack 26, climb to 3,000 feet and proceed to waypoint alpha."

Lieutenant Webster complied and moved the aircraft toward their first navigational waypoint.

"Any idea what this is about Web?" his backseater, Lieutenant Hackworth, asked.

"Your guess is as good as mine, Hack."

"Still not sure why they couldn't send a Greyhound. Seems like a waste of valuable government resources, if you ask me.

"Engine trouble and timing issues, from what I heard. I also heard the captain was on the horn with the president right before we got our marching orders, so I guess this is important."

"Well, I hear Africa is beautiful this time of year."

"Well, if someone decides to shoot a SAM at us, maybe you can see it for yourself."

Web didn't have to look to see the middle finger pointed at the back of his head. They passed through clouds as they climbed to their cruising altitude of 40,000 feet and leveled off for the trip to the small island nation. Web found himself wondering what the hell could possibly be important enough to send them. Normally, basic transport would be handled by the carriers C-2A Greyhound aircraft. It wasn't necessarily irregular that one would be pulled off a mission to address a maintenance issue. What was irregular was opting to use an alert aircraft to fulfill the mission of a completely different type of asset.

"Whatever it was they were picking up was important and small enough that they were supposed to grab it and push it at the best possible speed to Rota. They weren't expecting trouble, but they were also only carrying two AIM-120 AMRAAMs and two AIM-9 Sidewinders for self-defense. The rest of their loadout was in additional fuel tanks for the trip. If they did have to mix it up with someone, they'd run out of weapons fast and be outside the quick help of their peers until they got back closer to the carrier and Spain. But that was why they paid him the big bucks, he supposed.

An hour later, he decided to check and see if their cargo had landed in Cabo Verde yet. "Tower, this is Blackjack 26. Status check on precious cargo?"

"Standby, Blackjack 26," Web heard in response. It would take a second for the controller to gather the information from Cabo Verde if they weren't tracking the incoming flight directly with an E2-D Hawkeye.

A moment later, they responded, "Blackjack 26. Tower, incoming precious cargo is thirty minutes from arrival in Cabo Verde. They have declared an emergency and are down one engine. Will continue to monitor and provide updates to you."

"Blackjack 26 copies."

"Wonder what the emergency is," Hack said.

"You're the man with all the answers back there."

The backseater was the Weapons System Officer and, as such, had access to most of the situational awareness and operations data downlinked to their aircraft.

"Doesn't say, but it looks like the Agency blacklisted the flight, so whatever we're dealing with here is something spooky, most likely," Hack replied. Web was about to reply when an alarm blared in his helmet.

Hack spoke first. "Shit, something just locked onto us!"

60

Neues Berchtesgaden, Argentina

Colin's blood ran cold as he slowly raised his hands. He moved as slowly as possible, still staring at the back of the building. He was sure he'd heard the sounds of at least half a dozen weapons as the captain had spoken. *I'm really starting to hate this fucking place,* he thought to himself.

He heard Alina speak next to him. "What is it you think you're doing, Captain?" she asked commandingly. Colin was half expecting her to say she had caught him and was selling him out. But at the moment, she appeared to still be on his side.

"Drop the act. You have no business being here right now. I demand to know what you are doing," the captain replied. Alina slowly lowered her hands and turned toward the captain. Colin followed but kept his hands raised. Two bright flashlight beams painted their faces as they did, completely obscuring his vision. He closed his eyes to keep from being blinded.

"You will turn and leave now, or Colonel Sigfried will hear of this," Alina said, trying to sound commanding. Colin thought he could hear her voice faltering, though. Maybe he had been wrong about her, and she actually was on his side. Either way, it didn't matter at the moment. He needed to try and think of a way out of this.

"Will he? Well, perhaps you and this"—Colin could feel the captain's gaze on him through the bright lights, even though he couldn't see him—"man attacked me and my men, and we had no choice but to defend ourselves. I have a feeling even the SS will take my word over a dead woman's."

Colin wasn't sure what this guy's issue was, but he decided to try and take some of the heat off of Alina so she could talk her way out of it. "The lady said it's none of your business. And you haven't seen what I'm capable of yet. So, you might want to go back to the party before you wind up the dead one."

It was a hollow threat, Colin knew even as he said it. He was dead if he tried to charge these guys, and the odds of them believing him were even lower. Colin heard slow footsteps from the man's shiny black boots as he moved toward him. He could see him more clearly now, even with the light shining in his eyes. Malice dripped from his cold face. This man hated him. He opened his mouth to speak, and Colin knew they were in trouble. The captain lashed, connecting his fist with Colin's jaw. The blow sent stars across Colin's vision, but he didn't allow himself to stagger back.

"Oh, rea—" Suddenly, the front of his face exploded in a blast of red mist covering Colin and Alina. Colin fell backward, stunned as several more muted thwacks reverberated off the stone. Colin lay on the ground, stunned for a moment, listening to the raucous sounds of the party below them. When a powerful hand grabbed him and pulled him upright.

"Looks like I can cross killing a Nazi off my bucket list, Snowman," said Jester. Colin couldn't help but laugh as he reached up, wiping red out of his eyes. With the flashlights, no.

Longer pointed at him, he could make out the dark forms of Jester, Grinch, Panda, Ford, and the dog.

"Thank God you guys are here, brother."

"Eh, we were never far behind. Are you going to introduce us to your lady friend?"

Alina spoke first. "Alina Chapman, MI6. Pleased to meet you, and thanks for the hand."

"MI6, you're shitting me. Next thing you're going to tell me, there's a bunch of SAS dudes hiding behind the trashcans," Jester said.

"Unfortunately, it's just me."

"Damn, could have used a few more shooters. This place is crawling."

"Where's the rest of the team?" Colin asked.

"We're not sure. We lost comms a while back. We've been sticking close ever since. Any idea how we can get 'em back?"

Colin pointed up at the building behind them. We've got to turn off this jammer quietly. That should restore communications."

"Well, let's get to it. And oh, I've got something here for you." Jester replied. He pulled off his backpack and pulled Colin's beloved M1911A1.

"Thought you would miss this, so we grabbed it from the truck on the way in."

"You're a lifesaver," Colin replied. Jester grabbed a smaller 9-millimeter pistol and went to hand it to Alina, but Colin stopped him.

"Trouble in paradise?" Jester asked.

"No offense; just not sure if I trust you yet," Colin said.

"You're kidding me," she replied, an annoyed look on her face.

"I met you for the first time two hours ago in a secret Nazi village. Call me paranoid. But I need some time."

After a moment, her look eased, and she shrugged. "Fair enough."

Colin strapped on a vest he had been handed and attached a suppressor to the pistol, then moved to the door. Alina swiped the keycard and stepped away as Colin and the team moved inside.

Colin found an empty hallway and a set of stairs. He began climbing, the rest of the team close on his heels. They climbed three flights before arriving at the top, where a ladder led up the steeple. Colin began climbing, pistol still in his right hand. When he reached the top, he peered over the top of the floor and saw one guard sitting in a chair looking out toward the party raging below them. Even up here, the noise of the music and yelling was loud enough to obscure him climbing up behind the man.

He moved cautiously toward him, and when he was a foot away, he sprang. He grabbed the man's head, twisting it violently to the right and feeling the neck snap like a chiropractor visit gone wrong. He fell to the ground, silently suffocating. Colin hated killing men like this. It made him sick the way the neck popped with such ease. Bullets were cleaner. But they were also louder, and noise drew attention.

He turned to the jammer controls behind him—a complicated labyrinth of buttons on a computer screen. It was time to get back in touch with the world and end this.

61

The Mountain Bunker, Argentina

Colonel Sigfried Himmler noticed with satisfaction that his drink shook slightly in his hand. The bubbles in the glass of champagne ascended lazily, waving to the surface of his glass. The shaking was from the vigorous workout this morning, which had included a thousand push-ups and max-effort Romanian deadlifts. He always punished himself on the morning of a great celebration. The suffering made it more enjoyable.

He watched as the Obergruppenführer held court with his senior advisors. His fake smile and laugh irritated Sigfried to no end. This was his night, and the man was doing his best to take all the credit. Sigfried tried his best to push this from his mind, turning his attention to the large monitors on the walls around them. No matter what anyone said tonight, it was his operation, and he would see it through to its end, taking great pride in its results.

The monitors displayed a map of the ongoing information streaming onto America's social media and news sites. Graphs of sentiment shifted continuously as AI used the company's own tracking tools against them. Comments, pictures, and videos that attracted more attention were tracked, boosted, and pushed to more sites in an ongoing A/B test of despair. Botnets spun up and down, ensuring the latest posts came from hyper-local sources close to the incident while also simultaneously evading bot defenses from the platforms. Already hashtags like Ebola outbreak, plague of the century, and COVID 2.0 were. Trending on all social media sites.

He turned to another wall and tracked the location of the main thrust of tainted drugs moving across the border from Mexico to El Paso. Another bank of monitors showed the financial portion of the operation. Early sell-offs of key positions they had acquired large quantities of on the U.S. markets would serve as early warning signs to investors when the markets opened in the morning. Even if the U.S. attempted to halt trading, their systems would be unresponsive.

Even more, monitors showed mainstream television news outlets with red breaking news banners reporting live from the hospitals in Texas and California. The U.S. population was being swamped with fear. Sigfried watched with amusement as the pieces of his operation played like an orchestra in front of him. By morning, it would all be impossible to stop.

Gary Weider, the de facto seed of chaos responsible for so much of the carnage, sat at a desk behind a huge ultrawide monitor. Two menacing-looking guards stood behind him. "The political division hashtags are starting to trend," he commented sourly, looking from Sigfried to the guards behind him.

"Show me."

Gary tapped a few keys, and trending posts began to stream across the monitors. They stated things like do not comply, take off the masks, and never get vaxed. Another monitor showed posts from the other side. They said things like 'willing to do my part, let the non-vaxers die' and more comments along racial lines.

"Took most of these verbatim out of COVID posts," Gary said.

"How are they trending so fast?"

"Well, the algorithms prioritize engagement above all else. Nothing gets engagement like political arguments, fear porn, and fighting. It's human nature. We're taking that to the extreme by cross-posting hashtags to make sure posts from the opposite political camps infest the feeds of people who really won't like them. People can't help but respond. It might be to call someone a communist or a racist. It doesn't matter either way. Every comment, like, or repost boosts posts to reach up to a hundred times the original."

"Amazing," Sigfried said in awe of how fast things were moving.

"The real trick is all the fake news we're about to push into people's feeds. It gets sky-high engagement, and there's no way for the moderators to pull it down or label it fake without additional information. Sure, they might get some, but in general, the platforms are way more likely to leave something up, so they don't get labeled biased. We'll push petabytes of content over the next twenty-four hours. By the time they realize what it is, it won't matter anymore."

"Good work, Gary. The Fuhrer will be proud," said the Obergruppenführer coming up next to them.

"Sir," Sigfried replied tersely. It took everything in his soul to not turn and walk the other way. Or worse.

"You must be pleased with our progress," the Obergruppenführer said. Once again, the man insulted him by insinuating that he'd contributed to this operation. In truth, he'd done nothing but get in the way from the start. Constantly questioning Sigfried and inserting his own ideas. Several times he'd almost ruined everything. Sigfried wanted to kill him. But the Obergruppenführer was protected by a higher power. Too protected for Sigfried to risk finding a convenient accident for the man to meet with. There were just some things one couldn't do.

"Very pleased, yes, sir."

"Nothing can stop us now, it would appear."

"I would prefer not to put the cart before the horse, sir. There's still much work to be done," Sigfried responded. He finished his champagne in one gulp and placed the glass on the metal conference table in the middle of the room, then turned to walk toward a bank of monitors displaying yet more operational information.

"Aren't you forgetting something?" the infuriating man called after him.

Sigfried gritted his teeth. Some of the other officers in the room were watching now. As the Obergruppenführer would have known when he called the comment so loudly. Perhaps he would kill this man after all. Sigfried turned and snapped off a crisp, straight-arm salute. "Heil Hitler," he barked, knowing it was the ceremonial words to say on the man's birthday. The Obergruppen-führer's eyes widened.

"I would think on a day like today we can go with the new school. From this day forward," he called to the men around the table, "We no longer hide in the shadows. From this day forward, we are proud of who we are. From this day forward, we take back the world that was unrightfully stolen from us. The New Reich shall rise. Not the Fourth Reich. For ours is forever, brothers. When we have finished sucking the life from the most powerful nation in the world and taking all her strength, we will be the ultimate power. Heil Dominance!" he finished in a near scream. The room sounded off in echoed salutes and cheers.

Sigfried turned to get back to work. He would finish with America, then find a way to kill this man.

62

The Atlantic Ocean, Near Cabo Verde

J ack Connelly did his best to keep the Gulfstream G-450 moving in a straight line. Due to the engine failure, he had to make constant adjustments due to asymmetric thrust. This caused the aircraft to yaw toward the inoperable engine. In fact, judging by the lack of performance he was getting from the operable engine, he was pretty sure they were only going to get one shot at landing this thing. He could keep it level for now, but climbing out of a failed landing would likely be a no-go.

They had been flying dark, not communicating with the tower at Amilcar Cabral International Airport on Sal Island, or SID as they were calling it. Cabo Verde being an island nation was similar to Hawaii in that it was made up of many small volcanic islands.

"About time to call this thing Jack," Jim Reardon, his co-pilot, said.

"Couldn't agree more. Let's declare our emergency." He moved to the correct frequency and checked his instrumentation again before beginning his radio call.

"SAL Tower, this is Gulfstream N14875. We are declaring an emergency and have lost one engine due to primary and secondary fuel pump failure. Request immediate landing clearance."

The tower took a moment to acknowledge. And Jim looked at him nervously. Maybe they hadn't taken to kindly being snuck up on. Or maybe whatever they were carrying was expected.

"Gulfstream N14875, SAL Tower. Roger, your emergency cleared for immediate landing on Runway 3. Wind is 030 degrees at 20 knots. Do you require any assistance on the ground?"

Jim looked at him, relieved. "Do we need assistance?" he asked jokingly. Jack prayed they wouldn't, but he also knew they couldn't draw too much attention to themselves. He didn't know what their cargo was, but the last thing they needed was foreign emergency services and customs crawling through the plane.

"I think we both know the answer to that, Jim," he said.

Jack then toggled the microphone on his headset back to the tower. "Cleared to land on Runway 3, Gulfstream N14875. Emergency services are not required."

"Gulfstream N14875, roger. Report when you are on final approach."

Jack reported back that they were on final approach and hoped no one would ask too many questions about why their approach angle was so steep, or why they had declined emergency services. As a matter of principle, most aircraft in an emergency wanted emergency services present.

Jack now moved into landing procedures. "Gear down flaps 20, VREF plus 6 single-engine parameters normal," he said aloud, relaying the status to Jim. VREF was the reference speed of the aircraft for landing, so it had enough maneuverability. When landing with a single engine, it was imperative to build in additional speed for margin of error. Jack had no idea how much additional speed he needed in this scenario. He was doing it by feel, and the one engine that was left, combined with the 20-knot crosswind, was making life difficult.

"Gulfstream N14875 cleared to land Runway 3," the tower called. They were descending faster now, and Jack could see the white caps from the ocean beneath the aircraft. The wind picked up, pushing the aircraft slightly off course, and Jack compensated. The aircraft was really fighting him now, and he could hear the only engine they had left whining in protest as they continued their descent.

"This is going to be close, Jim."

"Hey, we've gotten out of worse."

"Stabilized approach, runway in sight, speed looks okay," he said as if willing his instruments to be the right speed.

"Gulfstream N14875, SAL Tower. We advise you pull up. You're coming in too low."

"SAL Tower, Gulfstream N14785, Roger," Jack responded, knowing he couldn't comply. They would either land on the runway or crash into the jettied rocks protecting the runway from the water a few hundred yards from its end.

Jack pulled up on the stick the best he could, attempting to get the aircraft to move upward slightly. But the engine whined more furiously in protest, and they continued to lose altitude. Jack felt every muscle in his body tense as they neared the ground. The crosswind and the thicker air from their descent were slowing them down too much. He throttled forward, trying to regain any speed he could. The tower continued to squawk instructions into his ear, but he couldn't hear them now. All his focus was on guiding the plane to the runway. He practically willed it to land.

Finally, *miraculously,* Jack thought they landed with only a few yards of runway under them. In fact, Jack was pretty sure they had kicked up a cloud of dirt from the rear wheels impacting just short of the runway.

"Shit, that was close," Jim exhaled.

"Yeah, let's not do that again, buddy."

Twenty minutes later, they had taxied to a private aircraft shelter on the opposite end of the airport. They had to talk the tower off the ledge for at least ten of those minutes, but at the moment, it didn't seem like anyone was coming to check the plane out. After another thirty minutes, both of them were even more surprised when an F/A-18 Super Hornet taxied up next to them.

"You jack?" the pilot asked as the canopy came off the aircraft over the roar of the engine.

"Yeah, who's asking?"

"Wendy Simons says you have something that belongs to us."

"Oh yeah?" he called back.

"Well, bring it over. We haven't got all day. We've got to boogie to Rota, and I've got to meet a tanker to get enough fuel to get there."

"Why not fill up here?" Jack yelled, walking the black pelican case up to the fighter and tossing it up to the pilot.

"Psht, yeah, sure, you put regular gas in your 55-million-dollar Corvette!"

The F/A-15F Super Hornet's canopy came back down, and the pilot motioned at Jack to get out of the way. Jack backed off to the Gulfstream's stairs and watched the magnificent fighter head back toward the runway.

"Weird day," Jim said, coming up behind him.

"Hope they get whatever it is there in time."

63

Neues Berchtesgaden, Argentina

"Whatever you're going to do, do it fast. It's started. We're out of time," the president said to Colin. He sat in the front seat of an ancient SUV they'd stolen from near the location of the jammer. They were heading toward the mountain where the bunker was. Witch and Sheriff were meeting them there with a truckload full of gear.

"People are getting sick already, sir?" Colin asked with a lump in his throat.

"Two confirmed cases already. Operation Hydra kicked off in full an hour ago. The entire internet's flooded with information, and we can't get a word in edge-wise. Not that the public would listen or trust us after COVID anyway. We need to shut it off at its source, or we're in trouble."

"My team's on it, sir. I'll radio with an update as soon as I have one."

The dark night flew past on the lonely mountain road. The lights of the small German village faded into the trees behind them as they climbed continuously toward the bunker. "Charlie, what's the status of the drone?"

"Orbiting the bunker now. There's nothing to see. Maybe one foot-mobile, but everyone else is inside. The front doors are huge. Like aircraft hangar huge. But if I get too low to take a peek, someone might see the drone and know we're coming. I can't tell you anything past that. I can't see through solid rock."

"Any other entrances?"

"I'm looking now. Give me five."

Colin swore under his breath. This situation kept getting worse. They were out of time, options, and didn't have shit for manpower. He decided then and there that if he made it out of this, he needed to rethink his choice of career.

"Snowman. There's a small vent stack a hundred yards or so from the hangar entrance. It's too small for any of you guys to fit in, though."

"How big?" Colin asked.

"About a foot and a half by two feet. Why?"

"If one of the guys can't fit down, why not one of the girls?" he asked, turning and looking at Alina.

"You want me to crawl down that thing?" she asked, mortified.

"Not claustrophobic, are you?" replied Colin, smiling.

"No, but also not in love with the idea of crawling down a small pipe with no idea where I'm going."

"You don't have to if you don't want to. But it would be a huge help to get someone inside to see what's going on."

She thought about this for a moment. She seemed torn between being terrified of enclosed spaces and wanting to stop the world from ending. Her eyes flicked back and forth as if considering an angel on one shoulder and a demon on the other. Finally, she spoke. "Are you going to give me a gun this time?"

"Two," Colin replied.

. . .

Twenty minutes later, they pulled to a stop in a small pull-off on the side of the gravel road. Tall pine trees surrounded them on one side and a drop off the side of the mountain with no guard rail on the other. The sky was so clear and black that the stars seemed to touch the ground of the valley floor in the distance. *One day I might come back here and really take in the sites,* Colin thought to himself. No matter the chaos he found himself wrapped up in, the world never ceased to amaze him when he just took a second to look.

Sheriff and Witch pulled up a minute later in the Range Rover Defender 130.

"Good to see you guys in one piece. Who's the girl?" Sheriff asked.

"MI6," Jester replied, raising his eyebrows.

"Alina Chapman," she replied to him, extending a hand for him to shake.

"Sheriff," he replied, shaking hers.

"You must have had some mother with a name like that," she replied in her odd accent.

"I wouldn't know she was abducted by aliens when I was six," he said, turning back to Colin.

"Ignore him," Colin said. "He gets sensitive when he hasn't slept in three days. They spent the next five minutes kitting up and preparing to assault the bunker. Their plan was simple. Alina would go through the air duct and try to get an idea of what was going on while the team circled around to the main entrance of the hanger in the mountainside. Depending on what they saw when they got there and what Alina saw from the inside, they planned to assault on the go.

Five minutes later, they were moving toward the air duct on the sides of the mountain. Colin felt much more comfortable geared up with an Ops Core helmet, Mithril body armor, and Sig Spear assault rifle. The vent itself was a silver upside-down J shape with a grate on the outside that Colin had no trouble pulling right off. They lacked rope, but a quick look inside with a flashlight revealed that the bottom of the vent was scarcely a five-foot drop. Alina carried nothing but two P-365 pistols that she had pulled from the team bags in the back of the SUV. She tucked these into the waistline of her pants, and Colin helped to lower her inside of the vent. When she reached the bottom, he tossed her a flashlight.

"Comm check," Colin said softly.

"I've got you loud and clear," she replied through the earpiece Witch had given her. He then dropped her a signal repeater, which ran by thin wire up to another module in Colin's hands. This he placed on the outside of the vent. It would be tough maintaining communications once she was inside, but this would hopefully help. Otherwise, Colin may have just truly sent Alina to her death.

"Let's move," he said urgently.

They took off, moving as fast as they dared. The 300 yards to the hanger door through the trees were rocky but parallel, so they mercifully didn't have to climb up the side of the mountain. Colin felt the wind pick up as they moved. It blew down from the peak overhead. The air was far more frigid this far above the village. Spring, it seemed, had come more slowly to this elevation, and a chill ran down Colin's spine. He wasn't sure if this was from the air or the situation, but he quickly tried to put the thought out of his mind by increasing his pace.

Ahead, Colin could now see soft red lighting, which seemed to glow out from the mouth of the mountain hanger. Colin knew red lights were used in tactical situations to help keep battlefield signatures low. They also worked to keep men's eyes well-adjusted to the dark. Colin's mind briefly flashed back to land navigation courses in basic training when he huddled under a poncho to try to read a map in the faint red light. Now they had night vision, but Colin hadn't pulled his GPNVG 18-night vision goggles down from his Op Core helmet yet the light of the stars and the clear thin air made it, so it was unnecessary at the moment.

Colin called a halt near the edge of the tree line. He could clearly see the hanger now that it was inside, bathed in red light, and it was truly a hanger. It appeared to Colin to be several hundred yards long and several hundred yards wide. Inside, Colin could see a few aircraft, including one very large one that looked suspiciously like a 747, but he was still too far to be sure. He also saw many stacks of supplies held in large crates, their contents a mystery. He saw several guards milling about, but the presence was lighter than he expected. Why he couldn't say perhaps they were all at the party or perhaps they were deeper inside.

What Colin didn't see was any kind of computer or anything that remotely resembled a data center. As stunning as the sites were in front of him, that was all he really cared about finding. If he didn't, the consequences would likely be too ghastly to contemplate. *If they weren't already,* he reminded himself.

"Alina, status check," Colin called into his earpiece.

"Coming up on the end of the vent now. It's—" She paused for a moment, leaving Colin on edge. "My God."

64

The Bunker, Argentina

"What is it?" Colin asked. Alina sounded panicked. Her voice shook like their connection was bad, but Colin knew fear when he heard it.

"The Obergruppenführer is here. Along with the other senior commanders for the area. I think they are overseeing the operation. It looks like they all just left some kind of meeting. I can see where the servers are located. It's clearly labeled on the wall here. But they are behind some kind of blast door. I don't think we can get in there without an access card."

"Do we have any C4?" Colin asked, turning to Jester. "Some. But if it's an actual blast door, like for a bunker, it's probably not enough to get through," Jester whispered.

Shit, Colin thought. "Alina, which one do we need to grab?"

"The one that's dressed like a general. You can't miss him. But it's possible the SS will be the only ones with the key. For that, you'll need to grab Colonel Himmler, but I don't see him," Alina replied.

"The president is asking for an update," Charlie said into his earpiece. *No time. Take a breath and make a call,* Colin thought.

"Tell him we're making entry now. Grinch, Ford, and Panda, take the left and work your way to the back. Jester, Sheriff, Witch, we're taking the right. Waste anyone you see in a uniform that doesn't look like an officer. If you can, try to capture anyone who does. We're looking for a key card to get us into the server room. Everything's on us now. Let's go!"

Colin stood up and bounded forward. Acknowledgment was not needed; the rest of the operators were hot on his heels. Colin sprinted toward the red light of the hangar like he was sprinting toward the red lights of Hell, knowing full well he probably wouldn't make it out. The team split in two as they went, with Colin and his element moving right while what was left of the Green Berets moved left.

Colin reached the edge of the hangar a moment later and peered around the corner. The guards stood conversing with each other twenty feet from the entrance. Colin made a hand motion to Jester, who was right behind him, and both spun out from around the corner. Colin went low, Jester went high, and both started firing immediately. The first two guards caught rounds center mass and went down hard. The third had enough time to fire off one round before Jester caught him in the throat with a suppressed .277 Fury round.

A moment later, an alarm klaxon began blaring throughout the hangar, and strobing lights added to the red ambiance. Colin heard shouting now in German and several dozen rifle shots from his left. The Green Berets were now in contact.

"Let's move!" Colin shouted over the deafening alarm. Witch fired three shots toward the center of the hangar and took down two more guards who were running toward the sound of the gunfire from the Green Berets.

Colin bounded forward, rifle up, looking for threats. The supply crates only covered the first hundred yards of their advance. Passed that, an array of aircraft and vehicles sat parked neatly along the hangar walls. Colin reached the end of the crates and peered around to check for threats. A guard collided with the front of his rifle as he did, clearly attempting the same as Colin in reverse. Colin fired several times into the man's chest and attempted to step backward, but the man collapsed onto him, pinning his rifle down. Ahead of him, Colin saw another guard behind the man bringing up a rifle to fire.

Colin allowed himself to fall back, reaching for his pistol as we fell. He grabbed it, brought it up, and unloaded an entire seven-round magazine from M1911A1 into the man. Colin dropped the magazine and reloaded with another from his belt. Jester and team had stepped over him to cover, and Sheriff gave him a hand back to his feet. Colin grabbed his rifle from beneath the dead man and wiped a mix of Kevlar and blood off the tip of the muzzle.

He didn't have time to think. Jester was already in contact with more Nazis firing a mix of MP7s and HK416s.

"Reloading," Jester called, spinning back behind the crates.

"We've got to move, or we'll get pinned here," Witch yelled.

"On me!" Colin yelled back. He pulled a fragmentation grenade from his vest and tossed it underhand in the direction of the incoming fire. He waited for five seconds. The grenade exploded to a cacophony of screaming, and Colin ran forward, firing through a haze of smoke from the explosion as he went. He charged toward a small prop plane using its tail as cover but only paused for a moment because he realized there was only enough room for two men to cover here.

Across the hangar, a furious gun battle raged. The echoes of the automatic weapons fire mingled and echoed with the alarm klaxons into a deafening melee of sound. Colin arrived at a second plane and paused for a second. He peered around the tail and saw two more men running toward him. He pivoted and fired, catching one man in the leg and sending him to the ground. The other dove to the side, and Colin missed.

Several shots from the man's MP7 sent Colin scurrying back behind the tail of the plane. Colin noted with alarm that the thin-skinned aluminum of the aircraft wouldn't stop anything from being fired at them and decided movement was his best protection at the moment. He pulled another grenade off his vest and tossed it underhand toward the source of the danger. Another quick count and another explosion echoed off the hangar walls around him. He ran toward the now-dying men and fired a round into both as he went.

When he arrived at the next bit of cover, he realized, in horror, it was a stack of barrels filled with fuel for the aircraft. He thanked God that his throwing arm sucked and that the grenade hadn't gone too far. He'd be dead right now if it had. He kept running. A stray round hitting those barrels could kill them all, and he didn't want to be anywhere near them.

Past the aircraft and the fuel Colin came into view of vehicles. This whole hangar seemed to be a supply depot for military operations, and Colin noticed with satisfaction that there was an armored car that looked like a JLTV in front of them. He bounded for it and dove just as an eruption of automatic weapons fire tore the concrete up beneath his feet. A second later, his team joined him. Colin stayed low, turned the corner around the vehicle, and fired in the direction of the oncoming rounds.

"Are there keys in that thing," he yelled to no one in particular before turning to fire again. A second later, he was greeted with the sound of a truck engine puttering to life. "Cover me," he said to Jester, who was next to him in line. He opened the rear door of the JLTV-like vehicle and looked up. There was the typical cut-out in the roof for the gunner, but no gun mounted to the top. *Shit that would have been too easy.*

"Get in. We're getting to that back of this hangar now!" Colin yelled over the maelstrom of sound. He went for the cutout in the roof and decided he'd use his rifle as the main gun. He reloaded as he went. A second later, everyone was in, and Sheriff drove the vehicle toward the center of the hangar. Bullets pinged off the side, and Colin fired at four more bad guys in the distance. He didn't hit them, but it sent them running for cover. Behind him, Colin could hear the sounds of a gun battle raging between the Green Berets and whatever opposition they were facing. Colin wanted to help, but there was no time.

He turned his attention back to the front of the vehicle in time to see Sheriff veer right directly into two sentries'. The crunch their bodies made as they collided with the enormous, armored vehicle was sickening. Colin squinted as the vehicle picked up speed. Trying to see in the distance. It took a moment, but he finally saw what he was looking for. A group of men was being hurried toward the back of the hangar toward what looked like a massive platform. *What the hell is that,* Colin thought as he let loose a barrage of fire at the guards around the men. Some scattered, but most stood their ground. Gunfire erupted back at him as Colin finally realized what it was. *Shit, it's an elevator.* Then Colin saw him. The Obergruppenführer.

65

Rota, Spain

J ake Lewis watched the F/A-18F Super Hornet descend through the clouds in the distance. Aboard it carried their last hope for saving Louisa Gomez's life. He tried to stay patient, watching the plane dip lower through the baby-blue morning sky. He leaned back against the frame of a doorless Humvee painted in woodland camouflage, tapping the heel of his foot continuously.

Finally, he saw the plane touch down in the distance. He'd been waiting over an hour. He couldn't bear to sit in the hospital any longer. Louisa looked too much like his daughter, and he hated the smell of the places anyway. It took another five minutes for the plane to taxi to a stop in front of him and another five minutes for the pilots to hop out and bring the pelican case to him.

"You, Jake?" the pilot asked. He noted the name tag on the man's flight suit.

"Sure, am. Lieutenant Webster?" he asked in return.

"Yup. Not sure what the hell this is, but it must be important."

"You have no idea," Jake said. "Thanks for giving it the

NASCAR treatment. You guys may have just saved a little girl's life."

Lieutenant Webster looked surprised at this revelation. "We did this for a kid? Not some urgent national security matter?"

Jake started the Humvee up and put it in gear. "What's the difference?" he called after them as he drove away.

The three-way video call between the situation room, hospital in Rota, and McRaven off the coast of South America entered its tenth minute as Jake watched eagerly to see what would happen next. Louisa had just been given the dose of the treatment that would hopefully prolong her life. *Hopefully,* Jake thought. He supposed when suicidal Nazi maniacs who wanted to kill everyone in America were involved, there was always the chance they wouldn't be true to their word.

"Mr. Gomez, you have what you asked for. Your daughter's been given the treatment. We've held up our end of the bargain; now it's time for you to hold up yours," the president said. In the bottom right corner of the screen, Jake could see the chubby Mexican man. He wasn't an expert at reading faces, especially over video calls and not hostage situations, but he was pretty sure the man was waffling. He kept knitting his eyebrows before beginning to speak and stopping.

Finally, he managed to get the words out. "I want immunity for me and my daughter from prosecution." *Bingo,* Jake thought.

To his credit, the president didn't waste any time. "Fine. But you will become a confidential informant to the United States government and help us dismantle the cartels."

"That was never part of our arrangement," Ernesto started, but the president cut him off in a tone that brooked no argument.

"Neither was immunity. Take it or leave it, or I'll have the captain shoot you and dump your body into the ocean."

It was harsh. Especially with the man's daughter on the line. But with everything currently at stake, Jake wasn't surprised, nor did he feel like it was uncalled for. He watched the man stare from the president's side of the screen to his daughter. There was true emotion there. Genuine sorrow for what he had put her through. Jake doubted the president would have the man shot. But Mr. Gomez didn't seem like a man who liked to gamble on things he didn't know he'd win.

"Fine. I'll provide the locations of the drugs to your captain." Jake watched with satisfaction as Ernesto began providing locations, times, and addresses for two locations. One in Los Angeles, the other in El Paso, Texas. The methods were simple and played on economic and racially sensitive smuggling methods. One was through automotive shipments, a critical trade link between the two countries; the other was through tortillas, something that might get an American cop in trouble for profiling for stopping. It reminded Jake of how the Soviets used to insert sleeper agents into Western Germany during the Cold War with Jewish names to keep the German authorities from profiling them.

When the proper locations were identified through the Palantir software the interagency task force was using, the president spoke again. "Mr. Gomez. Once we have the drugs in hand, you will be flown to the United States and remanded into the custody of the CIA to help identify everything else we need. If your cooperation is deemed anything less than stellar, we will revoke your deal. I will also have your daughter flown to the United States so you may see her. Do not mistake my kindness for weakness. It is only due to the direst of needs that I didn't have the team that captured you kill you. If you cross us, it will be the last thing you do."

Ernesto nodded. In a defeated sort of way, their link to the feed from the hospital ended.

"How are you feeling?" Jake asked Louisa.

She opened her eyes as wide as she could, barely being able to keep them open as it was. "A little better."

Jake turned to walk out of the room after giving her hand a small reassuring squeeze.

"Is my dad a bad man?"

Jake turned, thinking carefully about his response. He would have done anything for his daughter, no matter the consequences. It was genetic and unavoidable. But this girl's father truly was a monster. A victim of circumstance, perhaps, but a monster nonetheless.

"Your father did what he had to do to save you. But in life, there's right and wrong, and how your father did it was wrong." Jake was going to leave it there but had one more thought. "Not all heroes are good guys, Louisa."

With that, he turned and walked for the door.

66

The Bunker, Argentina

Colin ducked his head down into the JLTV as a smattering of bullets pinged off the side and crunched into the windshield.

"Sheriff, remember Mozambique?" he yelled over the roaring engine and impacting bullets.

"I don't think that's a good idea!" Sheriff yelled back.

"Do it!" Colin yelled.

"Oh shit," replied Jester grabbing the back of the seat. Colin reached out to grab something to hold onto, but it was too late. Sheriff grabbed the wheel and turned it hard left as he slammed the breaks. The JLTV's huge knobby off-road tires, which were excellent for off-roading but terrible for grappling surfaces like highly polished concrete, spun the vehicle like a top, whipping the rear end around and slamming into five of the guards protecting the officers. Colin went flying against the inside wall of the vehicle as it spun again, then finally came to a hard stop in the middle of the men.

Jester, who had maintained his perch by grabbing on in time, popped up through the hatch and emptied an entire magazine into the two remaining black-uniformed guards. Colin pulled himself up off the ground as the team began exiting the armored vehicle around him and screaming at the men in front of them. A second later, Colin followed, a little unsteady on his feet but ready to end this.

Jester began searching the men in front of him. While Witch climbed on top of the JLTV and aimed back down the hangar toward the still-raging gunfight. If Colin hadn't been wearing his Peltor ear protection, he was pretty sure he'd be deaf right now from the klaxons and the gunshots. "I'm not seeing any key cards here," Sheriff yelled.

"Charlie, what's the status of—"

A torrent of automatic fire from an archway to their right flew into the group in front of him, hitting the officers. Colin ducked and looked. A black uniformed man was turning on his shiny black boots and bolting through the archway.

Colin popped up from his position and tore after the man, "I've got him!" he yelled, unsure if any of his men had been hit. This guy might be their last chance to kill the data center. He ran, reloading his rifle as he went and jamming the spare magazine with three rounds left into his pants pocket. When he reached the archway, he saw dim lighting here and more red and strobing alarm claxons amplifying the sound. In front of him, he saw people with no weapons clamoring in different directions, trying to escape the gun battle raging outside.

He couldn't tell who was who in the uniformed mess, so he raised his rifle and fired around into the ceiling ahead. Instantly, people ducked, and Colin saw his prey sprinting thirty yards in front of him. He sprinted, hurtling a crouched man. When he got to the end of the hall, he made another right and passed what looked like a command center covered in glass walls behind him. The screens were black, but he'd seen intel fusion centers before.

"Team, some kind of command center down this hallway," he bellowed into his earpiece as he kept running, but with no response. The solid rock was killing their ability to communicate.

He rounded another corner and caught a glimpse of the man in the distance. He raised his rifle and snapped off two rounds at him, but they missed wide, chipping rock off the walls as they impacted. There were no more people here now, just a maze of doorways that led God knows where. Colin kept running. Knowing he should slow down and move more tactically but also knowing losing this guy spelled certain death for his country. He chose his country over his life and pushed himself even faster.

He could feel his lungs burning as he ran now. No amount of conditioning could have prepared him for today. The adrenaline kept him moving at top speed when, finally, he emerged out of the maze of hallways onto a catwalk. The edges of it spilled down into a bottomless darkness below, and Colin could hear water running in the distance. There in front of him was the SS Man with the black uniform. He was waiting for another vault-like blast door to open, but it was moving too slowly.

"Freeze, don't fucking move!" Colin yelled.

The man turned slowly but kept the MP7 in his right hand. "Drop that fucking gun," Colin yelled, stepping forward on the catwalk.

"And why would I do that?" asked the man almost lazily.

"Because if you don't, I'll shoot you," Colin replied just as lazily in return. He didn't have time for this asshole.

The man nodded. "I think the only one who will be getting shot today will be you, Mr. Frost."

This did take Colin aback. How did this asshole know his name? Almost no one knew his name. That wasn't good.

"Listen, fuckface, I don't—" he started, but the sound of a gun cocking behind him put the hairs on the back of his neck on edge.

"I think it is you who should drop the gun, Mr. Frost," a cold female voice said from behind him. It was full of venom but also familiarity. He heard soft footsteps on the metal grates from behind him, then the soft brush of hands on the back of his neck as she stepped around him on the catwalk. Her curly blonde hair bounced softly as she walked. When she reached the other side of him, she turned and pointed her pistol at him.

It was Alina.

67

M ick Aldridge couldn't stop sweating in the CBRN suite. Even if the temperature wasn't irregular for April, the circumstances certainly were. He was more nervous than he'd ever been in his life. The sun wouldn't even be up for hours, and Mick was beginning to worry if they waited any longer, his suit might fill with sweat until he drowned in it. His leg bounced up and down nervously, and he checked the Sig Sauer Romeo MSR sight for what felt like the hundredth time in the last hour. He was nervous he'd not turned on the red dot because this wasn't his usual optic. Usually, he ran an ACOG site, but he couldn't get a comfortable view through the optic with the gas mask on, so he'd opted for the reflex site.

He'd been in gunfights before. He'd even been wounded in Afghanistan during his time with the FAST teams due to shrapnel from an IED. But he'd never had the chance of contracting a deadly virus simply from his suite being knocked the wrong way or ripped. He'd seen the videos from the CDC representative. And he'd already decided that if it came down to it, he'd end it himself rather than going out that way.

He sat on the open trunk of a Chevrolet Suburban, waiting for the word to go. His legs dangled uselessly toward the ground. He felt helpless in a way, almost like their current efforts might be completely futile. Several cases had already been reported of the hemorrhagic fever. Three in El Paso now, and four in Los Angeles. Allegedly, it was contained according to his internal briefings, but according to social media and the news, the government had no idea what was going on, and the virus was already spreading.

Minor riots had already started in big cities, and fights over toilet paper and other essentials were all over social media. Mick had opted to put his phone down and not look at it anymore. It wouldn't do to focus anywhere but here. Maybe if they could stop this, it could be contained. Maybe not.

"Alpha Team, this is Phoenix standby to execute," came the call through his radio. Mick looked at Alan Swick sitting next to him, and they banged their helmets together.

"To Valhalla, brother," Alan said, keeping the nerves out of his voice. Mick flicked the safety on his M4 off and grabbed the handle next to his head, "To Valhalla."

As if in response to his statement, his radio squawked again. "All units. Execute. Execute. Execute."

The Suburban's tires squealed, and the vehicle's engine revved as it lurched forward. They were speeding straight for the garage door of the automotive warehouse in front of them. All Mick could do was hold on to the handle and breathe. The SUV bumped over the rise into the parking lot and caught air for a moment before bouncing back to earth. The engine revved louder. "Brace!" the driver called.

Metal and plastic exploded around Mick as the SUV drove straight through the garage door of the warehouse. The Suburban came screeching to a halt, and Jake popped off the back, bringing his M4 up and scanning for targets. For a moment, there was no sound. Then gunfire exploded around him. Mick couldn't tell if it was from his team or bad guys for a moment. The suit muffled his hearing, and he couldn't figure out how to make his typical hearing protection work with it.

A second later, a man to his right screamed and went down next to him in a spray of blood. Mick returned fire in the direction he thought the shot had come from, then crouched down and pulled the man back behind the SUV.

"Phoenix, this is Alpha Team. Man down!" he yelled into his radio. He knew it didn't matter. No one was coming to help them until the site was clear of bad guys and the CDC could walk safely in. Mick looked to his right and saw one of his men fire twice, then bounded toward a stack of boxes. He turned back to his left, but the suit killed his peripheral vision, so he couldn't make out anything past ten feet. The warehouse was filling with smoke, but he couldn't tell from where.

I need to fucking move, he thought, chastising himself for becoming a sitting duck. He yanked a flashbang off his vest, then thought better of throwing it. He didn't know where his men were. The gunfire around him echoed and boomed, further adding to the disorientation of the situation. He looked down at the man he had dragged to cover. He was bleeding from a bullet hole in his mask. *He's dead even if he survived that,* Jake thought. He stood into a low crouch and bounded for a set of metal stairs twenty feet to his right that ascended to a platform overlooking the warehouse floor.

He got twenty feet before gunfire made him duck for cover. He thought about diving but decided it was too much of a risk of knocking his protective gear out of place. *Slow down,* he thought. His right eye was fogging in his mask. He needed to end this quickly. He stood and fired five shots in the direction of the oncoming gunfire. It stopped mercifully, and he bounded for the stairs, this time making it all the way there. He jumped onto the first step, then made his way up them two at a time.

When he reached the top, he ran the length of the platform into a corner. Then he settled, catching his breath. The mask made it hard to breathe, and Mick could have been in better shape as it was. When he looked down, he saw the rest of his men pinned down by two separate machine guns on either side or a semi-truck. Mick had to take them out or his whole team was going to get massacred.

He pulled the flashbang back off his vest and tossed it over-hand at the far machine gunner. Mick simultaneously pulled his M4 and fired a series of three-round bursts into the closest gunman. The first burst didn't hit him, but the second two did, rewarding Mick with a spray of blood over a stack of white boxes. Mick then trained his weapon on the far gunner and fired again. One burst left the weapon, but it clicked dry. Mick ejected the magazine, pressed a new one in, and pressed the bolt catch. It locked forward and Mick fired again.

A few shots later, he was rewarded with more blood. He grinned in satisfaction, knowing he'd just saved his team. When the most horrific pain he ever felt tore through his thigh. Mick fell to the ground screaming. It was somehow hot and cold, and it felt like someone had torn his thigh in half muscle fiber by muscle fiber, like a piece of bread. He'd been hit. He tried to roll over but only made it halfway before the pain overwhelmed him. Out of the corner of his mask, he saw a man approaching with no protec-tive gear on.

He tried to bring up his weapon, but it was pinned under him in the fall. Mick went to reach for his pistol, but he knew he'd never get there in time. He was dead. *Better this way than from the virus,* he thought. The man leveled his rifle at him. Mick stared him dead in the eyes, not wanting to give him the satisfaction. A blast echoed from in front of him. Mick felt nothing. The man's chest exploded in front of him in a blast of bone and tissue.

Alan appeared a second later with his shotgun. "You know, 'To Valhalla' is just a figure of speech, man," he yelled. Mick's ears were ringing. Alan bent down and tied a tourniquet above the wound, then helped him up. "Looks like a through and through. You'll be fine. Teams got the drugs downstairs."

"Show me," Mick replied through gritted teeth with his arm slung over Alan's shoulder. He could see the blonde-haired man who'd been about to kill him staring wide-eyed up at the ceiling with his chest blown out. It made him want to vomit.

"I think we should keep you away from them. I don't want to infect you if they're not contained."

"Probably too late for that brother. At least let me finish the job."

68

The Bunker, Argentina

C olin didn't move his weapon's sight from the man in front of him. Alina could shoot him, but he'd make sure to take the man straight to hell with him. Where the rest of his team was, he couldn't say, but this was up to him now. Only one person was walking off this catwalk alive.

Colin did his best to slow his breathing, trying to take in the situation in all its details in the microseconds before he had to start taking action. He looked for a way out or through to the other side, but he couldn't see it, so he decided to stall.

"Guess our time in the truck didn't mean anything," Colin said. He had nothing, so he was just throwing stuff at the wall, hoping it stuck, buying time. Colin was surprised by the sudden flash of anger in the SS man's eyes.

"What did I tell you about playing with your food, Frauline?" the SS man asked. There was wickedness in his eyes.

Alina looked fearful but stayed calm. "Ignore him. He's stalling."

Colin pressed further. "I guess a kiss means nothing these

days. I really am getting old." Colin saw it more clearly now. They were lovers. The anger in his eyes and the fear in hers illustrated to him all the more clearly what kind of relationship they had.

"Lies!" she screamed at him. Her voice pitched up into a deeper German accent. Colin looked from her to him. There was ice in his expression. Pure hatred for her. Like a man who'd been cheated on, chosen to trust once more, only to be betrayed again.

"I'll deal with you later," he growled at her. She let out a muffled sob, the gun she had pointed at Colin shaking in her hand. He decided to change subjects, still looking for a way out. "How do you know who I am?"

The SS man smiled. "We know more about you than you could possibly imagine, Mr. Frost."

Colin's uneasiness grew to new heights. "How's that?"

"I'm afraid I don't have time to get into all of the details today, Mr. Frost. I have a country to destroy. And you won't be living long enough for it to matter. Now, Frauline, prove your love for me once more. We have a train to catch."

Colin looked back to Alina in alarm. He saw her reaching her finger toward the trigger, and he readied to fire at the SS man when a bang from behind him sounded off. The gun snapped out of Alina's hand, and she screamed in agony as it took two of her fingers with it. Blood sprayed across Colin's face as he turned his head in surprise. Walking up behind him was Alina. A second Alina. Colin's eyes darted back and forth between the screaming woman in front of him and the other behind him.

"You never could pick a man to save your life," the new woman said. She turned to Colin. "I see you've met my twin sister, Hilda."

Colin was stunned into silence. They were identical down to the last curl on their heads. The only difference now was the missing fingers. But Colin had taken his eyes off the ball for too long. Hilda's head snapped back as a torrent of fire from the SS man slammed into her, sending her falling into Colin. The rounds impacting her caused her to fire, and Colin felt a searing pain in his right arm as a bullet grazed him. The pain made his weapon temporarily slip in his hand, and before he knew it, the SS man had bolted. He turned to Alina to tell her to follow, but she was slumped on the edge of the catwalk, bleeding from her abdomen. The bullet that had grazed him had hit her. It was the lower left side. Likely not fatal, but not good either.

"Alina!" Colin yelled, running to her. She looked pale but determined. She was beautiful, and Colin regretted thinking it was her who'd betrayed him moments ago. Colin put pressure on the wound with one hand and reached for the XSTAT injector from his medical kit with the other. He shoved it in the wound and hit the plunger, sending a hundred foam balls into the wound to stop the hemorrhaging.

"You're going to be okay," he said.

She smiled, grasping his hand. "Go finish this."

Colin squeezed her hand and ran after the SS man.

He knew he had to hurry, so he used the searing pain in his arm as fuel to run faster. Alina would be fine—at least he hoped she would—but right now, only one thing mattered. He had to get the keycard and kill this data center to stop the attack. He crossed through the blast door and was greeted by a set of stone steps carved right into the mountain, and he started downward as fast as he dared.

The lighting was low here, and he could barely see ten feet ahead of him. When he hit the bottom, he stepped onto a dirt path with a low ceiling. In the distance, he could hear running, the alarm klaxons from above a distant memory now. All his focus was here. He used the flatter surface here to move to a dead sprint, trying to make up some ground. Up ahead, he could hear something odd. Like electrical charging or some kind of huge engine starting. *He said he had to catch a train,* Colin thought. *Shit, he's getting away.*

Colin put on a huge burst of speed, feeling his legs ache and his rib injury spiking in pain, and suddenly emerged from the passageway. The passage had given way to a huge, cavernous chamber with a train. At least it looked like a train. It was more of a huge cargo tram with several cars on some kind of Maglev sled, and it was moving. Colin chased after it. After another twenty feet of running, he managed to jump onto the last car, grabbing hold of a yellow railing.

He was on the move now to where he didn't know. Before he could think, the glass protecting the inside of the last car shattered around him, sending him diving for cover.

69

The Bunker, Argentina

Colin felt the train accelerating and knew he needed to get inside before he was thrown off the back. He couldn't hear the distinctive noise of metal wheels on tracks, which meant this train worked on magnets, and magnet trains were fast. Colin grabbed a flashbang off his vest and tossed it through the back window. A deafening pop blew out the rest of the glass a second later, and Colin stood vaulting the window into the rear car. He winced as glass from the broken pane sliced his brace hand. It stung, wrapping it back around his weapon.

He moved into the car with a half limp, in unbelievable pain from his hand, ribs, and bullet-grazed arm. He tried to push it from his mind. Two guards in black uniforms clutched their heads in front of him. Colin shot both and felt his weapons bolt lock back. He inserted another magazine. He only had one left. Then he'd be down to his pistol. Outside the train car, it was dark. They were moving through tunnels in the mountain. To where he didn't know.

Colin advanced up the train car, seeing some utilitarian seat-ing, like in the back of a cargo plane and supplies. The New Reich must use this to get supplies up to the town and bunker. The scale of it was unbelievable. As Colin moved, he felt the train sway to the side. The tunnel was turning.

He arrived at the bridge between the two cars and peered through. It looked dark, and he didn't see any men inside. He opened the door and was greeted with tremendous noise and wind. They must have been moving at over fifty miles an hour already. Colin didn't even want to think about what would happen if this thing derailed.

In the next car, he found hundreds of cardboard boxes and pelican cases stacked high on the periphery. The train continued to sway as he walked. When he reached the halfway point in the car, the door to the cabin opened from the other end, and three men walked in. Colin froze. Their flashlight beams were looking for him. He leveled his Sig Spear and fired as fast as he could.

The two men in the front who were grouped together went down immediately. The third was wiser and stepped back out of the car and to the side of the door. Colin aimed at the wall where he stepped and prayed the .277 Fury rounds had enough punch to go through the thin metal. He fired another ten rounds at the spot and ran to the door to peer through.

The man lay dying on the bridge between the two cars. Colin put a round into his head and felt the weapons bolt lock back again. *Fuck last mag,* he thought. He changed to it before entering the next car. This one had lights on and looked like more of a passenger cabin. It had wooden paneled walls and compartments for passengers. Colin thought this must be for the officers. He stepped forward, weapon up and scanning for more threats. The rhythmic rocking of the train as it moved, bouncing his rifle with it.

He arrived at the first compartment and peered in. Nothing. He started moving when he heard a strange sound behind him, like something had fallen off his vest. He looked down to see what it was. He knew immediately he was in trouble and closed his eyes. Someone had thrown a flashbang at him. Even with his eyes closed and his hearing protection on, it was bright and deafening. He staggered out of the way and opened his eyes just in time to see the SS man approaching. His vision was covered in bright spots, like he had looked at the sun. Before he could react, a punch connected with the side of his jaw, sending him into the wall.

Colin tried to bring his gun up, remembering to always bring a gun to a fistfight, but a monstrous kick hit it with such force it tore the sling from his body and sent the weapon to the floor. Colin stepped back, trying to regain his composure and protect himself from further strikes. He still had his pistol but didn't want to go for it until he was sure he could reach it. "I told you it was time to die, Mr. Frost," said the man advancing again.

Colin opted to try and throw the man off balance and charged, trying to tackle the man linebacker style. Colin succeeded and surprised him but couldn't get him to the ground in the small compartment. The man brought down a series of elbows onto his back, rattling Colin's already injured rib cage. Colin pushed off the wall behind the man going for separation again, thinking to go for his gun. The SS man charged at him before he could get to it. Colin sidestepped and threw an elbow at the back of the man's head, trying to run him into the wall.

The man caught himself and rolled out of the way of the kick Colin aimed at his ribs. Colin was gassed from his run to the train, and he breathed heavily, trying to get control of himself. Colin charged this time, hoping to catch the man before he could fully recover. He threw his full six-foot-two, two-hundred-and-forty pounds into the man, trying to body-check him to the floor. His momentum won, and the man went down under him. Colin arched up and began raining blows on the man's head, trying to knock him out.

But the train made a sharp movement to the left, and the SS man rolled with it, knocking Colin off balance and away from him. He stood, and Colin followed, moving back. The man advanced again, bringing his fists up. He threw a vicious right hook at Colin and followed up with two strikes to his left. Colin blocked all the strikes but failed to block the kick that connected with his injured ribs. The blow was tremendous, knocking the wind out of him and sending him into the wall. If Colin was out of breath before, he was in way worse shape now because he couldn't breathe.

He felt his brain screaming for oxygen as he tried to recover and get his diagram to open back up. The SS man moved in to finish him. Colin lunged up, slamming his Ops Core helmet into the man's face. He heard the man's nose snap just as he was finally able to get a much-needed breath into his lungs. The pain in his rib was so severe now he was pretty sure it was out of place, possibly poking into his lung. He needed to end this before his lungs filled with blood and he passed out.

"Enough of this!" the man screamed at him, blood pouring out of his nose. He pulled a knife from the small of his back. He held it with the blade out of the bottom of his palm and lunged forward at Colin, slashing at him. This guy knew what he was doing. You could always tell in a knife fight they'd been trained if they opted to slash instead of stab. Colin stepped back but was too slow. The blade connected with the part of his chest between his Mithril body armor vest straps, narrowly missing his neck. Searing pain radiated across his collarbones.

This was what Colin had been waiting for. Out of breath, he took a huge step back, fluidly drawing his M1911A1 pistol as he went. "Never bring a knife to a gunfight," he said as he pressed the trigger. He drilled the SS man straight through the bridge of his nose. Brains sprayed out of the back of his head onto the wood-paneled wall. The SS man fell to the floor, dead. Colin doubled over to catch his breath but stopped short when he felt the way his rib crunched with his movement.

Gingerly, he crouched down to the man and reached into his jacket pocket. The keycard came out. Colin had no idea how he was going to get it back to the team. Out of his pocket, he pulled out the Flipper Zero module Charlie had given him and cloned the keycards NFC signal for good measure.

A blinding light suddenly shone through the train car window. Colin ran forward to the front of the compartment and found himself in a small cockpit area. The train's conductor was dead. The instrumentation the train was controlled from was smashed, and the train seemed to be accelerating. They'd crossed out onto a bridge between this mountain and a smaller one. Below them, a hundred feet down, was a river.

"Charlie, can you hear me?" Colin said into his earpiece.

"I've got you, Snowman!"

"I'm sending you the key card codes now from the Flipper Zero," Colin said, triggering the transmit button on the small device that worked through his communications.

"Where are you?" Charlie asked.

"Not sure. But I'm on a train, and I need to get off. Look for a river and find me."

"I've got the codes, Snowman. Good luck."

Colin took a breath, opened the door next to him, and jumped.

70

The White House, Washington, D.C.

The president sat back in his chair, placing the half of his turkey sandwich he'd been eating back on the plate. He needed to go to the bathroom, but he couldn't seem to get a free moment, and he wasn't going to let any of his people see any weakness from him. He had to be better than human. They were waiting on a call from Fort Detrick in Maryland. The High Threat Pathogen Unit there was finishing analyzing the initial strains of the virus to give them more accurate spreading and lethality projections.

Operation Hydra was only just beginning, and securing the tainted drugs had been a major win. But it didn't help explain how people were already sick in hospitals. Eight confirmed cases so far in the two cities. All were expected to be fatal. The president decided while they were waiting for the call that he might be able to make it to the bathroom finally. He began to stand up when an aide from the other side of the room called out, "I have Fort Detrick, sir."

The president sat back down. "Put them up on the screen."

A second later, a tired-looking man in white appeared on the screen. "Mr. President, we have the results you requested."

"Get on with it," the president said. The man looked strange. The president felt the feeling of nervousness grow in the pit of his stomach. *That bad,* he thought to himself.

"Mr. President, have you heard of CRISPR?"

"I have, but I don't know anything about it. I worked in tech after the military, not science."

The man nodded. "How about a binned chip, sir?"

The president looked confused but answered, "You mean when a computer chip comes out of the factory and one of its compute cores doesn't work?"

"That's correct, sir. This virus is a binned chip."

There were looks of confusion in the room, the president included. "Elaborate," he said.

"Well, sir, it appears whoever created this virus took a normal Ebola virus—one of the deadlier strains, I might add—and took away one of its code's cores. In this case, the one that's responsible for letting it spread."

"You're saying this thing can't spread? Then how are cases already popping up?" the president asked.

"Well, sir, I'm not sure. But unless someone gets a dose of this virus and then is administered an RNA sequence to activate it, this thing can't spread. From the data we're getting from the hospitals, it appears the gene sequences are identical."

"You're positive?" the president asked.

"Sir, so positive I'd swallow the sample we have here."

"Why would someone attack us with a virus that can't spread?" Mack Tomlin asked. The table looked thoughtful but deeply confused.

Finally, Wendy slapped her hand on the table and smiled. "Don't you see, Mack? No one in their right mind would use a biological weapon. The whole world saw first-hand what happens when a virus gets loose with COVID. These things can't be effectively contained, and there's no telling how they might mutate in the wild. It's mutually assured destruction. All they needed to do was make the American people think there was another pandemic about to happen and ensure the narratives spun out of control. Then just step back and profit off the panic. They could destroy us with information and economic warfare far easier than physically attacking us."

The president looked thoughtful. "They used the pillars of our society against us—that is, free speech and the free market. Our very own democracy was weaponized to destroy us."

The room was deadly quiet. This was warfare as it had never been contemplated before. If no one could defeat us in the field, why bother? There were other ways to bring a nation to its knees.

"Even if we get this information out, unless we can cut the flood of misinformation and kill the short trades, they've won. Even though there won't be a nation-destroying pandemic, they've still won," the president finished with a bowed head. The rioting across major cities had gotten worse over the past two hours, and fighting online had reached a fever pitch. Even if they could get the mainstream news stations to report what they were saying, their audience was so small it wouldn't make a difference in time.

"Mr. President," the aide said from the end of the room. "I have the Echo Team!"

"Ah, Mr. President, this is, ah, Jester from Team Alien. We have the codes and are shutting off the data center now. Do you want us to blow it or just pull the plug?"

The room erupted into cheers around him as several people stood up, hugged, and high-fived. The president cracked his first smile in a week. "Damn good work, son. Pull the plug for now,

Jester. We'll send a team to dig through the code and ensure this never happens again."

"Ah, you got it, sir," the operator replied awkwardly.

"Where's Snowman?" the president asked. The room went quiet at this.

"We lost contact, sir."

71

Three Days Later, CIA Headquarters, Langley, Virginia

Wendy Simons watched rain beat down the glass windows of the director's office. She sat in a chair in the sitting area with the Director and his counterparts from the Five Eyes. The global intelligence alliance of the world's English-speaking nations included the United States, United Kingdom, Canada, Australia, and New Zealand. All five intelligence chiefs sat in comfortable armchairs or sofas, watching the ominous thunderstorm outside shake the windows.

The New Reich was the topic of discussion. How the global criminal syndicate had done so much and grown so large under the collective noses represented the largest intelligence failure since nine eleven.

"How's your agent?" Wendy asked Mary Jude, the United Kingdom's director of MI6. The woman with short-cropped gray hair and a serious face responded curtly.

"She's fine. She is recovering well in an American hospital before she can be transported back to England. The intelligence we recovered from that data center is the more vexing concern.

We've already uncovered five moles in our intelligence and military services."

"What are you doing with them?" the director of Canada's Security and Intelligence Service asked.

"That's our concern," she responded severely. A flash of lightning added an exclamation point to her words. Wendy was pretty sure she knew what that meant.

"What we should be concerned with is finishing processing all this information and dismantling or destroying every vestige of this group. We'll need to work together to do this right, or it will keep rearing its ugly head like Al-Qaeda."

"We'll try to help wherever we can, but our hands are full with China. They've infiltrated us far more severely than this New Reich group has," the director of the Australian Secret Intelligence Service said. The Director of New Zealand's Security and Intelligence Service agreed.

"What are you doing with the bunker and town?" Mary asked.

"The bunker is under our control. A new bilateral trade and security agreement with Argentina ensured that. The town is empty, and its residents are scattered. We have people hunting, but I'm not optimistic. We still have too few resources in the area to work effectively, and we've neglected our own backyard for far too long," Wendy replied.

The CIA director spoke up. "We're more concerned now with the other locations referred to in the IT map we pulled from the organization. There are sites globally. We need to hit as many of them at once as we can to kill the network. We'll also need to key in NATO allies to our operations to keep from ruffling any feathers."

Mary responded, "I think we need to keep this in-house. Europe is concerned with Ukraine and Russia. There's no telling how infiltrated our friends might be. Until we have a complete map of the situation and can strike as one, we need to sit. Otherwise, we'll have another Al-Qaeda or ISIS on our hands. Then the SAS and Ground Branch can kill as many of these people as you'd like."

"The operation needs to be limited to the people in this room and a few trusted underlings. Until we understand the depth of the compromise," Wendy said.

"Done," Mary replied. Of the five people in the room, the British and Americans held the most power in the alliance. Australia was a close third, and New Zealand and Canada were useful but lacked global striking power.

"Is anyone else going to ask the obvious question here?" the Australian said.

"How the hell did this happen right under our noses?" the Canadian replied. The room went quiet, as everyone thought.

Or maybe everyone knows the answer and doesn't want to say it, Wendy thought. The truth was the alliance had gotten so caught up looking at current threats it had stopped looking around corners and occasionally checking the rear-view mirror. With the world fracturing into ever smaller ideas and simultaneously combining into ever larger factions, there simply weren't enough intelligence resources to keep up with it. Wendy could barely keep up with the news. In the last three days, the cycle had gone from the end of the world global pandemic to incredible patriotism for enduring such a devastating attack to starting to blame those they thought were responsible. The world knew the New Reich now as a terrorist organization in a similar vein to ISIS. They had no idea of the scale of the organization, and they never would.

A few minutes later, the meeting broke up for lunch. They'd be here for the next two days deliberating on the best paths forward.

Mary hung back to speak with Wendy. She tucked an iPad under her arm as she approached.

"I never did get to ask you, Wendy. How's your team that was on the ground?"

"One dead DEA agent, one wounded but recovering and not infected."

"Thank God for that."

Wendy nodded in agreement, knowing all ten people who had ultimately been infected had already died. If the virus had been real, hundreds of millions would have been killed.

Mary spoke again. "That's not the team I was referring to, though. How's your team that was on the ground in Argentina? We'd like to express our gratitude for saving our agent's life."

Wendy smiled. "That's our concern."

Colin Frost will return in Code of Conspiracy!

Make sure to join our Discord
(https://discord.gg/5RccXhNgGb)
so you never miss a release!

THANK YOU FOR READING ECHOES OF DECEPTION

We hope you enjoyed it as much as we enjoyed bringing it to you. We just wanted to take a moment to encourage you to review the book. Follow this link: Echoes of Deception to be directed to the book's Amazon product page to leave your review.

Every review helps further the author's reach and, ultimately, helps them continue writing fantastic books for us all to enjoy.

Also in series:

COLIN FROST
Capital Murder
Echoes of Deception
Code of Conspiracy

Want to discuss our books with other readers and even the authors?

JOIN THE AETHON DISCORD!

You can also join our non-spam mailing list by visiting www.subscribepage.com/AethonReadersGroup and never miss out on future releases. You'll also receive three full books completely Free as our thanks to you.

Don't forget to follow us on socials to never miss a new release!

Facebook | Instagram | Twitter | Website

Looking for more great thrillers?

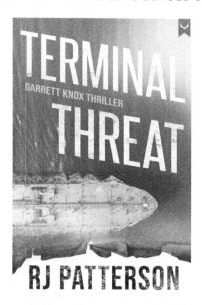

In a daring act of piracy, Yemeni terrorists have not only seized a special oil tanker but they've also captured a high-value asset. With President Lewis desperate to save his biggest donor's assets and protect his deepest secret, he orders Director of National Intelligence Camille Banks to deploy her secret team to recover the asset. Garrett Knox, along with his hand-picked team members of elite operatives, must attempt the impossible: infiltrate the treacherous Yemeni mountains and bring the asset home alive. Battling hostile terrain and relentless attacks, Knox and company close in on their target only to have the tables flipped on them as a far deadlier plot emerges. The terrorists offer a chilling ultimatum—the asset in exchange for a notorious bombmaker in U.S. custody. With time running out and the world watching, Knox and his team embark on a pulse-pounding mission to retrieve the bombmaker. But when a shocking betrayal threatens everything, Knox must make an unthinkable choice to save Rico and save the president. **From the Oval Office to the explosive climax, Terminal Threat is a non-stop thrill ride packed with jaw-dropping twists. As a sinister conspiracy tightens its grip, will Knox's team prevail, or will the President's dark secrets destroy them all? The clock is ticking in this electrifying novel by R.J. Patterson.**

Get Terminal Threat Now!

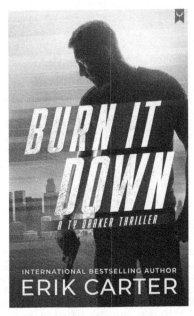

DISAVOWED. HUNTED. RUNNING OUT OF TIME. Ty Draker is a marked man with no idea why. Chased by ruthless operatives, Draker's sole ally is Beau—just a mysterious voice on the phone. In exchange for Beau's help clearing his name, Draker agrees to work as a fixer, crisscrossing the country to right wrongs. Draker plunges into a race against time after unearthing a terrorist plot with global implications. As he digs deeper, an unsettling realization dawns—shadowy threads seem to connect the terrorists, his pursuers, and the obscure events of his earlier life as a CIA operator. With the hunters closing in and catastrophe looming, Draker must solve the puzzle fast. Millions of lives depend on a man who can't trust his own history. **If you like action heroes with the steely resolve of Lee Child's Jack Reacher, the calculating will of Gregg Hurwitz's Orphan X, and the raw power of Mark Greaney's Gray Man, then you'll love Ty Draker, a new thriller series by Erik Carter, bestselling author of the Silence Jones Series.**

Get Burn It Down Now!

For all our Thriller books, visit our website.

ACKNOWLEDGMENTS

First off, I would like to say thank you to all of my readers. You taking the time to read my first book, Capital Murder, and making your way to my second is an incredible compliment. I hope your time spent has been entertaining. I want to thank my publisher, Aethon Books, for continuing to publish my stories and making my first book a success. I want to thank My editor Jakub for making my work polished and comprehensible. I want to thank Jack Stewart for helping me with some of my plot's more aviation-focused areas, even if I took some liberties... Please check out his incredible books.

I want to thank my four-legged friends for their insistence that a long walk is the best way to solve a plot problem. Lastly, I would like to thank my entire family for their support. It means everything.

Made in the USA
Las Vegas, NV
30 November 2024

12999733R00208